Second Chance City

by

L. A. Kelley

Second Chance City

Cover Art by *Tina Lynn Stout*

The Wild Rose Press, Inc.
PO Box 708
Adams Basin, NY 14410-0708
Visit us at www.thewildrosepress.com

Publishing History
First Fantasy Rose Edition, 2015
Print ISBN 978-1-5092-0230-0
Digital ISBN 978-1-5092-0231-7

Published in the United States of America

The building was silent

with the exception of a faint hum now emanating from the glow in the corner. Nate moved cautiously forward, shining the flashlight. "Debolt?" No one answered. "We'll check the rest of the store...Libby?"

Libby had stepped from his side, her attention drawn elsewhere. She stood in front of the display stand filled with comic books. Her respiration sharply increased. "What is that?" she asked. The eerie glow came directly from one of the books.

Nate's gaze widened. "I've no idea." The glow began to fluctuate, pulsing with a bright green neon light.

Libby squinted at the glare. She leaned in as if striving to discern the cover. "It's the latest Refractor issue. Why is it doing that?" On and off, on and off, the hypnotic beat flashed.

The light was oddly attractive. "It's not some marketing gimmick?" Nate asked.

"No way," insisted Libby. "I've never seen anything like it."

The tempo of the pulses increased, so did the hum. A little voice in Nate's head bleated a warning. *This isn't normal. You should do something...do something...do something.* His thoughts muddled with the incessant flash. The hand which had been resting on the gun, dropped to his side.

Libby clutched the pencil light to her chest. As if drawn by an irresistible impulse, the other hand reached for the Refractor comic.

Nate's confusion vanished, shoved aside by a powerful protective urge. "Libby, don't! It might be dangerous."

Dedication

For My Family

Acknowledgments

Many thanks to my editor, Lara Parker, for crossing the 't's' and dotting the 'i's'.

Special thanks to Doreen Alsen, who introduced me to Refractor and then encouraged me to run and play with him.

Chapter One

"Nate, how've you been?" Connor O'Reilly leaned over and filled Nate Hammond's coffee cup. "Haven't seen you in a while. Is that any way to treat a friend? All my old high school buddies are supposed to eat here at least once a week and support my business through the long cold winter. Buy an expensive breakfast, or I'll call your folks in Florida."

Nate grinned. "Hey, Connor. Judging by the crowd, you don't need my help, but I'll order a side of bacon to go with the pancakes."

"Coming right up."

As Connor jotted the order, Nate sipped his coffee and took a fleeting look around O'Reilly's Restaurant. Almost every booth was filled with strangers, and half the counter seats taken by teenage boys and girls. "Who are all these kids, anyway? I didn't see a bus outside—are they part of a school group?"

"Geez, some great cop you are," Connor replied with a deadpan expression. "I thought you were supposed to keep tabs on the local happenings. Don't you know a famous author arrives today to sign autographs at Write Away?"

"Someone is coming to the bookstore? Who?"

"Payton Debolt."

"Who's she?"

"He." Connor tsked. "Geez, I'm shocked. Despite

1

all those hours frittered away over comics as a boy, you are sadly out of touch with the youth of America. Payton Debolt writes the Refractor series."

"Seriously? That guy?"

"Uh-huh. He's doing some kind of publicity tour. Debolt will be in town this morning. It's quite a coup for Lorelei. Owners of small businesses don't usually get such a lucky break."

"What's he doing in Coldwater Bay? You'd figure a guy like him would hit the big cities."

Connor shrugged. "Beats me. It's all very sudden. Lorelei got a call yesterday from his assistant, and now Debolt is in town." He leaned over and whispered, "Maybe Lorelei used her publishing connections to dig up something juicy and blackmailed him to come— damn, I probably shouldn't have said that to a cop."

"Said what? I didn't hear a thing."

Connor grinned. "You are a one lousy officer of the law."

"Your customer service technique sucks big time," Nate threw back cheerfully. "I hope your remodeling skills are better, or the roof will collapse on Ellie's head. By the way, how's the house coming?" Connor had inherited his deceased grandmother's home and spent the last few months renovating the interior.

"All done except for some touch-ups. Ellie and I will give the outside a new coat of paint in the spring. It sure doesn't look like Nana's anymore."

Connor took off with order pad in hand. A few minutes later, he returned carrying a steaming platter of pancakes and bacon. Nate happily dug in. Before long nothing remained of breakfast other than a contented memory and a few maple syrup-soaked crumbs. He leaned back with a sigh and cradled his cup. A flash of color outside the window drew his attention. A woman in a bright red scarf skipped up the front steps and entered the restaurant.

Connor slapped the check down on the table. "Need anything else? Come on, I gotta make the light bill."

The girl in the red scarf walked behind Connor and jabbed him in the small of the back. "Are you trying to strong arm customers again? That is no way to run a business. Say the word, Nate, and I'll let him have it."

"He's very mean," said Nate with a straight face. "He almost made me cry, Ellie."

Connor grinned and planted a big kiss on Ellie Yoshida's lips. "Admit you're crazy about me."

His fiancée pushed him aside. "None of that now," Ellie scolded. I've got work to do. Nate, did you hear we set the date for the wedding? It'll be early April before tourist season starts."

"Not only the world's most beautiful business manager," said Connor, "but practical, too."

A pinprick of envy jabbed Nate in the heart. A wedding already? They had only started dating a few months ago.

Ellie went behind the counter and poured herself a cup of coffee. "Hey, Nate, how's Ashley? I haven't seen her lately."

Nate shifted in his seat. "Actually, we broke up. She got offered her dream job in Chicago."

Ellie regarded him sympathetically. "Oh, I'm sorry."

He shrugged. "I'm happy for her. It wasn't meant to be for us."

Connor shook his head. "Too Late Nate…still living up to his high school nickname."

Nate rolled his eyes as Ellie peered at Connor in confusion. "What?"

"That's what we used to call him. Nate always made a play for a girl a little too late. Like with Ashley." Connor turned to Nate. "Would it have killed you to move a little faster?"

Then I wouldn't be Too Late Nate. "If you don't quit sounding like my mother, I'm going to quit ordering bacon with the pancakes."

Ellie returned from behind the counter coffee cup in hand. Connor slipped an arm around her waist. "I'm just saying, a good woman doesn't hang around a man for long in Coldwater Bay unless he gives her a reason to stay. Look at me. I asked Ellie to marry me the day she came for the job interview as business manager for O'Reilly's."

"He sure did," said Ellie, shooting Connor a teasing glance. "I thought he was nuts. Lucky for him, he also had a cute butt, and I needed the job."

"You see," said Connor. "I'm right, Nate. You have to give a girl a reason to stay."

Nate paid for breakfast and left the restaurant with a promise to come to their newly remodeled place for dinner next week. The icy January wind off the bay clawed at any exposed skin. Nate zipped the coat collar tight to his neck and jogged across the park to the police station. The snow from last week's storm had melted in a brief warming trend, but judging by the menacing clouds gusting across the sky, another gale would blow in before the end of the day.

The gloomy weather matched Nate's mood

perfectly—not that he didn't wish Connor and Ellie well. In truth, he was happy for them. Nate was glad to have his old friend back in town. He and Connor had been close in high school, but then once he finished college Connor left Coldwater Bay for corporate America. When his grandmother died, he returned home to settle affairs, but stayed in town and bought the old rundown restaurant. Connor had worked his butt off to make O'Reilly's a success. He and Ellie certainly seemed to have an immediate connection. Nate sensed it the first time he saw them together. Why did others seem to have the knack for perfect timing? Why didn't any of his past relationships have staying power?

As Nate rounded the corner to the police station, a car's impatient beep drew his attention. In the off-season, parking was no problem in Coldwater Bay, but today spaces along Main Street and in the municipal lot had already filled. An expensive sports car idled in wait for Florence Peevey's sedan to exit a parking spot. The crusty clerk at Valenti's Automotive wasn't exactly in the stock car circuit and took her own sweet time on the road. Occasionally, Nate got a grumbled suggestion from townsfolk to ticket her for driving too slowly. He offered soothing words in return, but took no action. Florence's annoying driving habit hardly qualified as a safety hazard. Nate figured everyone was entitled to a few quirks, especially someone who had been around as long as Florence. Besides, Irina Duval would never forgive him. The police dispatcher and Florence were bingo buddies.

The sports car driver leaned on the horn. Florence rolled down the window, flipped him the finger, and then casually puttered along ten miles under the speed limit. The sports car parked in the empty spot, and a male driver and female passenger got out. As they crossed the street, the man returned Florence's one-finger salute. He then bent his head toward his companion to give her an obvious earful. She turned her head away. Tendrils of soft auburn curls around her neck blew in the wind before she mashed them under her hat.

Nate frowned. The glimpse of her profile reminded him of someone. Who was it now?

Libby Parish.

Despite the cold, wet flakes drifting down from the sky, warmth flooded in at the memory of the first girl to get away. He made a face. Wow, that was a totally deluded recollection. Nate never had a chance with Libby. None of the boys did. She'd made it plain even at thirteen her sights were set much higher than a life in Coldwater Bay. All Nate had ever gotten from her was a quick peck on the cheek and then she was gone. His lips unconsciously twisted into a smile. The sensation of his first kiss still lingered pleasantly in the back of his mind.

Nate scampered up the steps to the police station and turned his mind to the job. With all the people arriving in town for this book signing, traffic duty was high priority. As he entered, Irina Duval waved a cheery hello. "Morning, Nate—cookies by the coffee pot."

"Thanks, Irina. I'll grab some later. The chief in?"

"Waiting for you." She rolled her eyes good-naturedly. "He's in a mood."

He went immediately to the chief's office and rapped on the door.

Mike Williams barked, "Come in."

"I hear we have a celebrity in town," said Nate. "Visitors will be pouring in."

Mike took a slurp of coffee from a mug. "Big pain in the ass mucky mucks. Why the hell don't they stay home?"

"What's the matter, Chief?" said Nate lightly. "You anti-business?"

"Now you sound like Lorelei," he grunted. "I've already got a call this morning from her. She's worried all the fans might riot through the bookstore when the doors open or some such crap." He gave a disbelieving snort. "Comic book dweebs—they can't tie their own shoes let alone organize a riot."

"I like comic books," said Nate with a straight face. "And I can tie my shoes."

Mike eyed him askance. "As we speak, all the respect I have for you is leached from my body."

Nate grinned. "You want me on traffic?"

"Nope." The chief's dour expression lightened. "I'm saving that pleasure for myself. I'm going to go out with my citation book and ticket all their little asses for illegal parking. You get over to Write Away now and hold Lorelei's hand. Make sure all the comic geeks play nicey-nice and stay in line."

"It's Sunday morning, Chief. The store isn't open, yet."

"Lorelei wants to open early. Apparently, these people have no lives and are already leaving nose prints on the windows in anticipation of slobbering all over their hero."

Nate hesitated before leaving.

"Something on your mind, Officer Hammond?"

asked the chief mildly.

Nate shifted on his feet. "I wondered if anything was decided at the town council meeting last night."

"About what, pray tell?" he said, innocently.

Nate blew out his cheeks in frustration. Mike clearly didn't plan to volunteer any information. He would have to wheedle every last scrap out of him. "The amended budget request," Nate prodded impatiently.

The chief frowned. "Budget request? Budget request? Why yes, I do seem to recall something being said...what was it now?" He brightened. "I remember. A new metal pooper scooper was authorized for Animal Control. The old plastic one has a crack in it."

"Wow, so funny. Seriously, you're hysterical. How does your wife put up with you?"

"Geez, that's harsh," said the chief, feigning insult. "If I'd known you were so uptight with every little thing, I never would have hired you." He cracked a grin. "Relax, Nate. The council approved the request to add a new detective. The promotion won't go into effect for a month, so don't get cocky. You're still plain old Officer Hammond." He held out his hand. "But congratulations anyway."

"Thanks, Mike." Nate shook his hand warmly. "I appreciate all you've done."

"You did all the work," he grunted. "You passed all the tests. I only approved the request. Now get the hell out of my office and back on patrol, before I regret the promotion."

On Nate's way out, the county sheriff hailed him by the coffee pot.

Nate called out a greeting. "Hi, Abby, what are you

doing here today?"

"Dropping off paperwork from the county for Mike," said Abigail Franco, pouring herself a cup. "Excuse me, but is the rumor I hear true? Officer Nate Hammond will soon be promoted to detective? I didn't think you were old enough to vote."

"I voted for you two months ago, remember? I take it Irina spilled the beans."

"Naturally. No gossip gets by her." Abby shook her head in mock despair. "Officer Nate Hammond a detective...I'll have to speak to Mike about that. Coldwater Bay has certainly gone downhill since I ran for sheriff. Of course, you realize it's required that all new detectives spring for a round of drinks for the old-timers. You are old enough to drink, aren't you? We could go for ice cream instead."

"Gee, you are as seriously funny as Mike. Sure you want your constituents to see you in a bar?"

Abby shrugged and said cheerfully, "Think they're going to give me any lip? I carry a gun, you know." She grabbed her coffee cup and started toward the chief's office. "Don't forget those drinks, Hammond."

Whistling, Nate headed into the cold. Instead of scattered flurries, large lacy flakes now fluttered from the overcast sky. He rounded the corner to Main and even from the other end of the block spotted the crowd. Lorelei hadn't exaggerated. At least thirty people, shivering and stamping their feet, stood in a line outside Write Away. Many were parents shepherding pre-teens. Most clutched either comic books or packages of action figures. Nate politely edged past the queue and knocked on the glass. Lorelei hurried over. She shut the door behind him, eyeing the crowd with sympathy.

"I thought the plan was to open early," said Nate. "It's damn cold to force all those kids to wait outside."

"I can't," she whispered. "Debolt is making a big stink. He thought he was going to some mega-chain bookstore and wants to leave. He insists his time is more valuable than a side trip to Coldwater Bay. He's probably right," she admitted. "The truth is I only carry a few comic books for the kids, but man, I couldn't turn down a signing opportunity from someone like him. I only got the call from his assistant yesterday. All I had time to do was blitz social media, but look at the crowd. Word traveled fast." As they spoke, a dozen more people joined the end of the line. "I can't turn them away. A lot are bound to buy something once I let them in. It's off season, Nate. I need the business."

A man's heated voice carried from the rear of the store. "What the hell were you thinking dragging me to the middle of nowhere in this weather? Your ass is so fired."

"Poor girl," said Lorelei to Nate. "She's trying to calm him down right now."

"Want me to use my gun on him?" he asked in jest.

"Would you? Okay, probably not the best move. Come with me and help convince Debolt to stay so I can open the door and prevent any deaths from overexposure." Before Nate could object, Lorelei grabbed him by the arm and led him to the back.

A meticulously dressed man stood by the rear door. His red complexion resulted more from anger then any time spent in the biting cold. Nate immediately recognized Debolt as the driver of the expensive sports car. His companion stood behind him, blocked from view. Delicate hands had a firm grip on his sleeves.

10

Every time Debolt tried to shrug on his coat, she yanked it off his shoulders.

"Quit it," he snapped. "I'm leaving."

"No, you're not," said the woman. "You owe me this one, and you know it. So stop acting like a spoiled two year old or I swear to God I'll hogtie you to a chair and smack you silly."

Nate inhaled sharply. It had been years, but even the passage of time couldn't dull the determined timber of Libby Parish's voice.

Lorelei cleared her throat. "Excuse me, Mr. Debolt. Quite a line has already formed."

"You hear that, Payton?" said Libby. "Your adoring public awaits."

Debolt shot an irritated glance in Nate's direction. "Going to arrest me if I leave?" Libby suddenly appeared from around Debolt. She peered at Nate with a bemused expression.

For a moment, Nate found it difficult to draw a breath. He tore his gaze from Libby. "No," he said, "but I will politely ask you to stay. It's very cold and starting to snow. Lorelei wants to let everyone inside. A lot of kids are in line. I don't want to have to call in medical help for anyone." Nate decided a little white lie was appropriate. "Reporters and a photographer from *The Coldwater Bay Times* are waiting, too."

"I can read the social media feeds, now," chimed in Libby. "Payton Debolt abandons fans. Dozens of innocent children dead from overexposure. Even I can't help you smooth over a PR nightmare that big."

"Oh, all right," growled Debolt. "Elizabeth, I need coffee."

"Coming right up, Payton," Libby purred.

"I'll bring you both a cup," offered Lorelei. "The signing table is right over there."

Without a word, Libby grabbed Debolt by the arm and dragged him off. Lorelei did a little happy dance. "Finally," she said, heading for the door. "I'm going to open."

Nate's gaze followed Libby. She hadn't uttered a word to him and must not have remembered her old neighbor. It was just as well. What would a small town cop and a big city girl possibly have in common now?

Lorelei ushered in the crowd. More people had gathered, and the line eventually wove through the entire store. Nate ambled around. No riots. No pushing and shoving. Everyone was polite and well-behaved. It was going to be a long boring day.

By and by, he neared the signing table and cast a stealthy gaze over the crowd searching for Libby's curls. To his disappointment she was nowhere to be seen. Debolt probably sent her outside to brush the snowflakes off his car. How could she stand working for such an arrogant ass?

He half-expected to see Payton Debolt spitting on the masses, but to his surprise, the guest of honor had a wellspring of effusive charm stored in some hidden compartment. What a change from earlier. Debolt now flashed a charismatic smile at each adoring fan, signing his name with a felt tip flourish on the comic books and action figure packages clutched in their hands. Nate scrutinized his oily effusiveness with disapproval. What was that thing in his pocket? It resembled a fancy capped fountain pen. Why the hell would someone carry a pen and not use it? Who brought one to a signing just for show?

Debolt lapped up every bit of praise although he saved the most dazzling smiles for the few giggly twenty-something females in line. Nate snorted in disgust at his metrosexual perfection. He would bet a month's salary Debolt's manicured nails had never done a lick of manual labor.

Nate had enough. He wandered toward the front door to make another sweep through the store. The line continued to move smoothly, and he stifled a sigh. Boooring...his envy grew for Chief Williams in the cold, writing parking tickets.

He passed a stack of romance novels by Lorelei Del Fuego. The owner of Write Away had penned several bodice rippers. The latest, *Unhallowed Yearning,* was prominently displayed. The scantily dressed couple on the cover clung tight to each other. The hero's jaw jutted out, his hair tousled by an invisible wind. The heroine's eyes were wide, her mouth half-open. Her expression reminded Nate of a freshly caught mackerel. Rumor had it Lorelei based her characters on locals. Curious, Nate turned the book over and read the blurb on the back cover. *Passion forged his sword. Desire enflamed their hearts.* He snorted. That made no damn sense, not to mention sounding like the loving couple needed to be rushed to the ER.

Movement out the window caught Nate's eye. With gloved hands clutched tight around her collar, Cordelia Templeton pressed hard against the wind. More than likely the middle-aged woman was on the way to her real estate office. Nothing much slowed her down. Her son had recently joined the family business after his father passed away, but Nate was certain Bryce had more sense than to fight the elements on a day when no potential customers would likely drop by. He was probably staying toasty with his new squeeze, passion forging his sword.

Cordelia glanced at Nate. Her gaze went to the romance novel in his hand, and she raised an eyebrow. Flustered, he stuffed it in the rack.

Nate wandered toward the comic book display in the corner. He hadn't read one in a while. Out of curiosity, he selected the most recent edition of the Refractor's adventures and thumbed through the pages. There was the illuminated hero in skintight spandex tights fighting evil with Princess Arabella at his side. Her royal highness' costume didn't leave much to the imagination with boobs barely in check. How the hell could any male stand next to her in that outfit and not have a visible boner? Seriously, under all that glow Refractor must be a eunuch.

Nate flipped to the end where a fight with Mega Mole ended with a massive explosion. A woman in a police uniform announced Mega Mole and his associate Time Bomb were dead, along with a dozen innocent bystanders. Refractor had vanished. The suggestion was guilt would drive him from the city forever. Nate made a wry face. Who said guys didn't like soap operas? Comic books had melodrama in spades.

Holding the flimsy book in his hands released a flood of pleasant memories from the summer before ninth grade. In those days, given even the slightest opportunity, Nate would head for the big maple bordering Frenchman's Creek—a blissful sanctuary during a turbulent time in his life. A thirteen-year-old boy couldn't ask for a better place to idle away a few stolen hours with a pile of comic books.

Another image came to mind...that girl down the street with the wild curls, and the flash of anger in her teenage eyes when she discovered he had swiped her notebook.

"Nathan Hammond...my, my how you've grown."

Jerked back to reality, Nate turned around, and the years melted away. There she was—the little tomboy with the freckles sprinkled across the bridge of her nose. Only now, with her coat off, all the body parts he had remembered as flat were delightfully well-rounded. Color rose to his cheeks, once again the bashful schoolboy. "I didn't think you recognized me."

Libby regarded him with amusement. "How could I forget those dimples? Although, I seem to recall towering over you instead of the other way around. Glad to see you've been eating your vegetables."

"Glad to see you finally got rid of the braces, Libby," he teased. Nate's eyes unconsciously glanced at her left hand—no engagement or wedding ring. His smile widened.

She chuckled. "Oh, Lord, you would remember my crooked teeth...and no one's called me Libby in years."

"They should. It suits you better than Elizabeth."

"It's a kid's name. I'm not a kid anymore." A wistful expression passed so quickly over her face Nate assumed he had imagined it. "I see other things have changed in Coldwater Bay," she said, her good humor returning. "Lorelei is new. She seems vaguely familiar, though."

"Her aunt used to own the store. Lorelei has a family resemblance."

"Speaking of family how's your mom?" Her voice

softened. "Is everything okay with her now?"

Nate's heart warmed. She had remembered. "Yeah, she beat the cancer. She and Dad are both retired. They spend the winters in Florida near my sister and her husband and kids and return to Coldwater Bay in the summer. How are your folks?"

"Both remarried with new families and no longer shouting obscenities at each other...speaking of sunny personalities, I saw Florence Peevey is still gifted."

"Some things never change."

Libby motioned out the window at the swirling flakes. "Would you really have called in a medical alert for locals in a little bitty snowstorm? They're made of tougher stuff. Most of them probably don't even realize winter is here, yet. They would have laughed you out of Coldwater Bay."

His shrugged. "Debolt didn't know that."

She flashed a wicked grin. "Isn't it strange neither a reporter nor photographer from *The Coldwater Bay Times* has made an appearance? Someone who didn't know better would think Officer Hammond was a big fat fibber."

Nate plastered on an innocent look. "I could have sworn I saw Kristie Williams standing outside." He replaced the comic in the rack and motioned to the signing table. "You like working for him? He's kind of a prick."

"I know how to handle Payton," Libby said firmly. "This gig is a career maker for me."

"He doesn't treat you very well." The harshness of his tone came as a surprise to him, but Libby seemed unfazed.

"It's only business, Nate. I won't work with Payton

forever. Meanwhile, I'm making all sorts of important contacts. With the money I earn, I'll eventually be able to start my own PR firm."

"Making other people successful." As soon as the words were out, Nate wished he could reel them in.

Her shoulders stiffened. "It's a good living. I make more money in a year than you will in three."

Nate immediately backpedaled. "I'm sorry. I only meant you once had other dreams."

"That was a long time ago," Libby said sharply, "and neither of us are kids anymore. We grow up and get busy with real life."

Lorelei joined them. "Excuse me, Elizabeth, I got a call from *The Coldwater Bay Times*. Kristie Williams is on the way over to do a front page article on Mr. Debolt."

"I'll let Payton know." Libby ushered Lorelei away without as much as a goodbye to Nate.

He let out a curse under his breath. "Wow, that went really well. You're such a tool."

Despite the storm, legions of fans continued their orderly trek into Write Away. A short time later, someone at the door called out a cheerful greeting to Nate over the sea of heads. He spotted Mike's daughter, Kristie Williams, stomping her snow-covered boots at the door.

"Hey, Kristie, how's it going?"

"Cold," she said, blowing on her hands. "So we got us a real celebrity?"

"Payton Debolt thinks so."

"Judging from your less than enthusiastic tone," she said with mock horror, "he's not in awe of Coldwater Bay."

"The only thing he's in awe of is himself."

Kristie motioned to the camera bag slung over her shoulder. She had double duty as the newspaper's photographer. "Don't worry. I'll make his picture so pretty he'll be filled with undying gratitude for even setting his big toe in our fair town."

"Excuse me."

Nate turned around. Libby stood behind him. She introduced herself to Kristie and offered to take her directly to Payton. She didn't look once at Nate. He stifled a sigh.

As Kristie was led way, she turned to Nate and flashed a smile. "Don't forget our big date on Saturday." She let out an exuberant squeal. "I can't believe it's finally here. Cancel on me and you're dead meat."

"A zombie apocalypse couldn't keep me from your door." The past several weeks Kristie had been organizing a surprise party for her boyfriend, Dr. Logan Emory, a resident at the local hospital. Nate hoped the weather improved by then. Kristie was Type A to the max, planning events to the minutia. The word "reschedule" was not in her vocabulary, so a blizzard wouldn't stop the party. Even Nate's zombie apocalypse comment was only half in jest. If necessary, Kristie would stand on the front porch with a shotgun clearing a path for the caterers through the undead.

The door opened once more. A gust of snow blew in with the police chief. Mike scanned the orderly crowd with approval. He waved hello to his daughter and then with a satisfied grunt, ordered Nate to assist him on the streets. "The storm's developing into a real blizzard," he said. "Already got power outages on the north end of Main. The streetlight is out at the Center Street intersection, and I need you there to direct traffic. After it's working again, head to the station."

Nate shot a disappointed glance toward the signing table. He had hoped to speak with Libby and offer an apology before she left, maybe even talk her into dinner. He trudged down Main, his mood as gloomy as the weather. At the Center Street intersection, a utility crew was busy at work on a nearby transformer. Nate kept traffic moving smoothly. After the signal was running again, he returned to the police station.

The rest of the day, he answered emergency calls. A few times, Nate managed to cruise along Main Street past Write Away. He even once made it as far as the curb, hoping to run in and catch a quick word with Libby, but before Nate shut off the engine, he was summoned by Irina to respond to another call. It was nearly dark by the time he circled around to the store. A Closed sign perched in the window. Debolt's expensive sports car was no longer in its parking spot.

Too Late Nate struck out again.

Chapter Two

"Want some overtime?" asked Chief Williams after Nate finally returned to the station. "Everyone has settled in for the storm by now, but I'd like to keep an extra man on duty in case something unexpected happens."

"Sure," said Nate. "I've got nothing going on." He glanced out the window. "It sure blew in fast."

"Tell me about it. Seems like the blizzard came out of nowhere. Even the weathermen scratched their heads. All their reports predicted only a few flurries." He motioned to the door. "Grab something to eat while the phones are quiet."

"I'll call in an order to O'Reilly's before they close. Connor will probably shut down early. You want something?"

"Nope. Tania already dropped off dinner."

"Your wife is too good for you."

"Don't I know it," he said with a grin.

Nate trudged through the snow to O'Reilly's. Irina met him at the door on his return. "Sorry, Nate. A call came in from Raymond Quinn at the Breezy Point Inn on a missing guest. Ray's steamed. He figures the guy is probably banging one of the overnighters, but the girlfriend is making a stink. The chief wants you to check it out."

He handed her the take-out bag. "No problem. Eat

and enjoy. I don't have much of an appetite anyway."

"Be careful," she called. "It's nasty out there."

Nate got in the squad car and made his way slowly through the now empty streets to the Breezy Point Inn. As he drove along, the windshield wipers beat a furious tattoo clearing off the blowing snow. Lucky for him the SUV had four-wheel drive. Judging by the appearance of the streets already, he'd need it to return to the station. The plows in town wouldn't be able to keep up with this mess.

Over a dozen cars were in Breezy Point's parking lot, an unusual number for this time of year since Coldwater Bay was largely known as a summer resort. More than one comic fan must have decided not to chance the drive through the storm. Nate went directly to see Raymond Quinn. The middle-aged owner's office was right off the lobby. The door was open. Raymond sat at his desk. The tight lines on his brow signaled a man trying hard to hide exasperation. Bobbie, his wife and business partner, stood off to the side with an inscrutable expression.

Nate's heart skipped a beat. Libby perched in a neighboring chair, arms folded across her chest. Nate recognized the stance. Although seemingly calm and self-possessed, she was the equivalent of a human Mt. Vesuvius on the verge of an eruption.

"Libby?" he asked. "What's going on?"

"Nate?" She jumped up. "Thank God you're here. Something is wrong. Payton is missing. I can't get anyone to search for him."

"I've tried to explain," said Raymond, shifting in his seat. "I'm certain Mr. Debolt is somewhere in the inn. No one would wander outside in this weather. Even the interstate is closed. His car is in the parking lot. Several young ladies from the autograph session earlier booked rooms for the night instead of chancing the storm." His face reddened. "Mr. Debolt was most attentive to them at the bar." Bobbie bit her lip as if to keep from smiling.

"He's not with a girl," said Libby hotly.

Irina's descriptive phrase concerning a guest's girlfriend making a stink slapped Nate in the head. Had he totally misjudged Libby and Debolt's relationship? Was she involved with him? A sour feeling grew in the pit of his stomach. "What makes you so certain?"

"His cell phone is gone," said Libby. In response to Nate's bewilderment, she blurted out. "He never goes anywhere without it. It's still in his room."

"Couldn't he have simply forgotten to take it?"

"Not a chance. I swear he'd have it surgically implanted on his body, if he could."

No phone. Didn't wish to be disturbed. Nate sided with Raymond and dropped Libby a hint. "Perhaps he simply wanted some quiet time."

"Not a chance. He always picks up when I call, even if he's in the bathroom." She rolled her eyes. "You should hear some of the sounds I've had to shout over."

"If he's with a guest…" Nate cleared his throat. "A female guest?"

She bristled. "He's not."

Damn it, why was she was so insistent? Did they have a thing? A wave of intense dislike for Debolt washed over him like a tsunami.

"Please, Nate," Libby beseeched. "I've got a really bad feeling something happened to Payton. Will you help me look?"

"Perhaps," said Raymond, "you could assist Ms. Parish in her search without intruding on the other guests." His voice was low-key, but his body language practically begged.

Nate made a mental translation. *Please, get this woman out of my hair. When you find Debolt knocking knees with a fan girl, dear God, don't let her make a scene.* "Libby," Nate said, "why don't I go with you to Debolt's room and see if we can spot anything out of order?" The appearance of gratitude on the faces of both Libby and Raymond were quite satisfying. Bobbie bit her lip again.

Nate followed Libby upstairs to the Neptune Suite, the largest room in the inn. "I went to mine after dinner," said Libby. Nate's heart gave a leap. She and Debolt had separate rooms. "I told Payton I'd keep apprised of the weather," Libby continued, "and give him an update if we had to make schedule changes on the rest of the signing tour. It's odd now that I think back," she said with a frown. "Usually Payton throws a hissy with schedule changes, but he told me not to bother him for the rest of the night, and he'd see me in the morning."

"Why did you go to his room then?" asked Nate. He crossed his fingers, drumming out a mental wish. *It was only business…it was only business.*

"The weather got worse," said Libby. "I was afraid we wouldn't get out tomorrow, either. Payton had already given me a hard time over the last minute detour to Coldwater Bay."

"It was your idea?" said Nate.

Libby flustered, color rising to her cheeks. "I thought…well…it might be nice to see the old place again. Anyway, I didn't feel like waiting until morning to deliver the bad news, so I called, but the phone went to voicemail. I texted and no response. I thought maybe he wasn't getting a signal, so I tried the house phone in his room—nothing. Then I got worried so I ran down and knocked, but he didn't answer. The room was unlocked. I went in and Payton was gone."

Nate opened the door. The suite was undisturbed; nautical prints hung straight on the wall, blue silk curtains drawn, and every piece of furniture spotless. The bed hadn't been slept in. Debolt's wallet, car keys, cell phone, and room key lay on the nightstand. Nate frowned. "The door was unlocked?"

"Yes, but nothing is missing except his coat and don't even suggest he went out for a walk—not Mr. Squishy Southern California. Not in this weather."

Squishy...she called him squishy. She's definitely not sleeping with him. The sour feeling in the pit of his stomach vanished. "You know all his personal items?" Nate asked innocently.

"I should. I pack for him. I went through his suitcase. All his clothes are there including his underwear."

Damn. How close were they? Nate checked the wallet and raised an eyebrow as he made a rough count of the bills. "Not a robbery. Debolt has over a thousand bucks in here plus credit cards. Does he always carry so much cash?"

"Uh-huh. He loves flashing it around." Libby drew in a breath. "You don't think he was kidnapped, do you?"

Only by some half-drunk groupie hoping to score with Mr. Personality. "Doubtful. I don't see a ransom note, and why leave all this money?" He peeked into the bathroom. Men's toiletries were neatly laid in a row on the counter. "He has a monogramed toothbrush?"

Libby shot him a look full of wicked amusement. "They're fifty bucks apiece made from special bristles off a wild boar's rear end, or some crap like that. Payton swears it massages his gums."

"Fifty bucks for a toothbrush? That's crazy."

"Hey, we're dealing with a guy who can afford diamond encrusted toilet paper."

She is definitely not sleeping with him. Is she sleeping with anyone? Nate forced his mind on the job. "Did you notice anything strange at Write Away? Anyone loitering in the store who looked out of place?"

"Nobody hung around. People hurried home after the storm worsened. Lorelei told me the interstate closed, so I booked rooms at Breezy Point. Payton was the only one acting weird," she said with a puzzled frown. "He wasn't upset at all when we had to stay overnight in Coldwater Bay. After I hung up the phone, I found him toying with his pen by the Refractor display. He wore this strange, almost triumphant, expression. He immediately hustled me out of the store and seemed even more excessively pleased with himself than usual. I asked what was going on. All he said was that he was happy with the turnout." She glanced at the items on the nightstand. "That's funny. I don't see his pen."

"Pen?"

"A special fountain pen he always carries—you know the old-fashioned kind with the cap. Payton says it's his good luck charm, although I've never seen him use it. Actually, I've never even seen it with the cover off, but it's always on him. He had it today at the signing."

"I remember," said Nate. "It was in his pocket."

"He's totally anal with it; even more so than his cell phone. He never lets anyone touch it, even me. Can't you put out a what-do-you-call-it, an APB for Payton or something?"

"Not this soon, unless I see signs of foul play. There's no evidence of a struggle and, according to you, the only thing missing is a pen. I admit it's a little strange he left the room unlocked, but nothing is out of order, all his money and his car keys are here. Debolt is a grown man with no medical conditions. Isn't it more likely he shacked up in some lady's room?"

"Not without his—"

"I know, I know. Not without his cell phone."

"Please, Nate. I can't shake the feeling something is wrong."

Nate considered the options. Chief Williams would have a fit if his officer wasted valuable police time in a wild goose chase when he should be dealing with real emergencies, but Mike Williams didn't have pleading brown eyes. "I tell you what. Why don't you come with me, and we'll take a walk around the inn and ask if anyone has seen him?"

"Thank you, thank you!" Libby gave him an impulsive hug. She pulled back, flustered, but not before a pleasantly warm sensation traveled through Officer Hammond.

Before long they completed a full circuit. The comic book fans who booked rooms were still in the bar. To Nate's surprise no one had seen Debolt for several hours. It was as if he left the bar alone and vanished into the night. Nate retreated with Libby to the reception area by the front door. He peered out the window with growing unease. The grounds were pitch black. The only sound was the howling wind and the *tick-tick-tick* of ice crystals hitting the window. No one but a fool or a desperate person would be out tonight.

"Thanks for your time, Nate," Libby said with obvious disappointment. "I'm sure he'll turn up. Payton must be in someone's room."

"Yeah." A knot of anxiety tightened in his gut as he gazed out the window. Something was wrong. Despite continued reservations over Debolt's supposed disappearance, the whole situation didn't smell right.

Libby gasped. "You don't think Payton is outside?"

"His coat was missing." Nate drew his collar tight and took out a flashlight. "Wait here."

The brutal cold wind smacked him in the face, stealing his breath. Nate hunched over, pressing forward against the frigid gale and played his light across the yard—nothing but an unbroken layer of white snow. He trudged along the side of the building to the rear door cursing Debolt, and his own flawed instincts. "Son of a bitch," he muttered. "He's probably tucked in bed with some double-D fan-girl right now, sucking up gin from the minibar, and watching porn on cable."

As Nate approached the door, he put his foot down and nearly slipped on a patch of ice. Regaining his footing, the beam from the flashlight highlighted a series of regular indentations in the snow. "Son of a bitch." The footsteps led into a wooded area and down a hill. If they continued in the same direction, they'd intersect with the road into town.

"Debolt!" he yelled, shining the beam through the trees. "Payton Debolt! Can you hear me?" Only the howling wind responded. Drifting snow slowly blurred the mysterious footprints to indistinct shapes. Within a short time, they'd fill completely. Nate trudged to the parking lot to continue the search with the squad car. Along with four-wheel drive it had a powerful spotlight.

Libby stood by the front door, now bundled in her coat with a thin pencil flashlight clutched in her hand. She waved the small tight beam toward him. "Did you find anything?" she shouted over the wind.

"Footsteps from the rear leading to town."

"Oh my God," she cried out in horror. "What was he thinking?"

"I'm going to take the squad car and follow the trail."

"I'll come with you. Two sets of eyes are better than one."

Nate offered no objection. They got into the SUV. He turned on the engine and blasted the heater.

"I'd forgotten how cold the winters here can be," said Libby through chattering teeth.

Nate took her gloved hands between his, rubbing her fingers gently. "It will be warm in a minute...better?"

"Better." Libby chuckled. "A few years away and I've turned into a total wuss."

"It's good to have you back, Lib." Nate's voice dropped. His grip on her fingers increased. "I missed you."

A flash of something resembling regret passed over

her expression. Libby pulled her hands away and wiped off the condensation on the inside of the window. "Where could that idiot have possibly gone in this weather?"

"Not far," said Nate grimly. Libby responded with a stricken look. "I mean, I'm sure we'll find him soon," he offered as reassurance. "He probably got no farther than O'Reilly's Restaurant and called it quits."

"Why didn't he take his cell phone? He could have called for help…" Libby's voice trailed away. She peered out the window, distraught.

Nate reached over and squeezed her arm. "We'll find him."

Her gaze stayed fixed on the snow-covered landscape. "Thanks, Nate. I'm glad you're here."

So am I. Nate pulled out of the parking spot and headed to town. He drove at a crawl, scanning the landscape, and gave Libby the searchlight. She turned off the pencil light and placed it in her lap and then played the searchlight out the window. They reached the end of the Breezy Point Inn's driveway with no sign of Debolt.

Suddenly, Libby sat up straight. "Over there!"

The searchlight illuminated a distinct line of footprints coming from the woods. Nate followed, scrutinizing the area for any sign of Debolt. The trail led to Main Street, the now nearly-filled impressions growing more difficult to see by the minute.

As they got to Center Street, the footprints disappeared, buried in the snow. Nate made a right turn into the tourist district. The street was lined with bars and restaurants popular with out-of-towners. He scoured the block, but every building was buttoned up tight against the storm. The parking lots were empty, not a single car sat at the curb. Even O'Reilly's was dark. If Debolt made it here, he found no shelter.

Nate circled the block and turned on Main. "I'm going to the police station," he told Libby. "The trail is gone. We need more searchers. By now, all the locals are inside riding out the weather. No one would have seen Debolt pass by—"

"What's that?" Libby pointed ahead. Even through the blowing snow, a faint glow was visible.

"It looks like a light is on at Write Away," said Nate.

He parked at the curb. They stumbled through the drifts to the front door. Nate tried the handle. It turned freely. The interior of the store was dark except for one spot. A faint green glow illuminated the corner by the comic book display. The spotty power outages must have tripped an emergency light.

Little hairs on the nape of Nate's neck rose to attention. "Go to the car," he barked. "It's not like Lorelei to leave the door open. I'll check it out."

Libby followed, clutching the pencil light tightly in her hand. "No way. I'm coming with you. Payton may need help."

"Libby—"

"Unless you handcuff me to the car, I'm coming."

"Don't tempt me."

She shivered. "Can we please shut the door before we freeze to death?"

He hesitated only a second. "Stay behind me." Nate activated the radio and called the station. "Possible break-in at Write Away—" The only response was a static hiss. He swore under his breath, the raised hairs on his neck had now been joined by the incessant clanging of a mental alarm bell. Nate rested his hand lightly on his gun. He held his flashlight in his other hand and played it around the interior of the store. Nothing moved. Libby tried to brush ahead, but Nate grabbed her arm. "I told you to stay behind me."

"Payton may be hurt."

Libby was right. If Debolt had wandered this far through the storm, he was probably half-dead from exposure. The building offered shelter, but Debolt would need medical treatment pronto. Minutes counted in this weather. "All right, but stay behind me...Coldwater Bay Police!" he shouted. "Is anyone in here?"

"Payton," called Libby. "It's me. Where are you?"

The building was silent with the exception of a faint hum now emanating from the glow in the corner. Nate moved cautiously forward, shining the flashlight. "Debolt?" No one answered. "We'll check the rest of the store...Libby?"

Libby had stepped from his side, her attention drawn elsewhere. She stood in front of the display stand filled with comic books. Her respiration sharply increased. "What is that?" she asked. The eerie glow came directly from one of the books.

Nate's gaze widened. "I've no idea." The glow began to fluctuate, pulsing with a bright green neon light.

Libby squinted at the glare. She leaned in as if striving to discern the cover. "It's the latest Refractor issue. Why is it doing that?" On and off, on and off, the hypnotic beat flashed.

The light was oddly attractive. "It's not some

marketing gimmick?" Nate asked.

"No way," insisted Libby. "I've never seen anything like it."

The tempo of the pulses increased, so did the hum. A little voice in Nate's head bleated a warning. *This isn't normal. You should do something...do something...do something.* His thoughts muddled with the incessant flash. The hand which had been resting on the gun, dropped to his side.

Libby clutched the pencil light to her chest. As if drawn by an irresistible impulse, the other hand reached for the Refractor comic.

Nate's confusion vanished, shoved aside by a powerful protective urge. "Libby, don't! It might be dangerous." He grabbed her arm at the same time she touched the comic. For an instant, the world turned to green light.

Then total blackness enveloped them.

Chapter Three

Nate groaned. His eyelids fluttered open. Why did blinking hurt? Blinking shouldn't hurt. What the hell had happened? Scattered memories fluttered into his fogged brain. He was in Write Away. He saw a green light.

Libby...

Despite the pain, Nate opened his eyes. A bright beam forced them shut again. He grimaced and reached out his hand for the flashlight. He forced himself to his knees, nearly heaving as a wave of nausea swept over him. Nate's heart raced at the sight of the body huddled on the floor, one hand clutching a pencil light.

"Libby?" He felt for a pulse nearly crying out in relief at the strong steady beat.

"Nate?" She groaned. "Damn."

"Yeah, I know. Take it slow."

"What happened?"

"I'm not sure." He helped Libby to her feet and placed an arm around her shoulders. "The last thing I remember is that weird light. You okay?"

Libby drew in a breath and ran a shaky hand through her hair. "I've got a helluva headache, but am still in one piece. You?"

"The same."

She leaned her head against his chest. Without conscious thought, Nate pulled her close.

For several seconds, he reveled in contented silence until Libby gasped and took a step toward a nearby display. She gaped in astonishment. "I don't remember postcards. Where are the comics?"

The stand with comic books was gone. In its place was a circular rotating rack full of postcards. A few had pictures of buildings he didn't recognize.

Nate's mouth dropped open. "Not possible. That light must have done something weird to us. At least it's gone now."

"Payton—?"

"I'll call it in. We'll do a thorough search, but need medical personnel immediately." He activated his radio. "Dispatch, this is Hammond, come in. Irina, you there?" His spirits lifted when instead of the static hiss, he heard the reassuring crackle of a connection.

A long string of profanities erupted from the receiver. "Who the hell is on this line?" Irina barked.

Nate's spirits took an immediate nosedive. What was with her? "Irina?" He glanced at Libby with embarrassment. "It's me, Nate...Officer Hammond."

"Who the hell is that?" Another string of profanities unleashed. "This line is for official SCC business only."

SCC? What the hell was that?

"Sign off immediately," snarled Irina, "or I will hunt you down and shoot your ass dead."

Libby regarded him, bemused. "How long have you worked there?"

A faint pink color rose to his cheeks. "Irina, I need to speak to the chief. Is Mike nearby?"

Irina's voice rose to a screech. "You think that's funny? You are dead, ass-wipe. You are so dead."

"What's wrong with her?" whispered Libby.

"I don't know," said Nate, flustered. "She's never acted this way—"

"Who is that with you?" Irina demanded. "She's dead, too. Where the hell are you calling from?"

"I'm at…" Nate faltered. A knot of apprehension gripped his gut. He severed the connection.

"Why didn't you tell her where we were?" asked Libby.

How could Nate explain the growing edginess he didn't understand? "Let's get to the station and find out what's going on." He led her by the arm to the exit.

"What about Payton?"

Nate gritted his teeth. His head continued to pound, and he was growing deathly sick of hearing that name. "We'll come back for precious Payton," he snapped, the words unintentionally sharp.

Libby stiffened. "Was Irina a bad break-up?" she said coolly. "You want to stop for flowers?"

"She's like fifty," Nate sputtered in annoyance, "and married. We work together, is all."

"A woman doesn't get that miffed because you forgot to clean the breakroom coffee pot."

They reached the front door. Glowering, Nate yanked it open and ushered Libby ahead. "It must be Irina's idea of a joke—"

Libby froze on the threshold. "Where's the snow?" Her voice was barely above a whisper.

Nate walked outside in stunned disbelief. Not a single flake marked the ground. The brilliant light of a full moon shone down as a gust of balmy air brushed across his cheek. "It's not possible," he stammered. "Nearly a foot of snow had fallen." He walked to the curb as if in a trance. "My squad car is gone." He scrutinized the street in all directions. That wasn't the only obvious difference.

Next to Write Away was Cara Tyson Jewelry Design. Between the quaint converted bungalow and Frenchman's Creek was a public parking lot.

Only it wasn't.

Libby gulped. "Didn't that lot have a bunch of parking meters in it a few minutes ago?"

Cara Tyson Jewelry Design was in the same location, but the parking lot had disappeared, the grounds now surrounded by a black wrought iron fence. In one corner was a large oak tree dressed in leafy summer attire. It grew proudly erect as if it had always stood sentinel.

The fenced area enclosed a cobblestone plaza. In the center a fountain stood tall, made from an obelisk of polished black granite with a brass bowl affixed to the top. Water spilled from the bowl and trickled down the monument's sides leaving streaky tear-like marks. Carved in its surface was a dedication. A floodlight illuminated the inscription: Michael Williams Memorial Plaza, Rest in Peace Ever Faithful Guardian of Justice.

Libby gasped. "It can't be."

"Impossible," Nate whispered. The wrought iron fence was hard and cool to the touch. *Not a dream.*

A police siren wailed in the distance. From the far end of Main Street, a squad car with flashing lights rounded the corner. Nate grabbed Libby's arm and ushered her inside Write Away. "Get down," he hissed.

Without a word, she hunkered against a bookshelf. Nate pressed flat to the wall. As the siren approached, they both dared a peek. A modified black and white

SUV barreled past the window. The full moon clearly illuminated the Coldwater Bay logo on the side door panel, but underneath the words read *Second Chance City Police Department.* The modified machine gun turret on the roof was also new.

Nate gaped at the retreating squad car. Machine gun? Second Chance City? Why did that name ring a bell? "What the hell is going on?" he sputtered. "Any ideas, Libby? I'm open to suggestions, because trust me, I'm totally out."

Libby didn't answer. She leaned against the wall, her complexion pale, gazing blankly out the window. She turned to him and swallowed hard. "How open are you to the kind of ideas that get people sent to nice padded rooms?"

Nate gave a shaky laugh. "Checking into a mental hospital sounds pretty good right now."

"Okay then..." She took a deep breath. "I think we've been sucked into the Refractor comic book."

"Say what now?"

"Refractor lives in Second Chance City."

"That's why the name sounds familiar." Nate gave her the eye. "People don't get sucked into comic books."

Libby gestured outside. "The memorial next door is identical to the one Payton drew in the comic for the police chief. I mean absolutely identical, right down to the scrollwork on the wrought iron fence and the oak tree near the fountain. Even the inscription is the same. Citizens donated funds to construct the plaza as a tribute after the chief was murdered by Time Bomb in Issue 21: Countdown to Doom."

Nate took off his hat and ran a shaky hand through

his close-cropped hair. "The chief in Second Chance City was Mike Williams?"

"Not exactly," she admitted hesitantly. "In the comic, he was referred to as Michael."

"Mike, Michael, what's the difference?" Nate sputtered.

"I don't know," Libby asserted in annoyance. "Anyway, he wasn't a real person. Second Chance City wasn't a real place. At least, I never thought so. Besides, the name is common. There must be a million Michael Williams in the country. I never thought of Chief Williams in Coldwater Bay. I didn't even remember his first name."

"How about Write Away?"

"Definitely not mentioned. Payton never wrote a bookstore into the series. He never wrote Breezy Point Inn, either. He kept to a straight cast of characters and locations. I wanted him to expand, but he never would." Libby waved her arm around the room. "All this...it's like we're in this weird mash-up of the two. Well, that's my crazy theory. Have you got a better idea?"

"Head trauma? CIA mind control experiments?" Would either explain the bizarre conversation with Irina, and the extraordinary change in the weather? Except for a lingering headache, Nate felt perfectly normal. He pinched himself.

"Did you just pinch yourself?" asked Libby.

He shifted on his feet. "Maybe."

"Did it hurt?"

"Yes."

Libby snorted out a wry chuckle. "Must not be a hallucination, then. Darn, I was rooting for head trauma." She held out her wrists. "Nevertheless, I volunteer to be cuffed and taken to a nice padded cell."

"Tempting, but I'll save the cuffs for a last resort." His lips twitched in a slight smile. "I don't remember you being this much trouble when we were kids."

"Trouble? Me?" Libby grasped at her heart with mock insult. "Watch your back, Hammond. I can still throw a pretty mean rock."

Nate chuckled and rubbed the nape of his neck. "Now, I remember. You were always trouble." A sudden idea occurred to him. "Let's check the post card rack."

Brightly-colored cards filled the display. Nate and Libby each grabbed a handful, and Nate shined the flashlight over the photographs on the front. "All the local tourist spots are here; Coldwater Bay Lighthouse, Willow Lake, the art district, plus a few I don't recognize. Are all these in the comic book?"

"No," said Libby, "at least Payton never mentioned them." She gulped. "The newspaper is called *The Second Chance City Times*, though."

"That's too close for comfort."

Libby selected a card with a picture of the memorial plaza and read the description, "In honor of the massacre at O'Reilly's…Payton and I passed a restaurant named O'Reilly's on the way in."

"Yeah, it belongs to my friend Connor. He just opened it. Do you remember him? He went to school here…" He startled as her words sank in. "What massacre?"

Her face paled. "The location of the final fight in Refractor's last issue was at a tavern called O'Reilly's."

Nate was taken aback. "You didn't draw the connection?"

She made a disbelieving face. "Why would I? O'Reilly's in Coldwater Bay is a restaurant, and you just said Connor only opened the place a short time ago. The name O'Reilly is as common as Williams." Libby reached for a street map for sale at the top of the rack. "I wonder what else changed."

Libby spread out the map, and Nate peered over her shoulder. "Wow. Coldwater Bay sure has grown."

"Technically, it's Second Chance City," said Libby. She ran her finger down a line fronting the harbor. "There's Main Street."

"Oak Avenue, First Street, Second Street," Nate murmured. "The layout of the downtown area is exactly the same. Growth spread north, west, and south, but the streets in this area haven't changed at all. Main Street is still right outside. Peregrine Island is offshore in the same spot, too." He jabbed his finger at a large patch of development at the edge of the point. "This whole area past the docks used to be way over town limits, but now, according to the map, is incorporated land."

Libby ran her finger down the lines representing roads. "Funny how I never noticed the similarity in names. All these downtown streets; First, Second, Main, Oak, and the others. They also occur in the comic."

"That's not surprising," said Nate. "Those names are probably even more common than O'Reilly and Williams." He held the map and shook his head in disbelief. "Is Second Chance City really based on Coldwater Bay? How did Payton know?"

"You got me," said Libby, clearly dazed. "Payton never claimed the city was real, and when we drove into Coldwater Bay, I swear he didn't recognize anything. He passed right by O'Reilly's without blinking. Mostly, he was ticked because it was a small town." Her brow wrinkled in thought. "In comic books, many super heroes are headquartered in a real city or at least a stylized version of someplace like New York or Chicago. Funny," she mused. "I always had the sense Second Chance City was neither of those. Unfortunately, another thing Payton never drew was a map—Payton! I forgot all about him."

Nate stifled the irritation at the mention of his name. "We'll check the rest of the store." Nate shone his flashlight under every table and display, but found no sign of Debolt.

"He obviously isn't here," said Nate. "We should concentrate on getting home."

"I'm open to suggestions."

"Yeah, um, I don't exactly have any. Man, this reads like a comic book adventure, hero and heroine trapped in an alternate universe."

She snickered. "So we're the hero and heroine, now?"

Nate flashed a cheeky grin. "Why not? You could write them a happy ending. You've even done it before for a couple of freaks."

"Oh my God," she gasped. "I can't believe you remember that."

"Of course, I remember. How many other eighth graders actually wrote and illustrated their own comic book? *Crazy Ass Freaks*... It was a great story."

She punched him in the arm.

"Ow. What was that for?"

"For reading the notebook without my permission."

"That was over ten years ago, and, as I recall, you

got payback when you beaned me with a rock."

"It was a pebble, you big baby. You deserved it. I can't believe you turned out to be a straight arrow cop. You were such a little stinker. I was sure you'd end up in prison."

"Because I swiped your notebook?"

"Aha!" She shook her finger at him. "You said you found it."

"I may have exaggerated a little," he admitted slyly. "I couldn't help it, Lib. You drove me crazy, scribbling under that tree and refusing to show me what you wrote. I was curious, so I took the notebook from your backpack when you were distracted. The story was awesome, so were the illustrations. I couldn't put it down. I read through it five times."

His praise brought a pink tint to her cheeks. "Thanks. Just kid's stuff, though."

"It was ten times better than anything else out there. Why didn't you publish?"

She stared down at the floor. "Who'd want to read about a group of plucky eighth-graders?"

"Plucky eighth-graders," he reminded her, "serving as spies for a rebel force—the last hope of an enslaved Earth conquered by aliens. What were the code names of the kid leaders again…?" He thought for a moment. "Red and Bluecoat."

Her face lit up. "I'm flattered you remember."

"Are you kidding? The story was amazing. The aliens had all the superpowers and technology, the kids only had their brains and skills and guts to get them out of danger." He ticked off his fingers. "The writer who laid out the strategy, the kid with the slingshot, the one who did slight-of-hand, a math geek, a gamer, and all the others…where'd you get the idea?"

Libby shrugged. "Kids are perfect spies. Nobody notices them. Nobody thinks they're smart enough to understand or keep a secret." Her voice held a wistful quality. "Anyway, that's in the past. I'm done with all that."

"Can't you figure out a way to write us out of this mess?" Nate joshed. "We could use a comic book hero."

Libby started. "That's it, Nate. We have to find Refractor."

He regarded her with disbelief. "You're not serious."

"Of course, it all makes sense. If Second Chance City is real, then he must be, too. Refactor and his team are superheroes. If anybody has an idea how to send us home, it would be one of them."

"Things aren't exactly the same in this universe as in the comic book," he reminded her. "What if instead of special powers, they own a deli?"

She offered a weak smile. "We'll order two pastramis on rye and then ask if they're hiring."

"Seeing as I don't have any better ideas, let's give it a shot." Nate scratched his head. "How do we track down Refractor? Doesn't he have some sort of secret lair?"

"Yeah, all superheroes have secret lairs. Refractor's is hidden at the top of a penthouse on the waterfront."

"No penthouses on the waterfront, unless something new has been built. We'll walk down there and check it out." A sudden thought occurred to Nate. "I don't suppose we could call? Do you know the phone number for his secret identity?"

"Actually, Refractor doesn't have one. He emits a constant bright light and can bend the rays around him to veil his appearance, but only for a short while. He has to stay hidden when not out battling supervillains. I've always thought that was a major weakness in the story. Poor Refractor. A trip to the grocery store is about all he can manage. A good superhero should never lose his compassion for others, but it's hard to connect to people when circumstances in your life always keep you apart. To me, Refractor came across as cold and aloof."

"You'd have written it better," Nate stated with confidence.

Libby flashed a smile. "Yeah, I would have. I sure hated stuffing Princess Arabella into that ridiculous costume. She's the leader of a planet, for heaven's sake. She should have had some dignity, but Payton likes big boobs."

"You illustrated it?" said Nate.

She brushed off the question. "I helped with the inking once Payton saw I could draw. No big deal..." Libby frowned in thought. "Pierce Powers is an associate of Refractor. According to the comic, he is a physicist and a multi-gazillionaire owner of a dot com, so he might be in the phone book. The building where Refractor lives belongs to him."

Nate whipped out his phone. "No bars. Our cell phones must not work in this universe. Let's try the store phone." He called information, but they had no listing for either Pierce Powers or Pierce Powers, Inc. "That was a waste of time. I say we search the waterfront for this penthouse."

They doffed their coats in the balmy air outside and stuffed them out of sight under a bush in the memorial park. Libby kept a tight grip on the pencil flashlight. Nate grinned at her, and she flushed. "Well, you get to carry a gun for protection. I can at least poke someone in the eye with this if they get fresh." She waved it at him with a smirk. "So watch yourself, buster."

"Thanks for the warning," he chuckled and then glanced around, filled with sudden edginess. The sky had lightened considerably in the east. If Second Chance City was anything like Coldwater Bay, the waterfront wouldn't be empty for long.

"What's wrong?" asked Libby.

"I feel naked out in the open." He motioned to a strip of trodden ground running along the outside of the fence bordering the memorial park. "Lucky for us in this reality the path next to Frenchman's Creek is still here. We'll stay off the main roads and keep a low profile until we figure things out."

They entered the wooded area and followed the burbling water as it splashed toward the bay. "You're smiling," said Nate.

"Am I?" said Libby, bemused. "Frenchman's Creek holds good memories. When Mom and Dad got into another shouting match, this place was my escape."

"I'm sorry about your folks," said Nate. "After you left Coldwater Bay, Dad told me they divorced, and you wouldn't be back. Must have been tough."

"At least the screaming stopped. They both remarried and started other families. I got bounced between. I know they love me and I love them, but I never felt like I fit anywhere." Libby scanned the area with a slight smile as if reliving a fond memory and then abruptly let out a cry. "I can't believe it's here." She pointed to an old maple. "I used to sit under that tree when I needed time to think. It was my own secret lair…until some pesky annoying kid arrived to bug me about my writing."

"Hey, you're the one who intruded on my private fishing spot."

"Where did you come from anyway?" she protested with a chuckle. "Everyone in Coldwater Bay knew you couldn't catch fish in Frenchman's Creek."

"Florida," he said mildly. "Hey, cut me some slack, I was new in town. By the time I realized my line would always come up empty, it was too late. I couldn't get that girl with the fierce expression and headful of wild curls out of my head. What was she writing? You wouldn't show it to me so I had to swipe it. Thus began my life of crime. All your fault."

"Very short lived, I take it?" Libby said, amused.

"Yup. Right after you left, Chief Williams caught me carving on a tree. He gave a stern lecture about defacing public property and then drove me home. That's how we handle major crime waves in Coldwater Bay."

Rosy streaks colored the sky. Dawn would break any moment. They reached the end of the path and arrived at the waterfront. Libby's gaze strayed along the pier. "It's a lot like I remember," she said. "You'd know better, though."

Nate peered through the dim morning light, scrutinizing the surroundings. Similarities certainly abounded. The long public boardwalk stretched across the waterfront with the same wooden benches and planters now bursting with brightly colored flowers.

The seafood market and retail shops remained in the same spots, but the marina had tripled in size. Coldwater Bay never had million-dollar sailing yachts moored at its pier, either.

Nate and Libby wandered farther down the harbor, away from the heart of the tourist area. Fisherman on the commercial docks prepared for the day. One boat pulled from its slip. On another, several men tossed fishing gear aboard. A couple of them shot Nate a curious glance, and he hurried Libby along. His Coldwater Bay police uniform was painfully out of place.

"No penthouses," he said, eyeing a gleaming chrome-and-glass, three-story building on the waterfront. "That's different, though. Templeton Real Estate is now TIDC: Templeton International Development Corporation. Looks like business is good. Back in Coldwater Bay, the firm is run out of a converted Victorian."

"What's that place?" asked Libby. Right next to TIDC was a large bunker-like structure. A glowing neon sign on the roof said The Factory. "Didn't that used to be empty?"

"Weird," Nate murmured. "The shoe factory closed even before you left and has been vacant ever since. Last month, Cordelia Templeton and her son bought the property for a condo conversion. They'll break ground in the spring."

Libby studied the building. "I don't think the Second Chance City owners plan to make shoes."

The old boarded-up windows were gone. The entrance off the parking lot sported an elegant maroon canopy over a solid mahogany door with polished brass handles. A placard on the wall announced upcoming band performances. "The old factory is now a club," said Nate in surprise.

Libby read the placards. "Not only that. The dates for all these performances are in July. No wonder the air is warmer. We jumped a few months."

"Does this place ring any bells for you?" asked Nate.

"Not the location, for sure, but like I said Payton never drew a map of Second Chance City." She frowned. "The comic referenced several bars and nightclubs on or near the waterfront. Want to knock on the door? The light is still on. Someone may be inside. This is the type of classy place Arabella might visit. She's a princess, after all. We could ask if anyone knows how to get in touch with her."

Nate considered the exterior of the building. He spotted a security camera barely visible, affixed underneath the awning. Another one on the light pole pointed toward the parking lot. Edginess increased with the notion someone could secretly watch their movements from inside. "I don't think we should announce our arrival yet."

The headlights of a lone car turned down the access road heading their way. Nate grabbed Libby's elbow, and they jogged across to TIDC and flattened against the wall. A silver luxury sedan stopped in front of The Factory and a middle-aged woman got out. Nate recognized her immediately. "Cordelia Templeton. Wow, this is strange. She looks exactly like the one in Coldwater Bay."

Despite the early hour, Cordelia was immaculately dressed with not a hair out of place. She glanced around. As if satisfied no one observed her actions, she went directly to the front door and knocked. It opened immediately, and she slipped inside.

"Well, there's one difference," said Nate. "Coldwater Bay's Cordelia Templeton wouldn't be caught dead sneaking into a club at the crack of dawn."

Libby frowned. "Cordelia Templeton? I remember that name. She's loaded, isn't she? Or at least she was."

"Still is, if Templeton International Development Corporation is as successful here as Templeton Real Estate in Coldwater Bay. The Templeton's have been in the town for generations and own a lot of property in the area. Cordelia had it rough this past year, though. Her husband recently died in a car accident."

"Maybe Cordelia is our new supervillain," said Libby with a grin. "They're always rich and having a tragic backstory is a plus."

"That would fit. I almost see her as a crime boss. She's very organized and likes to get her own way. She's not a bad person, but can be overbearing. Her personality has mellowed a bit, though, since her son came back to town to join the business. I think she was lonely. Hey, maybe she's plotting a takeover of the Founder's Day festival."

Libby made a disbelieving face. "By rigging the watermelon eating contest? That doesn't sound very evil." All at once, she shot Nate an anxious glance. "It just occurred to me, the villains' headquarters was also on Second Chance City's waterfront."

He folded his arms and regarded her with disapproval. "Now you decide to share?"

"Hey, I'm winging this…but if you have a hero, you also must have a villain. I don't see any old warehouses, though. That's where Mega Mole and his minions hide."

"All right," said Nate, "we've proved we're definitely not in Coldwater Bay, and I prefer to think neither one of us has gone crazy, so we need to get off the street and decide our next move."

"I'm willing," said Libby. "Where do we go? You know you stick out like a sore thumb in that cop suit."

"Yeah," he said dryly, "and you blend in wearing fleece-lined boots in July and waving a pencil light." He thought for a moment. "There are plenty of B&Bs with rooms for rent."

Her doubt was apparent. "You think our money and credit cards are good here? It also might be a tad suspicious if we show up at the door with no luggage or car."

"Point taken…a few bungalows were on the market and currently sitting empty in Coldwater Bay. I made a sweep by them while on patrol. The same ones may be for sale here. We can break in and squat for a while. With luck, we won't need a place to hide for long and will be on our way home soon."

"What do you know?" said Libby lightly. "I'm leading you into a life of crime again."

Nate grinned. "Yeah, you're nothing but trouble, Parish. Come on, let's grab the stuff we left at the memorial."

They followed the path along Frenchman's Creek and retrieved their gear from underneath the bushes. "We'll head down Pine Avenue," said Nate, as they exited the plaza. "The first vacant house isn't far—"

The pavement swayed underneath their feet, rolling and heaving like cascading ripples from a stone tossed in a pond.

Nate reeled, striving to keep his footing. "What the hell was that?" he stammered after the earth settled down. "Earthquake?"

Libby stared at the ground. "No," she whispered, half to herself. "It can't be."

"Can't be what?" An alarm sounded next door at Cara Tyson Jewelry Design. The ground pitched again. From inside the store came a woman's scream. Nate dropped the coat and drew his gun. "Wait here!"

The front door of the jewelry store was gone, replaced by a gaping hole. Without warning, Nate was hit with a foul odor reminiscent of a rotting compost heap. He stifled a gag.

Out of the hole clambered a walking nightmare. The macabre figure was large and hairy and stood on two legs. The shoulders and arms sported massive muscles, the legs spindly by comparison. Knife-like talons sprouted from the tips of its fingers, the eyes mere pinpricks buried deep in the skull. The creature was a clone of the illustration of Mega Mole in the Refractor comics, right down to an identical pair of boxer shorts slit in the rear to release a stubby tail.

Cara Tyson huddled against a counter inside the store. She gaped in horror as Mega Mole heaved his tremendous bulk onto the sidewalk. Clutching her chest, she let out another scream.

"Police!" Nate barked, aiming his weapon at the monstrosity. "Don't move."

The creature swiveled his head. At the sight of Nate, it wrinkled its muzzle, and then with a low gravely hiss, dove into the hole. Nate crept forward and peeked over the edge into a dark empty tunnel. "What the hell?" he murmured. "Where'd it go?"

The ground exploded underneath Nate's feet.

Chapter Four

Nate flew into the air and landed hard on Main Street. The gun fell from his hand. Stunned, he staggered to his feet. A second hole appeared where he stood a moment ago.

Mega Mole vaulted from the depths and let out a rasping growl. "You interrupted my business, little man." The lips pulled back in a sneer to display a long pink tongue and razor-sharp teeth. "I'm not pleased."

A man in a silver spandex body suit crawled from the hole and motioned toward Nate. "Who the hell is he?"

"Dead meat," said the creature. Its massive bulk lurched toward Nate, moving with surprising speed. The powerful talons swung at his head. Nate dodged and they swished harmlessly past his ear. He hit the ground with a roll. Snatching the gun, he fired three rapid shots.

The creature stumbled as the bullets struck and let out a high-pitch squeal. "Time Bomb!"

From inside the store, Cara Tyson dove to the floor. An instant later, the man in the silver suit exploded.

Nate fell backwards as the shock wave knocked him across the pavement. The front windows of the jewelry store shattered. Somewhere nearby a car alarm blared. Nate scrambled up as a misty shape coalesced in the middle of the street. He gaped in stunned amazement as the silver man reformed.

The beast clutched his bleeding arm and screamed in rage, "Get him!"

A light beam blasted from behind Nate. The glow spread out to form a protective barrier an instant before the silver man detonated again. The explosive wave slammed into the light. Energy rippled and danced across the surface, but none of the devastating effects made it through.

Libby drew alongside Nate, her face a study of intense concentration. Beads of sweat trickled down her forehead. She clutched the pencil light tight in her hands. Only now, instead of a normal LED, the end pointed toward Mega Mole and Time Bomb blazed at the tip with a little hovering star.

"Libby?" Nate gasped. "What are you doing?"

"Not...exactly...sure," she spit out between clenched teeth. Her arms trembled as if she held the flashlight steady with great effort.

The silver man reintegrated again. "Can't break the shield," he barked.

"Let's get out of here!" yelled Mega Mole. He plunged down the hole with Time Bomb right behind him. A geyser of dirt spewed from the opening. When it settled, both holes had completely filled in.

The energy shield created by the star collapsed. Libby's arms dropped to her side. Her knees sagged. Nate rammed the gun in the holster. He put his arm around her shoulders to offer support. "You okay?"

Libby leaned against him. "I-I think so." She tucked the flashlight under one arm and then shook her hands as if to restore circulation. "Man, that smarts."

Nate tried to formulate a rational series of questions, but the only words that tumbled out were, "Libby, what the hell?"

"I know," she stammered.

"Were they...they couldn't be...tell me they weren't...were they?" Nate couldn't bring himself to say it.

Libby could. "They were. Mega Mole and Time Bomb, villains from the Refractor comic in the flesh."

"Your flashlight? How? Why?"

"I-I don't know. It just blinked on."

Cara stumbled from the shop, regarding the filled-in holes with joyous relief. "They're gone."

"You okay, Cara?" asked Nate.

Her eyes widened in surprise. "How do you know my name?"

Nate decided now was not the best time to mention Coldwater Bay. "That doesn't matter. You're certain you're all right?"

"Yes, yes, of course." She gaped in amazement. "You shot Mega Mole. I can't believe you shot him. Thank you, thank you! The police said he was dead, but we've all heard the rumors he and Time Bomb have returned to their usual tricks—" She gawked at Nate and Libby in confusion. "Who are you? You're not with the police. Are you with HIM?" The way she breathed out the word made Nate instantly visualize all capital letters.

"Who him?" asked Libby.

Cara's voice dropped to a whisper. She peered around as if nervous to be overheard. "Has Refractor returned?"

Nate and Libby exchanged uneasy glances. "He's

been gone?" said Nate.

Cara was obviously bewildered at his response. "It's common knowledge. No one has seen him for months. Aren't you on Refractor's team?"

"His team?" echoed Nate.

"The masked man and woman he's seen with," she flustered. "Why don't you know this? Who are you two? Where did you come from?" Down the street a siren wailed. Cara let out a derisive snort. "The police—too late as usual."

Nate whispered to Libby, "It might not be the best idea to run into them, yet—not until we figure things out."

"You think they're looking for us?" said Libby nervously.

"I don't want to hang around and find out."

She nodded an accord. "Lead the way." They snatched their coats and ran toward Pine Avenue.

Cara called after them. "Wait! I don't even know your name."

"Just a couple of good citizens," Nate shouted as they rounded the corner.

They ran for a block. As they crossed the street, more sirens blared out, the wail closing in on their position. After another block, Nate directed her north. "There was a home for sale this way—" He pulled Libby to a halt in front of a one-story bungalow and peered in confusion at the For Sale sign in the window.

Libby tugged at his sleeve. "Is this it?"

"No...I mean yes. This is...was...Connor and Ellie's house, but it doesn't look like anyone lives here now."

Libby shot an uneasy glance behind. "Nate, we

should either go inside or keep moving. Those cops will be here any second."

Nate hesitated only a moment before taking Libby's arm and leading her to the back door. He scanned the ground.

"What are you looking for?" she asked, puzzled.

"The house used to be owned by Connor's grandmother. She willed it to him after she died. That's when he returned to town. I hope it's still here—aha!" Nate pounced on a rock half buried in the earth. It made a rattling sound as he pried it from the dirt.

Libby peered over his shoulder. "What is that?"

"Mrs. O'Reilly always kept a spare key in one of those containers resembling a rock." Nate unlocked the door. They slipped inside the kitchen as a squad car turned the corner. Flattening against the wall, both held their breaths until the wailing siren faded in the distance.

Nate exhaled with relief. "They're gone." He examined the interior in disbelief. "Wow, I'd forgotten what it was like before Connor and Ellie remodeled. The house still looks exactly the same as when Mrs. O'Reilly lived here." He ran his hand along the wall. "Connor took this place down to the studs. He removed most of the walls and modernized the kitchen and bathrooms. Both Connor and Ellie worked their butts off," he added wistfully, "and did a great job. I wonder what happened in Second Chance City to change things."

Libby ran a finger across the kitchen counter. It came away covered in dust. "No one has lived here for a while." She fiddled with a knob on the stove and then went to the faucet. "Gas still works. Water is on.

57

Somebody must pay the bills." She opened a pantry door. "Hey, it's still full of canned goods. No one bothered to clean it out." Libby snatched at a jar. "Instant coffee!"

"Is there anything to eat?" Nate asked. "I'm starved."

Libby shot him a look. "A few minutes ago you were nearly blown to pieces by a comic book villain, and the only thing you can think of is your stomach?"

"Not exactly." He cleared his throat. "What's also running through my mind is, apparently, I got saved by a comic book superhero." He motioned to both Libby and the flashlight. "Thanks."

She flushed. "You're welcome, but I'm no heroine."

"Sure felt like it to me when you charged to the rescue. What happened, Lib? What is that thing?"

Libby sank down on a chair at the kitchen table and stared in fascination at the flashlight in her hand. "I-I'm not sure. Everything happened so fast. Mega Mole attacked. Time Bomb exploded. I ran to help you—"

"You ran to help me before the flashlight activated?" His voice tightened. "Libby, you could have been killed."

Libby dropped her gaze and shifted in the seat. A slight smile tugged at her lips. "I never claimed to be bright. Anyway, as I ran toward you the LED bulb began to glow. Suddenly, it wasn't an LED anymore. You saw…it looked like a little star. I felt a build-up of energy, like a static electric charge against my skin. Then this sensation of tugging inside me—as if the flashlight needed to be powered up and I was the battery pack. Then these words appeared in glowing print on the casing." She held out the light. Etched on the side in a flowery script was *Write Your Own Ending.*

Nate wrinkled his brow. "What the hell does that mean?"

"You got me. Next thing I know, the beam shot out and made the shield. All I did was hold on."

Nate cupped her hand between his own. "It hurt you. I saw."

"I'm fine now." She rubbed her forehead. "Okay, maybe a little headache. My hands sting some..."

Nate opened her palm and stroked the skin gently with his finger. The deepening pink in her cheeks highlighted the freckles. "You're sure that's all? Maybe you should lie down."

"I'm all right." The silence grew between them, and Libby drew her hand away. "Although, once you mentioned food, my stomach growled."

Nate jumped up from his chair. "Right...food and coffee." Libby put a pot of water on for coffee while Nate opened two cans of chili and dumped them in a pot. While the meal heated, she moved a stack of newspapers and brochures on the table to the side and set out dishes and flatware. A few minutes later, they sat down to eat.

Libby's spoon hovered over the bowl of chili. "Do you think Mrs. O'Reilly would have minded?" she said with a guilty look. "I got sucked into an alternate reality. For all I know, ghosts are real here. I don't want to offend the dead by stealing her food."

Nate grinned. "Trust me. Mrs. O'Reilly would have been happy we raided her kitchen. No one ever left her house hungry. Frankly, she'd probably haunt us if we didn't eat something."

After his last spoonful of chili, Nate leaned back with a contented sigh. "The sign on the window said For Sale so we should be able to crash here. We'll have to be wary of potential home buyers, but it doesn't seem as if this place gets much foot traffic. It's lucky the utilities were left on. I guess it makes the house easier to show." Nate glanced around. "I wonder what happened to Connor."

Libby thumbed through the papers left on top of the kitchen table. "Some law firm is in charge of the sale." She slid a stack of real estate flyers over to Nate.

He scanned a brochure. "Regina Morales—she's a local attorney in Coldwater Bay, too." Nate squinted at the small print on the bottom. "The proceeds go to..." A lump formed in his throat.

Libby leaned over the table. "What is it?"

He swallowed hard. "All proceeds from the sale go to the Connor O'Reilly Memorial Scholarship Fund." Nate stared in shock. "He's dead."

"Wait a minute," said Libby, rifling through a stack of newspapers on the table. "I saw something in one of these detailing a fund drive for a scholarship...here it is." She retrieved an edition of *The Second Chance City Times* dated several months ago. Her face paled. "More people other than just Chief Williams and Connor died at O'Reilly's that night."

Nate skimmed the article, running his finger along a line of print listing all the fatalities. "Ellie Yoshida's name is here, too—" He found it difficult to speak. "So are my folks and my sister. Damn..." he murmured sadly. "They're all gone."

Libby reached over and laid a consoling hand on

his arm. "They weren't killed in our reality. Connor and Ellie and your family are alive and well."

Nate's voice filled with bitterness. "Somehow that doesn't make me feel better."

Libby gave him a comforting pat and spread the papers across the table. "According to the article on the explosion at O'Reilly's, Mega Mole and Time Bomb died. It looks like they're not mentioned at all for several months. However, the most recent editions note a suspicious increase in criminal activity, hinting Mega Mole and Time Bomb were responsible. Nothing regarding any sightings of Refractor, either."

"That jives with what Cara told us." First, Mike Williams and now, Connor, Ellie, and his parents and sister. All these deaths of people close to Nate cut unbelievably sharp. How many others had disappeared? His fingers clenched tight, and he forced them to relax. "We don't belong here. We need to return to our own world. Where the hell did Refractor go, Libby?" he demanded.

She seemed taken aback by his harsh tone. "How should I know?"

"You've read all those stupid comics," said Nate, irritation growing. "You're the big expert. You must have some idea."

"If I did," Libby snapped, "don't you think I'd tell you?"

Nate glowered at her. All of a sudden, his shoulders sagged. He ran his hands through his close-cropped hair. "Sorry, I didn't mean to jump all over you. This isn't your fault."

Libby reached over and gently squeezed his arm. "It not your fault, either. I'm sorry about your friends and your folks."

Nate sighed. "You're right. They're not my people here."

"But still…?"

"Yeah…but still." He rose to his feet. "Why don't we have some more coffee, and you can fill me in on the life and times of Refractor? Maybe if we put our heads together, we can figure out where he went." Nate fixed two more cups. They moved to the living room and sat on the sofa.

Libby slipped off her snow boots with a sigh and propped her feet on the coffee table. "Like I told you already, Refractor has no backstory so I don't know where or when he got his power. He has a constant glow and can shoot these awesome laser-like beams from his hands. He can also bend light around himself to create an appearance for a short time, but not long enough to maintain a secret identity. Refractor arrives in the first issue to interrupt Mega Mole's attempt to kidnap Princess Arabella."

Nate shuddered. "Why did that big disgusting thing want her? Tell me quick it wasn't anything sexual, so I can wipe that image from my mind."

Libby chuckled. "It wasn't. The reason has to do with the princess' backstory. She actually has one. Arabella came from the planet Mo'R'ees Six."

Nate shook his head. "What idiot names a planet Maurice?"

"It's actually more guttural than that when Payton pronounces it and the accent is on the second syllable, but I agree. It's a stupid name. Arabella was a member of the royal family—big deals in their part of the galaxy. General Syr was the military dictator in a neighboring system. He wanted to gain access to the rich asteroid mining belt circling Mo'R'ees Six and then extend his power throughout the sector. He has a large following because the helmet he wears allows him to sway people's thoughts."

Nate raised an eyebrow. "Like super ESP or something?"

"Exactly. The royal family stood in his way. He killed them all in an attempted coup, but Arabella escaped. As the last surviving member, the people rallied to her name."

"Which is conveniently human," said Nate smugly.

"Yeah, Payton originally dubbed her Robella, but the publisher insisted on a change because it sounded too much like rubella. Payton didn't care." Libby snorted. "Payton was never bothered by any edits—kind of strange when you think about it. Most authors are so vested in their characters that even simple name changes can be hard…anyway, Syr discovered Arabella hid on Earth."

"Again, not to belabor the point," said Nate, "but even though she's an alien, she looks human and speaks English. Syr's name is stupid, too."

Libby made a face. "It's a comic. Go with it. As I was saying before being rudely interrupted, Syr arrived on Earth to hunt her down. To maintain control over Mo'R'ees Six, Arabella must die. He put a bounty on her head, and Mega Mole aims to collect."

"What are Arabella's superpowers?" asked Nate.

"She has supernatural control over weather patterns. In effect, she can call down rain, lightning, or a windstorm. The only other person of note in the comic is Pierce Powers."

"The gazillionaire physicist."

"Right. He invented a device that runs on zayton radiation—"

"Zayton? Oh please…"

"Zayton," Libby reiterated firmly, shooting him a "pipe down" look. "The invention enables Powers to enhance or weaken others' super abilities. By manipulating the effect of zayton radiation on inter-dimensional space-time waves, Powers intercepted Arabella's distress call and guided her to Earth. He and Refractor pledged to help her capture General Syr."

Nate sat back to think. Nothing Libby told him generated any ideas how to get them home. "Didn't Refractor disappear in the last issue—the one that shanghaied us?"

"Not exactly. The story ended with his disappearance, the suggestion being he was emotionally scarred by witnessing the explosion." Libby wrinkled her nose. "Superheroes spend a lot of time in a good solid mope. Apparently, Refractor blamed himself for the deaths of all the citizens in O'Reilly's Tavern."

"Was he responsible?" asked Nate.

"No. The dead were simply innocent bystanders caught in the ambush. Strange," she mused, "Payton kept delaying the start of the next issue. The first stories flowed, but after this last one, his writing came to a dead stop. Our hero was due to return in the next issue entitled, wait for it, The Return of Refractor, but I know for a fact Payton hasn't worked in weeks. He didn't even give me an outline. It's like he had nothing left to say."

"Writer's block?" suggested Nate. "He killed off Mega Mole and Time Bomb, too."

Libby chuckled. "Have you forgotten death in comic books is less fatal than death in real life? It's entirely possible they could return. You'll note that although both the newspaper articles and Cara Tyson mentioned Mega Mole and Time Bomb had vanished from Second Chance City, both also expressed doubts pertaining to their permanent demise."

"It figures. What's the point of being either a superhero or supervillain," kidded Nate, "if a teensy explosion can wipe you out forever?"

"Ah," said Libby with a smirk, "so you are a fan of the genre, after all."

"I read my share, if you recall." Nate rubbed his chin. "So we're back to square one. In the comic, Refractor hid in his lair, but we don't know where the lair is in this world."

"Comic books," Libby mused, "any fiction for that matter, always involve some sort of call to action. The hero or heroine discovers something needs to be done. The meat of the story is how they accomplish the task and get to the happy ending."

"Like Hamlet?" said Nate wryly.

"Yeah—kind of sucked for him. Happy endings aren't guaranteed, I'm afraid." Libby drummed her fingers idly on the arm of the sofa. "Could we have been sent here on a mission?"

"Damned if I have a clue," said Nate.

Libby let out an amused snort. "What we need is someone who knows everybody's business and can give us a lead."

"In Coldwater Bay it would be Irina, the dispatcher at the police station, but she didn't sound very happy to talk to me before."

Libby rolled her eyes with an innocent expression. "If you treated ex-girlfriends better, you wouldn't be so nervous to run into them again. I'm only saying…"

"I told you, she wasn't a girlfriend—" An idea slapped Nate in the head. He darted from the sofa and retrieved one of the newspapers from the table. His finger pointed to a familiar name. "Aha!"

"Find something?" Libby said eagerly.

"The byline on all these Refractor stories is the same…Kristie Williams."

"I remember her," Libby murmured flatly. "She was the reporter at Payton's signing."

"Kristie is Mike's daughter. She's smart, fair, and hard-working—always tries to get two sides to the story. If Second Chance City has a plucky reporter in league with the good guys, it would have to be Kristie." He blew out his cheeks in relief. "Man, this is a bit of luck. I can't tell you how glad I am she's here."

Libby shifted in her seat. "She must be a good friend."

"Yeah, Kristie is great."

She gazed down at her lap. "Your relationship would be different. After all, she doesn't know you."

"I have to get acquainted then. I need her." Some undefined emotion flashed across Libby's expression. "Are you okay?"

Libby squared her shoulders. "Yes, of course. You're right. You must make contact."

"Don't worry," Nate said with all the assurance he could muster. "If Kristie is anything like her counterpart, she'll help me."

"I'm sure she will," Libby replied with a wan smile.

"She would be at *The Second Chance City Times*. The address on the newspaper's masthead is the same—Oak Avenue."

"That's right downtown," said Libby, "and if I remember correctly, not far from the police station. What if the police stop us? We don't carry any ID that makes sense. What do we tell them?"

"Yeah, you're right." Nate scrutinized his Coldwater Bay uniform, and Libby's heavy winter clothes. "We kind of stick out. Let's check the closets. No one hauled off the furnishings. Maybe they left clothes, too."

"I'm in luck," said Nate, opening the closet in the first bedroom. "It looks like Connor kept some things at his grandmother's." A shadow passed over his face. "I feel wrong going through his stuff."

"I don't think he'd mind," said Libby, kindly, "considering the circumstances."

Nate motioned out the door. "Mrs. O'Reilly's room must be at the end of the hall."

Libby left while Nate rooted through the clothing. Fortunately, he and Connor had been the same size. He grabbed a pair of well-worn jeans, sneakers, and a t-shirt. He changed and hung up his uniform, but removed the gun and tucked it in his belt, stuffing the extra clips into the pocket. Nate slipped on an old hoodie jacket, pulled up the zipper and gave himself a good once-over in the mirror on the door. He nodded in approval. The gun wasn't apparent.

The door to Mrs. O'Reilly's old bedroom was shut. Nate knocked. "You ready?"

"Aw, geez," came the disgruntled response.

"Libby?" Nate wrinkled his forehead, confused.

"Are you coming out?"

"Maybe."

"Lib?"

"Oh, all right," she grunted. "Don't laugh, or I'll smack you."

"Sheesh, I promise."

The handle turned. The door slowly opened. Libby was dressed in polyester blend flowered Capri pants with an elastic waist. The pale pink cotton polo shirt had an alligator on the pocket and a fitted band at the bottom that, unfortunately, bloused around her smaller frame making her appear twenty pounds heavier with a pot belly. On her feet were sturdy, dependable, slight orthopedic-looking, white walking shoes. She carried a nylon yellow windbreaker with a matching floppy sun hat.

She cocked her head. "Well?"

Nate bit his lip. "You look nice...real nice."

Libby glared. "No, I don't. These are old lady clothes. I look like Meemaw Parish in this getup." She punched him in the arm. "Stop laughing."

"Ow! I wasn't laughing." Nate forced on his best innocent expression. It didn't fool her for a second.

"You're thinking about it," she said accusingly.

Nate couldn't hold the guffaw in any longer. "Sorry, can't help it." To Nate's consternation, the little star reappeared on the top of the flashlight. "Uh, Lib?"

"Must be tied to my emotional state," she said testily. "Maybe if I smack you again, I'll feel better and it will shut off."

As she drew back her fist, Nate raised his hands in mock surrender. "Seeing as how I don't want to explode or fry or whatever else that thing can do, I give up."

Libby's dour mood softened. She let out a chuckle, and the star vanished. "I accept your surrender, but you better erase that smile, pronto, if you know what's good for you." She examined her clothes with a sigh. "They're really bad, aren't they?"

Nate decided this was one time agreement was not a viable option. "On the plus side," he offered cheerfully. "That's a great disguise. Nobody would suspect a superhero hides underneath."

Libby slipped on the windbreaker, jammed her auburn curls under the sun hat, and tucked the flashlight in the waist band. With a sharp tug, she adjusted the jacket to make certain the flashlight was completely hidden. "Let's go find the plucky reporter. The sooner I'm home with my own closet, the better. I swear to God, I'm going to hug every article of clothing I own."

They made their way to Oak Avenue, keeping an eye out for the police. As they approached downtown, foot traffic substantially increased. It was nearly noon and the sidewalks were crowded. They walked briskly with their heads down, but no one appeared to pay them any attention. As they rounded the corner to the newspaper office, Nate halted, gaping in astonishment at the three-story edifice, headquarters of *The Second Chance City Times*.

"Wow, things have changed," he murmured. "It makes sense a big city newspaper would have larger staff than a small town, but I didn't expect this."

"What are you going to tell your friend?" asked Libby, as they walked into the lobby. "I don't want to be shipped to a mental hospital."

"Me neither, but I know Kristie and hope she still

can't resist a good story. Of course, in Coldwater Bay headlines are usually something on the order of 'Tensions Rise at the Sudden Death Spell-off at the Regional Elementary School Bee.' " Nate paused to consider an approach. "I'll play it cool—drop a few hints on witnessing the attack on Cara Tyson Jewelry Design this morning and then ask for the lowdown on Refractor's disappearance."

A listing by the elevators said Kristie Williams' office was on the top floor. "Her own office," Nate murmured. "Nice. In Coldwater Bay, she had a cubby by the restrooms."

They stepped out of the elevator to a large open space crammed full of desks pushed together with short space dividers in between. The whole floor thrummed with activity. Libby stood on tiptoes to scan the area. "Do you see her?" she said.

"No, but she has an office. I'll ask—"

Out of nowhere, Kristie Williams ran to him, an anxious expression on her face. "What are you doing here?"

Nate was momentarily dumbfounded by the sight of Kristie Part II. Except for the smartly tailored business suit, she was an identical twin to the girl he'd talked to less than twenty-four hours ago. "Kristie? I mean…we need to talk."

"It's not safe." Nate and Libby exchanged confused glances as Kristie hustled them down a corridor.

"You know us?" said Nate.

"Not by your real names, of course," said Kristie smartly, "but I got the description from Cara Tyson. I'll have a big write-up in the afternoon edition." She flashed an admiring smile at Nate. "May I be the first to welcome Good Citizen and his sidekick to Second Chance City."

Chapter Five

Nate gaped at her. Good Citizen?

"Sidekick?" Libby's eyes blazed fire. "I'm only a sidekick?"

Nate flashbacked to age thirteen, right before he was beaned in the head with a rock. "This is...uh...Mighty Light." Nate quickly added, "She is my partner, not sidekick." The fire in Libby's eyes shrunk to an ember.

Kristie regarded Libby with doubt. "Dressed like that?"

"I'm in disguise," she growled.

"Well, it's a darn good one," said Kristie cheerfully. "No one would suspect." She stopped in front of an office and turned to Nate. "You shouldn't have come here. It's too dangerous to be out in public."

Nate blinked in surprise at the name on the door. "You're editor-in-chief? Wow, I'm impressed."

A pleased smile spread across her face. Kristie ushered them inside and then shut the door. To Nate's astonishment, she threw her arms around his waist, hugging tight. "Cara Tyson said the new superhero escaped. I'm so relieved."

"Uh, thanks." His cheeks reddened. Kristie latched on like a drowning man clinging to a life raft and showed no signs of letting go.

"Excuse me," said Libby, tapping her foot in

annoyance. "I hate to interrupt, but we're trying to find Refractor."

Kristie reluctantly released her grip and regarded Libby in surprise. "I assumed you were part of his team sent to hunt Mega Mole."

"Actually," Nate said. "We only arrived in town and are searching for him."

"I don't know where Refractor is. Nobody has seen him in months—not since the explosion at O'Reilly's." Her voice turned bitter. "That was an awful day."

"We read one of your articles in the paper," said Libby. "You hinted Refractor was missing, but the police don't seem to think so."

"The police," she spit out in disgust, "don't want to admit anything in town is wrong. The chief is afraid panic will spread if people know Refractor is gone, so she created a big cover-up to hide the truth. The official line is Refractor retreated to his secret lair, but keeps silent watch over the city. He isn't needed at the moment since Mega Mole and Time Bomb died, too. What a crock."

Libby cocked her head. Her brow wrinkled as if in thought. "Makes sense. I can see where a random attack with that many casualties would spook people."

"Over a dozen were killed," said Kristie, her voice hardening, "including my father."

Nate's gaze softened. "I'm really sorry about Mike."

"You knew Dad?"

"Yeah," he admitted awkwardly. "We'd met. He was a good man."

Kristie's chin trembled. She grabbed a tissue off the desk and dabbed at her eyes. "Damn it. I swore at his grave no more tears."

"What happened that night?" said Nate.

"Refractor kept a low profile around town, but he and Dad were friends. Every now and then they'd get together and share information on criminal activity. That night they planned to meet at O'Reilly's. Mega Mole and Time Bomb must have spotted them going inside. The next thing you know, there was a massive explosion. Everyone said Mega Mole and Time Bomb died, but I never believed it and swore to use the power of the press to obtain justice for my father's murder."

"Avenge the death of a parent," muttered Libby under her breath to Nate. "Typical comic book trope." She turned to Kristie. "What do you know about Pierce Powers and Princess Arabella?"

Kristie wrinkled her brow. "Who?"

"They're Refractor's teammates," said Nate. "Ever hear of them?"

"No." Her confusion was obvious. "A masked couple was often seen with him, but no one ever mentioned names. Do you think those two know where he is?"

"More than likely," said Libby. All of a sudden, her gaze widened. "Hold on a sec...I've got an idea how to track them down—"

Her words were cut off by the wail of multiple sirens. They peered out the window down to the street. Several squad cars screeched to a halt in front of the building. "Damn it," muttered Kristie. "It's the cops. The chief has spies everywhere. Someone must have noticed your arrival."

"What do they want with us?" said Nate.

"To take you into custody. You've upset the status

quo. Don't worry," she declared. "The power of the press is behind you. I'll fight for your freedom."

Nate made a quick decision. "Hide in here, Lib. I'll turn myself in."

"I'm not hiding," Libby sputtered. The star lit on top of the light and emitted a soft glow.

Nate pressed his gun and the clips into Libby's hand. "You have an idea how to find Powers and Arabella. The building is surrounded by now. These are cops doing a job, not villains. Comic book or not, I won't fight my way out of here or shoot at them."

She regarded him anxiously. "What if they start shooting at you?"

"They won't," he assured her. "I'll be fine. I speak cop. At most, they'll hold me for twenty-four hours. I'll meet you at Connor's." Before Libby could offer an additional argument, Nate stepped into the hallway and shut the door. The elevator at the end of the corridor dinged. Three Second Chance City uniformed police piled out. They spotted Nate and pulled their guns.

Nate raised his hands as his heartbeat ratcheted up. "I'm unarmed!" he shouted, walking toward them. He'd spoken brave words to Libby. What if these cops had orders to shoot first and ask questions later?

"Are you the one called Good Citizen?" demanded a female officer, obviously in charge.

"Yes—" Nate was confounded by the sight of Sheriff Abigail Franco in a police sergeant's uniform.

"You're under arrest for disturbing the peace," said Abigail. "Put your hands against the wall." Nate complied without protest. He had known Abby for several years and always admired her professionalism. He made a silent wish the same qualities held true for her counterpart. She patted him down and slipped on a pair of handcuffs.

A prickle of unease jabbed at Nate. She didn't read him any rights. "You know this charge is bogus, Abby," he said.

Her head jerked toward him in surprise. "How do you know my name?"

"Doesn't matter. I'm right, aren't I?"

"That doesn't matter, either." For an instant, Nate caught the impression of sympathy.

"Where's your sidekick?" said another officer. "The report said there were two of you."

"I don't know who you mean," Nate said smoothly. He blessed his good fortune this was not a real comic book page. Libby's angry thought arrows at the word "sidekick" would have burst through Kristie's closed door and been a dead giveaway to her location.

"You want us to search the building, Sarge?" the patrolman asked Abigail. "She couldn't have gotten far."

"No."

"But the chief—"

"I said, no," she barked. "Let's get the hell out of here." She escorted Nate by the arm to the backseat of a squad car parked in front of the building. "I'll take in the prisoner and make the report," she said to the others. "You two return to patrol." Abigail slid behind the wheel and started the engine. She regarded Nate sharply in the rearview mirror. "How did you know my name? We've never met."

"I know lots of things about you, Abby. I know you're a good cop."

"I like to think so." Her voice sounded bitter. "At

least I used to be." She put the car in gear and drove away from the curb.

Nate hazarded a guess. "You don't buy it that Mega Mole is dead."

Abigail inhaled sharply. "Are you with Refractor?"

"I'm trying to find him. Do you have any idea where he is?"

"Then you're not a friend of his," she snapped. "Who are you?"

"Someone who wants to help. I know Refractor hasn't been seen in months. Lately, the crime rate has risen. I saw Mega Mole and Time Bomb today. So did Cara Tyson. They attacked her store."

Abigail shifted uneasily in her seat. "You're mistaken. The chief already took her statement. It was a sinkhole, not Mega Mole. Cara has a wild imagination—"

"A sinkhole?" Nate shot back in disbelief. "Here? Do you really believe that or isn't it more likely someone pressured Cara to change her story?"

Abigail parked the car in front of the police station. Her hands clenched the wheel. "It doesn't matter what I believe."

"You can't bury the truth, Abby. Secrets always find a way to dig themselves out and then bite you in the ass. I know you care about this place, but no one is safe any longer. You don't want another massacre like O'Reilly's."

"What do you expect me to do? If you're hunting Refractor, I can't help you. No one knows his hideout's location." She got out of the car and opened the rear door.

Nate slid out. "Find proof the uptick in crime is due

to Mega Mole and Time Bomb. People need to be warned if they're back in business. Maybe the knowledge will flush Refractor, or people that know his hiding place, into the open."

Strong emotions played across her face. "Turn around." Abigail unlocked the handcuffs. "Get out of here. I'll make up some story to tell the chief."

Nate rubbed his wrists. "You'll get in trouble."

"No more than usual—"

"Sergeant Franco!" A shrill yet oddly familiar voice came from the open door of the police station. "What the hell are you doing? Is that any way to transport a prisoner?" A cold chill swept through Nate. No…it couldn't be.

"God damn it," Abigail murmured tightly under her breath. She called out, "He came peacefully, Chief. I thought—"

"You're not paid to think, Sergeant Franco. Put the cuffs on." A middle-aged woman with the countenance of a constipated bulldog stood at the top of the stairs. "Escort the prisoner to the interrogation room," snapped Chief Florence Peevey.

Abigail relocked the cuffs. She joined the police escort and led Nate up the steps and into the interrogation room. Like the newspaper, the station had also undergone significant changes. The building was even larger than *The Second Chance City Times*. Dozens of uniformed officers sat at the desks, but only one was familiar.

"Is that the son of a bitch who thinks a joke about Chief Williams is funny?" snarled Irina.

Irina, the dispatcher? With a weapon? Nate couldn't tear his gaze from her.

"What are you staring at?" she snarled, resting her hand lightly on the gun butt. "I'm watching a dead man walking."

Irina never could hide her feelings.

To Nate's dismay, Florence ordered Abigail and the officers to deposit him directly in an interrogation room; no fingerprinting, no processing, no paperwork, no official record of Nate inside the police station. If he never made it out again, who would care? Judging from the hastily turned faces of the men and women at their desks, not a single one of them.

Abigail stood guard outside. Florence shut the door and then took the seat across the table. She made no move to remove the cuffs, her expression set in a glower. Florence had a damn good glower. It had brought lesser men to their knees, but Nate had known Florence for years. She was a pill, rough around the edges, but her gruff exterior belied a warm caring heart underneath. As Florence continued to shoot eyeball daggers in his direction, a cold chill came over Nate. How different was this Florence?

"Who are you?" she demanded, "What the hell are you doing in my town, piss ant? Speak up—I'm waiting for an excuse not to kill you right now."

Okay, so any kindness was buried way, way underneath. Better go easy. Florence could do more harm to him here than simply flipping a finger. "All I did was stop a robbery," he answered mildly.

"Oh, yeah," she sneered. "I heard. You're Good Citizen." She leaned over the table. "I don't need some superhero wanna-be spreading lies and causing panic and unrest."

"Are you serious, Florence?" Nate sputtered. "You

can't ignore what's going on here."

"It's Chief Peevey to you, boy, and nothing goes on in my city without my knowledge."

Nate matched her scowl for scowl. "Whether you admit it or not, Mega Mole didn't die at O'Reilly's Tavern and Refractor hasn't come to the rescue lately. I've read the newspapers. I've seen the crime stats on the rise. I know what's going on."

"Newspapers," she snorted out in disgust. "*The Second Chance City Times* is nothing but a lot of crazed posturing from fear mongers like Kristie Williams. All she wants to do is grow circulation."

"Mega Mole and others are testing the waters," argued Nate. "Until now, they haven't been certain Refractor was gone, but once they're sure no one will stop them. Second Chance City will erupt in flames."

"If...and I do say *if*, Mega Mole has returned, then Refractor will reappear and defeat him like he always has."

"If he doesn't? What then? Is Second Chance City's police force a match for them?"

The chief's jaw clenched. "I will not have you spreading panic. People will get hurt."

"People will get hurt if you hide the truth and convince them they're safe. Plenty of good folk live here. If you let it be known Mega Mole has returned, the whole of Second Chance City will be your eyes and ears. All it takes is one good tip to track down the gang's new hideout. It must be close. Someone must know something."

Florence shot him a sly look that tightened the knot in Nate's stomach. "Oh, someone does. I've already gotten an anonymous tip on the attempted robbery at

Cara Tyson Jewelry Design and plan to arrest the real perpetrator—you! Jail will shut your mouth just fine."

Nate half rose from the seat, enraged. "That's totally bogus, and you know it. Cara saw what happened. She'll stand up for me and never press charges."

"Perhaps you're right." Florence placidly examined her fingernails. "However, it can take a surprisingly long time for paperwork to clear and an innocent man to be freed."

"I want a lawyer," Nate demanded.

Florence pushed the chair away from the table and walked to the door. "Whatever for?" she said coolly. "We're not charging you, yet. You're obviously deranged—running around and calling yourself Good Citizen. I'll park your ass in a jail cell until you simmer down."

"You can't do that," cried Nate.

"Sonny," she snarled, yanking open the door. "This is my town. I can do whatever the hell I want." Although, Florence had scoffed at the idea of Mega Mole's return, she obviously had concerns for Nate's own abilities. She handed him over to Abigail and signaled to three other officers as additional escort. "Put him in a cell until he decides to be reasonable."

Abigail raised an eyebrow. "You want me to book him?"

Florence glared. "Did I ask you to book him? Just throw him in a damn cell."

Abigail flushed and pressed her lips together in a thin tight line. She and the others led Nate down the corridor. Instead of the small compact jail in the rear of the Coldwater Bay PD, this cell block occupied half of the building. One of the other officers opened the door to an end unit with a small barred window. Abigail unlocked Nate's cuffs and motioned him inside.

"The chief may want to play dumb," said Nate, "but you all should know Mega Mole and Time Bomb have returned. Watch your backs out there." The other officers exchanged a quick anxious glance with Abigail.

After they left, Nate peered through the solitary window. "Great view of the parking lot," he groused. "Wouldn't exactly recommend it to a tourist though."

He threw himself on the cot in a funk. What a mess. So much for his fine words to Libby on talking the same language as the other cops. The legal system evidently worked differently in Second Chance City. Nobody seemed hot to fulfill his request for a lawyer. He could be stuck here for days. His stomach soured. Or maybe months? Or years? What happened to Libby? Was she safe? The idea she had fallen into trouble without him to help changed the sour knot to a tight ball of anger.

Footsteps approached the cell, and Nate jumped to his feet. Abigail returned with a tray she shoved through a slot in the bars. "Thanks," he said. "I figured the chief would be happy for me to starve to death."

"That's not the way we treat prisoners here." Her voice tightened. "At least not the way we used to." She glanced over her shoulder down the corridor. Her voice dropped to a whisper. "It won't be easy to prove Mega Mole and Time Bomb are alive."

"What about the official report on the explosion at O'Reilly's? I'll bet it doesn't mention their bodies."

"That doesn't mean anything. I've seen what explosions and fires can do. Lots of people were inside.

Not everyone could be identified."

"Ask Cara Tyson, then. She'll back my story. She saw everything go down." He grabbed the bars. "Trust your gut, Abby. What does it tell you?"

Her voice hardened. "Second Chance City is in danger."

A door opened down the hall and Irina's voice called out, "Franco, what's the problem?"

"Coming, Lieutenant," she yelled and then murmured to Nate, "I have to go."

"Call Kristie Williams," he whispered. "Tell her what happened to me."

Without a word Abigail hurried down the cell block. Nate watched her go with a heavy heart. Had he gotten through? Would she listen? He placed the food tray on the desk, any appetite gone, and paced the floor. With nothing to pass the time, minutes ticked by with agonizing slowness. Sunlight filtered through the window facing the parking lot. Shadows lengthened and stretched as afternoon faded into evening.

Eventually, rosy streaks tinted the sky. Soon it would be dark; a light fog might roll in off the bay. Nate had always enjoyed summer nights like this. They filled him with calm serenity. Not from a jail cell, though. Fatigue cramped his shoulders. He raised his arms and stretched. How long had it been since he slept? Nearly a day must have gone by from the time he and Libby left Coldwater Bay. The thought of Libby tore at his heart. What had happened to her? After all these years, Libby Parish had waltzed into his life and then as quickly, he lost her. Talk about timing…

No. Not again. Nate lay on the bed, arms behind his head, his mind drifting. "I'll get out of here, Libby.

I'll find you, and we'll make it back to Coldwater Bay, and then I swear to God I'll ask you to dinner. We'll go to Smuggler's Cove, the fanciest place in town. Nate will not be late again." He fell into a light sleep.

"Psst!"

Nate stirred on the cot.

"Psst! Nate!" A harsh whisper called to him, "Wake up."

"Wha…?" Half asleep, he rolled out of bed rubbing his eyes. The cell was empty. He was enveloped by an eerie feeling and fought hard to remember any villains in the Refractor series gifted with invisibility. The fact no one came immediately to mind, offered surprisingly little comfort.

"Who's there?" he called out.

"Shhh… Over here at the window."

The top of a yellow sunhat barely peeked above the sill.

"Lib!" he cried out in relief. "Man, it's good to see you. What are you doing here?"

Libby stood on tiptoes eyeballing him with a big grin. She clutched the flashlight tight in one hand. Dusk had settled, and the little star at the tip glimmered faintly in the dark.

"It's a prison break," she said cheerfully.

He blinked. "What?"

"Stand back. I'm not too good at this, yet."

He blinked again. "What?"

The star's intensity increased. Immediately, Nate pressed flat against the wall. Underneath his fingertips, the cinderblocks vibrated. He jumped aside as a ceiling tile jarred loose and fell to the floor. Through the barred window, light grew ever brighter. A section of wall bulged out, as if distorted by an incredible force pushing from outside. Nate dove for the corner and covered his head.

Seconds later came a horrific roar. A section of cinderblock, separated from the wall, flew across the floor and slammed into the cell door, knocking it off its hinges.

"Oopsie."

Libby poked her head inside from the now substantial hole to the parking lot. She waved a hand back and forth to waft away the plaster dust swirling in the air. "Sorry," she added contritely. "I have a few control issues to iron out."

An alarm blared somewhere in the building. Footsteps pounded toward the cell block. "Don't apologize," said Nate, darting through the hole. "Let's get the hell out of here."

"This way. I scored a ride."

Second Chance City police officers poured through the rear exit as Libby and Nate raced across the parking lot. Nate expected to see Kristie, but instead a petite woman around thirty years old with chestnut hair waited in the driver's seat of an idling sedan. Although decades younger, the features of Breezy Point Inn's co-owner was unmistakable.

"Bobbie Quinn?" cried Nate. "What's she doing here?"

"No time to explain," said Libby as they piled into the back seat. "Punch it, Bobbie!"

Instead of burning rubber like Nate expected, they drove out of the parking lot at a leisurely pace.

"Uh, Libby?" he muttered, casting a nervous glance behind them. "This isn't exactly a blistering getaway speed." From nearby came the roar of a dozen engines turning over. The entire police force would be on them in seconds.

She settled in her seat with a wily half-smile. "Watch."

Nate peered out the rear window. Weird...the fog rolled in much faster than expected—much faster than he'd ever seen. He gawked in astonishment as, within seconds, a thick gray blanket settled on the street and then rose in height to form a smoothly surfaced wall. It completely blocked the view of the police station. Not even a muted glow from the streetlights was visible.

"How long can you keep it going?" asked Libby.

"Not long," Bobbie replied. "My device only has a limited range." On one wrist, she wore a peculiar metal band with some sort of electronic readout. She glanced at the display and tapped her fingers as if to make an adjustment. "The fog now extends completely around the station house. The police are locked into a one block radius, too thick to drive through at anything other than a crawl. By the time visibility returns, we'll be long gone." From somewhere in the direction of the jail came the sound of squealing brakes followed by a tinny crash.

He gaped at Libby. "She's doing this?"

Libby grinned. "Nate Hammond, allow me to introduce you to Bobbie Ballard—otherwise known as Princess Robella, aka Arabella, last survivor of the royal house of the planet Mo'R'ees Six."

Chapter Six

"Ballard?" Nate whispered to Libby. "That's Bobbie's maiden name."

Bobbie caught his astonished gaze in the rearview mirror. "Pleased to make your acquaintance, Good Citizen. Mighty Light told me so much about you."

"Bobbie is Princess Arabella?" Nate gawked at Libby in disbelief. "You know, I should be totally jaded and blasé by now with anything that occurs here, but I cannot wrap my head around this."

Libby chuckled. "I know, isn't it crazy? When Robella came to Earth, she took on the identity of Bobbie Ballard and bought the Write Away bookstore. She's been hiding under an alias ever since."

He was out of jail. Libby was safe and unharmed. All the tension Nate carried melted away. He fought an urge to reach over and kiss her. Instead, he blurted out, "What happened after I was picked up? How did you discover the location of my cell?"

"Simmer down, Good Citizen," Libby said brightly. "One thing at a time." She reached under the seat and retrieved his gun.

"Thanks." He tucked it in the waistband of his jeans. "Kind of felt naked without it."

Bobbie shot Libby a teasing glance. "Good Citizen naked? Interesting visual image, eh Mighty Light?"

Libby shifted in her seat. "Zip it, Bobbie."

"Bobbie?" Nate eyed her quizzically. "Not Your Highness? Or Your Royalness? Or Your Most Illustrious Perfection? Or whatever it is they call rulers of planets here?"

Bobbie let out a sigh. "Please, just Bobbie. I prefer it to Robella—never did like the name."

Nate turned to Libby. "How did you track her down?"

"Once the police left," she explained, "Kristie and I snuck out an emergency exit to her place. I figured if Arabella had a secret identity, she would be easier to find if I stripped off all the comic book tropes. Not a bad job, if I do say so myself." Libby took a folded paper from her pocket and handed Nate a character sketch of Princess Arabella, except her highness was in street clothes, without an elaborate hairstyle, costume, mask, and the exaggerated super heroine physique.

Nate examined the drawing in disbelief. Bobbie's haircut and hair color were different. The body shape had changed, too. Princess Arabella had the figure of a large-breasted Olympic athlete in a push-up bra, while Bobbie was normally proportioned. However, by removing all the cartoony attributes, a remarkable facial resemblance became apparent. "Wow. How come I never noticed before?"

"It's Superhero Syndrome," said Libby dryly. "No one recognizes anyone out of uniform. How do you think a certain caped wonder's alter ego managed to evade detection all those years with only a pair of black horned-rimmed glasses?"

She peered at the paper. "I showed the sketch to Kristie. She thought it was Bobbie Ballard, the owner of Write Away, so I went to the store and confronted her. She admitted to being Princess Robella in disguise. By the way, she has no idea how we got here, either."

"Mighty Light believes an interdimensional portal was involved," said Bobbie. "Unfortunately, the bridge between worlds has vanished. I can find no trace of residual radiation in the area where you materialized."

"Interdimensional portal?" he murmured to Libby.

She leaned over and whispered, "It made more sense than to say we came via comic book."

"How did you know I was in jail," Nate said, "and in that particular cell?"

"You can thank Kristie Williams and your new friend at the police station."

"Abby called?"

"Women seem to have a way of quickly falling under your spell, Good Citizen," Libby responded tartly.

"Not everyone," Nate said, uncomfortable with the conversation's direction. "Florence Peevey is the new chief. She didn't take to me at all."

Libby gasped. "Good God. How'd she get the job?"

"Florence was appointed chief by the city council after Williams died," chimed in Bobbie. "Maybe they felt sorry for her because she and the chief were lovers."

A disturbing visual image of naked Florence and Mike rolling around in the sheets like wrestling squirrels popped unbidden into Nate's mind. He shuddered. "Yeesh. I did not need to hear that."

"No monkey business between the two of them in Coldwater Bay?" said Libby with a grin.

"Hell, no. Mike is completely devoted to his

sweetheart of a wife and Florence…well, she's Florence. The idea of the two of them together is too horrible to contemplate."

"Did you see any sign of Payton at the police station?" said Libby.

"No. He wasn't in any of the other cells, and Florence didn't mention another out-of-towner getting thrown in jail. I'm sorry, Lib. He must have either got left in Coldwater Bay or dumped somewhere else." She appeared so upset, he quickly changed the subject. "Where are we going?"

"This world's version of Pierce Powers. He'll lead us to Refractor."

Nate perked up. "Great! So where has Refractor been all these months?"

Libby folded her arms and regarded Bobbie with clear disapproval. "She won't say."

Bobbie shot a glance at them in the rearview mirror. "It's best you talk to Ray." Nate got the distinct impression she was uncomfortable discussing Refractor.

"Ray?"

Libby flashed a wicked grin. "There is no Pierce Powers here. Ramón Quintero is the other person on Refractor's team. I'm not saying any more. We'll arrive soon, and I don't want to spoil the surprise."

Despite persistent cajoling from Nate, Libby refused to divulge more details. He finally quit when she threatened to use the flashlight on him. He thought he glimpsed the beginning of a star. It may only have been his imagination, but he decided not to chance it.

Nate checked out the window. They were well beyond Bobbie's fog barrier with no sign of pursuit.

The car now approached the outskirts of Second Chance City. Bobbie turned onto the coast road and headed directly to a building overlooking the bay.

"Breezy Point?" Nate sat back with an incredulous expression on his face. "I thought Refractor's other sidekick was supposed to be a zillionaire dot com magnate, not an innkeeper."

Libby chuckled. "Yeah, things are a little different here. Princess Robella is a scientist with no supernatural gifts and Pierce Powers...well, he's a moderately successful inventor named Ramón Quintero with a knack for electronics. You'll have to see the rest for yourself."

Except for the absence of snow, the house had the same general appearance as yesterday. A rock foundation still supported the clapboard-sided walls, but the parking lot by the front door was now a tree-filled yard. A crushed shell driveway led to a detached garage where only a storage shed used to be.

Flowers bloomed around the perimeter of the building. A full moon shone down casting silver light on the colorful borders. An expansive lawn spread out across the front, although not manicured to perfection like the one in Coldwater Bay. The inn still fronted the sea, though. Nate wondered idly if the same chaise lounges and Adirondack chairs had been set out for guests after the climb from the public beach.

"Except for the lack of parking," observed Nate, "the front is pretty much the same. "Wait...the welcome sign for visitors is no longer by the door."

"Breezy Point is a private home," said Libby, "not an inn." Her eyes twinkled. "That's not the only difference. Wait until you meet Ramón."

The door opened, and a man motioned them inside. As they neared, the interior light allowed Nate to discern his features. Instead of the balding, middle-aged innkeeper, Ramón Quintero was in his early thirties. Thick, wavy, dark brown hair showed no sign of a receding hairline, and his skin tone sported a deep tan. Despite the age and ethnic shift, however, the core resemblance to Raymond Quinn remained.

Nate gawked in surprise. "Ray?" Libby pressed her lips together, as if striving to hold in a laugh.

Ramón Quintero peered at him in bewilderment. "Have we met?"

"Never mind," said Nate quickly. "It's not important. Bobbie said you could help us."

His softened gaze turned in Bobbie's direction. "I thought at our last meeting we had parted for the final time. It's good to see you, again."

"And you." A faint pink color rose to her cheeks. She gestured to Nate and Libby. "Mighty Light and Good Citizen arrived in Second Chance City only recently, and they've already garnered enemies. It's an emergency, Ray. Otherwise, I wouldn't have broken the agreement."

Ray turned to Nate. "Who wishes you harm?"

"Mega Mole, Time Bomb, Florence Peevey…Irina Duval isn't too crazy with me either at the moment. Take your pick."

Ray drew in a breath. "The police reported Time Bomb and Mega Mole were dead."

"The chief lied," said Libby. "They're very much alive."

"Cara Tyson saw them, too," added Bobbie. "You have to take them to see *him*."

Ray stiffened. "You know that's not possible."

"Refractor is the only one who can help."

"You've wasted your time. Refractor can't help anyone any more—not even himself."

"What's wrong with him?" demanded Nate.

"Who knows?" Ray's words came sharp. "I tried talking to him, but got nowhere."

"Listen to their story and then decide." Bobbie squared her shoulders, a determined light in her eye. "Maybe it's time for everyone to stop hiding. I already helped Mighty Light break Good Citizen out of prison."

Ray's expression filled with disapproval. "Bobbie! I thought we agreed—"

"We did, but trouble has returned to Second Chance City." She grinned sheepishly. "Besides, it was fun—like the old days."

Ray's lips twitched in a slight smile. He ushered them into the same room used as an office in Coldwater Bay. As everyone settled into their seats, Nate did a discreet survey. The furnishings were exactly the same, although paintings of seascapes decorated the walls instead of photographs of Ray and Bobbie's children.

Nate and Libby recapped the events leading to their arrival at Breezy Point's front door. Ray listened in rapt fascination. When they described the fight with Mega Mole and Time Bomb, he clenched his jaw. "I had doubts from the beginning they were dead, but hoped I was wrong. Chief Peevey will stay blind to the truth until Mega Mole and Time Bomb bring the entire station down around her knees." Ray rubbed his chin. "Fascinating…an interdimensional portal materialized in Write Away. I've heard tales of such devices, but never actually saw one…Bobbie?"

"My people don't have any such mechanism, and we're more technically advanced than here. I'd like to get my hands on it." She turned to Nate and Libby. "Can you describe the device?"

They exchanged hesitant looks. How could they explain this part and not sound crazy? "Green pulsing light," Libby answered, uneasily, "it formed in a comic book."

Ray wrinkled his brow. "A what?" Bobbie also appeared puzzled.

"You know," Nate said, with growing confusion. "A type of soft-cover magazine...a story with colored drawings." His fumbled attempts at an explanation brought no signs of understanding. He peered helplessly at Libby, silently begging for assistance.

She jumped in. "The action is laid out in illustrations and a series of panels...plots involve heroes and villains...dialog inside balloon shapes..." She grew more flustered as Ray and Bobbie continued to stare blankly at them.

"Big fight scenes," added Nate weakly. "Sound effects spelled out. Oof! Arrrgh! Wham! Anything ring a bell?"

"Arrrgh?" said Ray. He turned to Bobbie. "Wham?"

"Intriguing concept," she said. "I've never heard of it."

"Me neither."

"Nate, they don't have comics," Libby blurted in shock. "If that is what brought us here, but none exist in this universe, how will we get home?" A sinking feeling enveloped Nate.

Ray had a faraway look. "I wonder...Refractor told

me once of someone who could supposedly mine information from even the darkest recesses. Clients called him Scribe. He fulfilled contracts in the way you described—a buyer paid for a particular item of information; state secrets, secured patents, the location of a person in hiding, whatever. He or she then received a flimsy book detailing the requested material. It always had schematics coupled with descriptions—words and pictures, if you will."

"How did Scribe get the information?" said Nate.

"No one knows."

"Was he hero or villain?" said Libby.

"Depends on your point of view. Scribe was amoral, driven by the desire for wealth. He put his skills to work for the highest bidder, no matter the client's underlying intention. To my knowledge, Scribe never killed anyone with his own two hands, but the people who bought secrets from him certainly had no such qualms. Many deaths resulted from the information he sold."

Nate nodded with understanding. "Like an arms dealer."

"Exactly."

"Scribe is well known," added Bobbie, "even in my section of the galaxy. What became of him, Ray?"

"Refractor said he was banished—as a matter of fact, that's one of the last things he said before shutting himself away."

"Why?" said Bobbie. "Where did Refractor send him?"

"I'm not sure. He wouldn't give details. You know how Refractor is...was."

She sighed. "Nothing has changed?" Ray merely

shrugged with a helpless expression.

"If Scribe knows how to pry out secrets," said Nate with growing excitement, "maybe he came across a way to travel through dimensions."

Ray looked doubtful. "I can't guarantee you'll get any answers from Refractor, and even if you find Scribe, he may not be able to supply the information you seek."

His obvious reluctance to talk about Refractor bugged Nate. Some indefinable emotion flitted across Ray's demeanor each time the superhero's name was mentioned. Was it anger? Frustration? Pity? A combination of all three. Nate couldn't quite place it.

"We'll take our chances," stated Libby without hesitation. "Scribe may be our only way home. At the very least, Refractor needs to know Mega Mole and Time Bomb aren't dead."

Bobbie clasped Ray's hand. "Take them to Refractor, Ray. He can't bury himself forever. Something has to change. I'll go, too."

They traded tender gazes. Ray rose to his feet, a new determination in his stance. "You're right. This self-imposed exile has gone on long enough."

Instead of heading out the front door, Ray led them through the house and down the steps to the water. "The police will be watching the streets," he said, "so we'll take my boat to the southern end of Second Chance City. The place we're going is right on the coast just past the public docks and Frenchman's Creek."

Moored at the end of a dock was a sailboat with a diesel engine. Nate stopped in his tracks. The name on the stern was Sea Spray.

"What is it?" asked Libby.

"I know this boat. It belongs...belonged to my parents. They sailed it down to Florida and kept it at my sister's house."

Libby eyed him tenderly and patted his arm. "It's still there."

Ray started the engine. They sailed south along the coast, paralleling Second Chance City harbor. The night was clear, no fog to block their view of twinkling city lights.

Libby stood next to Nate on the stern of the boat, peering over the water. "I'd forgotten the bay was so pretty."

"One of my favorite views," he said. "Although, it sure is whack to see Coldwater Bay with a nighttime skyline complete with high rises. Can't say I approve."

"Don't tell me you're one of those reactionaries who glorifies the good old days. Trust me, they weren't that good."

"Nope. I'm all for progress. I'm banking on it, actually." Nate pointed to the neon sign of The Factory shining in the darkness. "That's where the new condos will be built. Other homes are under construction, new businesses moving in every day. The town is growing bit by bit. That's a good thing—still small, but with more opportunities for folks. Hopefully, all the appeal of a close-knit community will remain. That's one of the reasons I came home."

Libby regarded him with interest. "Where did you go?"

"I went to college in Boston and signed on with the PD after graduation."

Her surprise was evident. "You were a patrol cop

in Boston?"

"Uh-huh. I wanted to be a cop since my folks moved to Coldwater Bay. I thought I also wanted the excitement of a big city, too, but something was missing. I didn't figure it out until Mike Williams called and offered me a job."

"You're satisfied writing parking tickets in Coldwater Bay for the rest of your life?" Libby scoffed; her skepticism plain. "After Boston, it doesn't seem like enough."

"I won't be a patrol officer much longer," said Nate. "My promotion to detective becomes effective in a month. Mike and I have talked about my future. He plans to retire in the next ten years and wants me to step in and take over. My career will grow along with the town."

"But still," argued Libby. "Coldwater Bay must be pretty dull compared to Boston. I'd think you miss all the action."

"Don't get me wrong," he said. "I loved Boston. Still do. It's a great city. I loved being a cop there, too. Nothing gets the adrenaline pumping better than running down bad guys." He leaned against the railing. "The problem was I never got much follow through with anything. I'd arrest some kid for shoplifting. He disappeared into the system, and I'd never find out what happened. I tried to stop by local businesses and make myself known, become a part of the community, but it's a lot harder to do in a big city."

His musing stirred a memory. "I actually became a cop because of Mike Williams. He caught me carving initials in a tree on public property. Instead of a lecture, he sat me down to ask about my mom." Nate made a wry face. "You can't keep any secrets in a small town. We were new arrivals, but word got out she had been diagnosed with cancer. Mike told me not to worry, her doctor was excellent. He never mentioned the tree again, but we both understood my career defacing public property was over. Then, he drove me home. The next day his wife, Tania, arrived at our house with a casserole. Once a week, Mike would drive by and stop me on my way home from school to ask how I was doing. That's the kind of cop I wanted to be—and I couldn't be him in Boston."

"That's a nice memory," murmured Libby. "When I flashback to Coldwater Bay, mostly I hear yelling and screaming between my parents." She leaned against the railing next to him. "You know, Mike Williams spoke to them, too."

"He did?" said Nate in surprise.

"Uh-huh. One of the neighbors must have called because of all the noise. I was in my bedroom with the door shut, wishing they'd both disappear, so I'd have the house to myself. Then a police car parked outside." She turned to him, chuckling. "Scared me for moment, I thought I got my wish, but Chief Williams only took my dad outside to talk. I don't know what was said, but Dad moved out that day, and the folks filed for divorce soon after. We all left Coldwater Bay, and I bounced between the two of them and their new families. I never wanted to live in a small town ever again. My one goal was to reinvent myself in a big city."

"You didn't need to," said Nate stoutly. "Nothing was wrong with the original Libby Parish. She made that summer bearable. Sitting against that tree with you meant, for a few hours, I didn't have to watch my mom ravaged by chemotherapy, or see the fear in my dad and sister. Talking about comic books and superheroes untied the anxious knots in my stomach—at least for a little while. Underneath that tree was the one place in town during that whole summer where I didn't feel afraid and helpless."

Libby turned her head away. "That tree was special for me, too. I felt safe there. You were the only one who ever understood me."

Nate wished he could see her face. Did she feel the same yearning for those emotions left behind so many years ago? What would he give to have Libby at his side again, but as a man this time, not a fumbling adolescent?

As if in answer to his wish, a gust of wind canted the sailboat hard to starboard. With the sudden change in direction, Libby stumbled. Instantly, Nate had his arms around her.

"Sorry," she said, red-faced. "I don't have my sea legs yet."

He pulled her close. "I won't let go."

They moved together in a steady rhythm with the waves; no thought, no effort into maintaining balance. Every shift of her body, every altered direction instantly reflected his. She turned her face toward him. His hand stroked her cheek, wet with spray. "Libby…"

Tell her now. Tell her what's in your heart.

Ray cut the engine. "We're here."

Libby stepped from Nate's side. Whatever moment they shared was gone. The boat approached a dock jutting from the shore. Perched on a cliff overhead was an elegant one-story building with an expansive view of the bay.

100

She leaned against the railing. "Hey, that's Smuggler's Cove Restaurant. I remember that place. It was the fanciest one in town."

"Still is," said Nate. "Strange hideout for Refractor. You'd think he'd be a tad conspicuous waiting tables. Although," he added lightly, "I hear the tips are good." He was rewarded with Libby's soft chuckle. Perhaps the moment wasn't lost forever, only this time and place weren't right. The desire to return home with her pressed against him stronger than ever.

After securing the boat, Ray switched on a flashlight, and the four of them climbed the steps to the restaurant. They reached the top, and circled the building to the front door. Obviously, Smuggler's Cove hadn't been open for some time. The canopy over the front door was torn, every window shuttered.

"I bought Smuggler's Cove when it went out of business several years ago," said Ray. "I needed space for my lab, but haven't returned since Refractor asked me to keep my distance." He motioned to the lighthouse a hundred yards away. Unlike the structure in Coldwater Bay, this was not in a public park, but surrounded by a chain link fence topped with barbed wire. "He's in there."

Nate scrutinized the fence. "How do we get on the grounds? I don't see a gate."

"The entrance is at the front, but a tunnel also connects this building with the lighthouse."

"The lighthouse keeper is in on it?"

Ray sported an impish grin. "Refractor is the lighthouse keeper. When George Styles, the old keeper died, Chief Williams hushed it up. He and I smuggled out the body and buried him in the woods. Refractor took over his identity."

Nate raised an eyebrow. "Seriously? No one got suspicious?"

"Refractor can form an image of George long enough to fool anyone who happens by," said Bobbie. "He was a known recluse, so didn't often get visitors."

"Yeah," said Ray, "Everyone in town knew George hardly ever left the lighthouse. Plus, this area is isolated and off limits to the public, so no one comes out here. Any random glow emitted from Refractor at the top of the tower wouldn't attract any attention, either."

"What happened to George's sons, Jake and Paul?" asked Nate.

"Never heard of Paul. Jake died years ago, killed during a bank robbery. The death tore his father up inside. Refractor tracked the murderer down. In gratitude, George offered the lighthouse as a hideout. He died soon after, and Refractor stayed on to watch over Second Chance City."

Nate's thoughts were in turmoil. More people he knew dead. He started as a gentle hand rested lightly on his arm. "I know," he said. "The people in Coldwater Bay are alive and well, but…"

Libby finished his sentence. "It doesn't feel that way."

Ray unlocked the door. He flicked on the lights and waved them inside. Nate had been to Smuggler's Cove a few times. The interior continued to hold faint remnants of the elegant dining establishment. The same crystal chandeliers hung high overhead. The polished wood floors were intact, if a little dusty. Most of the tables were gone, though. Those that remained had been pushed to the center of the room and covered with computers and lab equipment. Bookshelves instead of serving carts lined the walls. A bed, couch, and chairs shoved against shuttered windows made makeshift living quarters.

"Same old laboratory," said Bobbie. She pointed to a table with a slight smile. "I miss the fresh flowers, though. You always had a big vase full waiting for me right there. They made the place warmer."

"It wasn't flowers that made the place warmer." For an instant, their gazes locked. A flush rose to Bobbie's cheeks, and she looked away.

"Huh," whispered Libby to Nate. "I didn't see that coming."

"So in the comics they don't...you know."

"Nope. They don't 'you know.' Pierce Powers is all scientist. I'm not even sure he understands what 'you know' is."

"Maybe not," Nate quipped, "but I'll bet Ray and Bobbie don't need an instruction manual."

Ray touched a decorative molding on the wall. A section slid aside to reveal wooden stairs leading down an opening in the floor. Gentle illumination filtered up from the bottom.

"Mind your step," Ray cautioned.

The stairway led to a tunnel entrance. A row of lights, strung along the ceiling, lit the passageway.

Nate ran his hand against the wall as they walked along. "You carved all this out of solid rock?"

"The tunnel was already here," said Ray. "Styles showed it to us before he died. In the 1920's, Smuggler's Cove was a speakeasy. The tunnel was used by rumrunners to smuggle booze in from Canada." They passed a fork in the path. "That way goes to the sea and a hidden cave. A camouflaged door hides the entrance from any curious boaters passing by. This way leads to the lighthouse."

After a hundred yards, they came to a solid metal door. Ray slowly eased it open. They flinched as a loud squeak broke the silence.

Bobbie shot him a warning. "Careful, Ray!" she scolded. "You don't want to startle him."

Nate leaned over and whispered in Libby's ear, "Why is that bad?" She shot him a damned-if-I-know expression. An uneasy feeling took hold. Nate's hand moved to the grip of his 9mm.

They stepped into a small circular space. A metal ladder secured to the wall led up to a trap door. Ray went first with Bobbie right behind him. He pushed lightly on the hatch. It swung open freely, and he shouted, "It's Ray and Bobbie. We're coming in!"

Bobbie tugged on his pants leg. "It's not locked. That's a good sign, don't you think?" The apprehensive look he shot back did nothing to appease Nate's jitters.

The trapdoor was in the kitchen. This section of the lighthouse served as the gift shop in Coldwater Bay, but here was the keeper's quarters. The kitchen led into a living room. Visible through an open door on the far wall was the bottom of a spiral staircase—the only access point up the tower to the giant lens in the dome.

Bobbie stepped to the center of the room. Neither she nor Ray appeared eager to proceed any farther. "Refractor?" she called. "We've brought people to see you."

After several seconds of silence, an irritated shout echoed down from somewhere at the top of the spiral staircase. "Go away!"

Ray tugged at his collar. "Well, that's it then. We'll try again tomorrow." He and Bobbie took several steps back.

Nate's mouth dropped open. "What do you mean, that's it?" he snapped in annoyance. "You're calling it quits already?"

"He doesn't appear willing to speak at the moment," said Bobbie weakly.

Nate had reached his limit. "Well, he damn well better speak to us." Good Citizen was tired, hungry, and had it up to his neck with Second Chance City and its inhabitants. He stormed over to the opening. "Hey you! Get down here!" Nothing but silence greeted him.

Libby tugged at his sleeve. "Maybe a softer approach—"

"I'm soft," he sputtered, temper rising at the continued silence. "Look at how god-damned soft I am." Nate shouted up the stairway to Refractor. "What the hell is wrong with you? I said, get down here. We've come a long way—"

A sudden bright light issued from the open door. The little star blinked into existence at the top of Libby's flashlight.

"Wrong?" thundered a voice from somewhere above. "I'll tell you what's wrong. No one will leave me the hell alone!"

A silver beam coiled down from above, following the exact arc of the staircase before taking a hard right turn into the wall. It burned a neat little hole through the plaster a few inches from Nate's head.

Chapter Seven

Nate drew his weapon, and pushed Libby to the floor. To his horror, she immediately wiggled free and jumped to her feet. Clutching the flashlight, she went directly to the bottom of the spiral staircase. He grabbed for her, but she sidestepped. "Come back here," he whispered.

Libby ignored him and shouted, "My name is Elizabeth Parish..." She held the flashlight out in front. "Um...Mighty Light."

Nate grabbed her arm. "What are you doing? He tried to kill us."

"No, he didn't," she scoffed, shaking off his grip. "Refractor can shoot laser beams from his hand with pinpoint accuracy. You saw...he can even bend light around corners. If he wanted you dead, that hole would be through your forehead right now and not the wall."

"She's right." Ray's voice came from somewhere behind the couch. "That was a warning shot."

"Technically," added Bobbie, her voice issuing from the same location, "he wasn't shooting at Mighty Light, only you. He's rather an old-fashioned gentleman in that way. He always gives women a sporting chance."

Nothing anyone said improved Nate's disposition. Getting shot at always made him cranky. "You tell me right now," he snarled at the couch. "What the hell is wrong with that guy?"

"He's a little depressed," offered Ray.

"Depressed?" Nate gaped at the small smoking hole in the wall. "What do you mean, depressed?"

Bobbie peeked over the cushion top. "You know, mopey and down in dumps. It's been coming on for a while, but several months ago Refractor snapped. Now, he's shut himself in the lighthouse and won't talk to anyone. Ray and I figured he needed time alone, so we let him be."

Libby's expression softened with a wave of intense pity. "The worst thing for someone who's depressed is to be ignored by the very people who are supposed to care the most." Her voice hardened. "I'm going up there, Nate. You can either come with me or stay behind."

Nate glowered, but the stubborn tone told him no argument would change her mind. Holding tight to his gun, he stepped cautiously on the first tread.

"Listen up, Refractor!" he shouted. "Libby and I are coming to talk. She seems to think you're not going to kill us. I'm not so sure, but she has a flashlight that will knock you totally on your ass. I have a gun that may not do you much damage, but makes me feel better. You harm one hair on Libby's head and if nothing less, I'll shove my gun in your butthole…if you have a butthole. If not, I will make one in your butt and then shove it in."

Libby bit her lip. "Thank you. That was very threatening."

The radiance issuing from the top of the winding staircase diminished in intensity. "Whatever," said a doleful voice.

Bobbie and Ray stood up behind the couch. "You got him to communicate," said Ray with what smacked of false heartiness. "That's great."

"Good luck," said Bobbie. Without a glance back, they scurried to the trapdoor.

Nate and Libby cautiously climbed the stairs. Nate's heart hammered as they neared the top, but no other laser bolts issued from above. They reached the platform encircling the giant lens. An illuminated figure sank against the wall next to a rumpled bedroll and some plates with dried-on food. Refractor's shape was human. He had two eyes, a mouth, and a nose, but his facial features were smooth, more like a plastic mask, as if the light had evened out any irregularities. He was Generic Man.

Nate squinted against the glare. Generic Man was right. Refractor had fingers and toes and heavily muscled body parts in all the right places. He also appeared to be wearing a skintight swimsuit commonly referred to as a banana sling. Judging by the bulge, he wasn't a eunuch, after all.

"Hi," said Libby. "I'm Elizabeth Parish. This is Nate Hammond."

"Right," Refractor said bitterly. "The one who's going to shove the gun up my ass. Good luck with that, cowboy."

"He's not a cowboy," said Libby. "He's a cop. They call him Good Citizen," she added helpfully.

Refractor wasn't impressed. "Ridiculous name," he muttered and turned his head toward Libby. "Your costume is also absurd. Why do you dress as if you are headed for bingo night at the local Catholic Church?"

Libby laughed. "We're both a little new to the hero

gig. Any advice?"

For a moment, Refractor seemed drawn in by the sound of Libby's laughter. Then he turned his head away. "Give it up while you still retain the semblance of a normal life. Now leave me in peace." His shoulders hunched over, the picture of despair.

Nate shoved the gun in his belt. "This is a complete waste of time, Lib. How the hell can he help us? Let's get out of here."

Libby's attention remained focused on Refractor. She sat down on the floor next to him. Her hand touched his. "I'm so sorry," she whispered. "I know you're in a lot of pain. Tell me what happened. I want to help."

"It doesn't matter anymore."

"It does to me." She shot Nate a withering look. "To us."

He sighed in resignation and sat next to Libby. "Yeah, it does."

"We're not leaving," said Libby gently, "so you may as well talk." She clasped his glowing fingers in hers.

Refractor gazed down at their entwined hands. "What point is the fight when in the end innocents continue to suffer?"

"You're referring to what happened at O'Reilly's," said Libby. "That's where this all started, didn't it?"

"No, that's where it ended." He leaned against the wall and closed his glowing eyes. "Mike Williams...and others. They were all good people." His voice was heavy with grief. "Do you know how long it's been since I've had such closeness—felt part of a community? Do you have any idea how old I am?"

Nate and Libby exchanged puzzled glances. "Not really," she admitted. "Payton never wrote a backstory issue."

"A what?" said Refractor, clearly bewildered. "Who is Payton?"

"Never mind." Libby quickly changed the subject. "How old are you?"

"Many years," he said wryly. "I barely recall my true name."

"What is it?" asked Libby.

"Caleb." His lips formed a smile. "You are the first person to ask in a while."

Libby smiled at him. "Caleb is a nice name. My I call you that?"

"She said the same—" He broke abruptly off as if not wishing to stir a painful memory. "I would be pleased if you did."

"What happened to you?" asked Nate. "How did you become Refractor?"

"The fateful day occurred during the war."

"In the Middle East?" he guessed. It was tough to pin an age on someone who glowed all over.

"No," said Refractor. "The War for Independence."

Nate blinked. "From Great Britain?"

"That's the only one I recall," he said in obvious confusion. "Did I miss another? As I said, memories of events occurring during my origin are sometimes unclear."

"Go on," urged Libby.

Through the windows, the clear night sky twinkled with stars. "I remember a night like this," he said. "I walked along the shore. It was late, an unusual time to travel, but the moon was high, and I knew the territory better than any man. I had a short leave from the army and was anxious to see my wife."

Nate raised an eyebrow. "You were married?"

"Yes. I left to fight the British. Grace remained here in Coldwater Bay—"

"Coldwater Bay?" cried out Nate and Libby in unison.

"That was Second Chance City's original name. It was rechristened many years ago, but no one else remembers now except me."

Refractor stretched out a hand to the night sky. "I heard a strange whistling sound from above. A glowing rock streaked across the darkness and plowed into the sand at my feet with such force, the resultant upheaval of earth knocked me aside. It was so beautiful; I had never seen the like. I reached out as if it called for my touch. Then came an explosion, and I lost consciousness. When I awoke, my countenance and form were as you see now."

"What did you do?" asked Libby, enthralled.

"I staggered into town. No one recognized me, of course. All thought I was some manner of demon, come to destroy Coldwater Bay. They came at me with guns and pitchforks. A force like lightning exploded from my hands. It struck the side of a house and reduced a wall to ash. Terrified at this awful power, I ran. I had no desire to harm anyone. They were all good people, frightened by something they didn't understand. I lingered in a cave along the shore for days, hoping the effect would disappear, and I could go home."

Refractor hung his head. "Nothing changed. Then Grace found me. She had been searching. Even under all this," he gestured to his body, "she perceived my true self. Grace begged me to come with her. It was then I realized I had to leave. Other people would never see me as a man. My existence put her in danger. What would they do to Grace if they found her consorting with a demon? I said goodbye and bid her tell the townsfolk she received word of my death. She must forget me and find happiness with another."

He rose to his feet and gazed at the lights of Second Chance City. "I wandered for many years, learning to control my new powers. Eventually, I was able to bend the light, form an illusion of a shape, and hold it for a short while. It gave me a semblance of a life."

Libby regarded him with intense sympathy. "Did you ever see Grace again?"

"Once, but I only watched from afar. It brought my soul some peace to see her happily remarried with children. I left Coldwater Bay, swearing never to set foot within its boundary. Over the years, my reputation for fighting evil grew. People became less fearful. Along the way, someone gifted me with the name Refractor. Caleb died that night. It seemed as good an identity as any."

"How sad," said Libby softly. "What convinced you to return?"

"In my travels, I chanced upon a postcard for Second Chance City," said Refractor. "It tugged at buried memories of home. I had not planned to remain, but upon arrival found trouble had not left a place once held so dear. I met Ray who also was committed to fighting evil. We became friends. He vowed to search for a cure to my condition. Robella arrived on Earth and joined us. I made other friends, too—and enemies who took revenge. Now many good people are dead because of me."

Libby listened, wide-eyed. "Crisis of conscience," she whispered to Nate. "Typical comic book trope."

"I don't see how moping in a lighthouse helps," he muttered.

Libby responded tartly. "That's not very sympathetic."

Nate silently stewed. He had listened to Refractor's tale and was plenty sympathetic, damn it. He was also tired and fresh out of ideas how to get home.

Refractor hung his head. "People think immortality is a gift, but it is a curse. I have watched so many dear friends pass on. I no longer wish to be a part of life and have prayed my light will dim forever. However, it seems I am chained to an eternal existence."

That did it. The one person in this whole universe Nate had counted on for help was having a major pity party. "Well, I no longer wish to be a part of Second Chance City, either." Libby jabbed him in the side in a futile effort to shut him up, but Nate was on a roll.

"Other people have had it rough, too, you know," Nate grumbled. "I've been here less than a day. I discovered a lot of people important to me have been wiped from existence. I had my keister tossed in jail for no good reason, and, oh yes," he added sarcastically, "battled a giant mole and an exploding guy who tried to kill us. Right now I'm fed up with doing your job—"

Refractor eyed him sharply. "What's that, you say?"

"Mega Mole and Time Bomb are alive," said Libby.

"Not possible." The astonishment in his voice was

plain.

"Big, fat, ugly, hairy dude," sniped Nate. "Exploding guy in a silver suit? Sound familiar?"

Even through the radiance, Refractor was visibly shaken. "I was assured no one survived the fire and explosion at O'Reilly's Tavern."

"Did you see their bodies?" asked Libby.

"I-I had no need. It was too difficult. I couldn't look at her, I mean, at them...Officer Peevey assured me—"

Nate grunted. "Officer Peevey is now the chief."

Refractor eyed him askance. "That seems like poor judgment on the part of the town council. Florence Peevey hardly has a leader's temperament."

"No, kidding. Guess who threw me in jail solely for doing your damn job?"

"Perhaps, then," he responded coolly, "not a mistake. Her judgment now appears sound."

"Funny, real funny."

Nate glowered as Libby linked her arm with Refractor's. "We need your help."

"I'm not sure what assistance an old warrior like myself can offer," he said softly.

"Let me be the judge of that." Her gentle smile directed at the glowing figure raised Nate's hackles even more. "Listen to our story," Libby urged. "Perhaps we can find a way to help each other." Refractor bowed his head in acquiescence. His face lingered near Libby's. In expectation of a kiss?

Nate stepped between them. "Downstairs," he growled. "Libby and I aren't sitting on this cold stone floor any longer."

"Is Good Citizen always this rude, Mighty Light?"

asked Refractor as they descended the circular staircase.

"Yup," she cooed. "I usually pitch a rock at his head—straightens him right out...and please call me Elizabeth."

"Thank you, Elizabeth. I shall remember your advice."

The three of them sat at the kitchen table. Libby did most of the talking, wrapped up in the story. Nate's mood improved as she no longer seemed inclined to reach over and take Refractor's hand again.

"You showed great courage to stand against Mega Mole and Time Bomb," Refractor said to Libby with admiration. "Not many who battled them alone have lived to tell the tale."

Nate bristled. "Libby wasn't alone. I wouldn't let her fight them alone."

"A gun is hardly a suitable weapon against such enemies."

"Mega Mole would disagree," Nate huffed, irked by his dismissive attitude. "I hit him three times."

"But didn't stop him. Bullets inflict no permanent damage." Refractor motioned toward the flashlight. "May I?" Libby handed it to him. Refractor ran his fingers lightly across the surface. "A true object of power. I sense hidden energy. Keep it close. I wish no harm to come to you." As he pressed it into her grasp, his hand rested lightly on hers.

Libby smiled at him. "Thanks. I will."

"Back to this comic book that kidnaped us," Nate said, trying hard not to scowl at their hands. "Ray thought it might be connected to someone called Scribe."

"Scribe?" Refractor murmured, leaning back in his

seat. "I hadn't considered that. It's possible he arrived in your dimension."

"Ray told us you banished him," said Libby.

"No, I said he *vanished*. Scribe had barricaded himself behind a closed door. When I broke through, I caught a glimpse of his figure surrounded by a strange green pulsing light. Then both he and the light were gone."

"We saw the same green light!" Libby cried out.

Nate thoughts whirled. Their little unplanned side trip to Second Chance City began to make sense. "What does Scribe look like?"

"A youngish man, roughly one score and ten years, dark hair, always mindful of his appearance. Arrogant, wealthy, enjoys the finer things in life."

Nate caught Libby's gaze. Her wide eyes told Nate she had come to the same conclusion. "You don't think…" she stammered.

"Yeah," Nate said grimly. "I do. Payton Debolt and Scribe are one and the same."

"You know of Scribe?" asked Refractor.

"We believe he came to Earth from Second Chance City and assumed another identity," said Libby. "I worked for him actually," she added weakly. "He was always a douche, but I never expected anything like this."

"Do not blame yourself," said Refractor. "Lack of cleverness was never one of Scribe's faults."

Libby's jaw tightened. "How could I have been so stupid? All those times I helped him with the Refractor stories. I practically wrote the damn things for him. I was so desperate for my big break, I did whatever he wanted. He knew it, too. He played me, Nate, and I fell for it."

"You're not to blame, Lib," said Nate. "You couldn't have known."

"I should have known," she spit out in disgust. "I should have suspected something was fishy. Payton never even liked comic books. He made fun of people who read them. He didn't even feel a connection to any of his characters. He and his stupid little fountain pen—"

"Fountain pen?" Refractor leaned forward with growing excitement. "Describe it."

"Shiny black, tube-shaped, had a silver cap on the end."

"I've seen him with such an object," said Refractor. "It's not a pen. It is a type of interspace transporter. It was how he stole secrets and made his escape. The device allowed him to open a bridge between great distances or into secured areas—theft and escape made easy. The object was in his hand when he disappeared, emitting the green light you describe. It must be how he traveled to your dimension."

"We have to find Debolt," said Nate. "He brought us here. He can send us home."

"Alas," said Refractor. "Scribe could be anywhere. It was only by chance I spotted him. He was never known to stay in one place very long."

Libby slumped in her seat. "That's it then? There's no way home?"

Nate gaped at Refractor with incredulity. "We're stuck here?" Never to see his family and friends again? Never to walk the streets of Coldwater Bay? A wave of despair washed over him. "We can't be."

Libby's voice was barely above a whisper. "What

do we do now?"

Refractor's tone filled with tender concern. "I won't let any harm come to you." She smiled at him.

Nate's hackles rose straight to attention. Damn it. He should be the one offering solace to Libby. She should be smiling at him. How had Too Late Nate allowed this guy to jump the gun already? "Neither will I," he growled. "Libby doesn't need your help."

"Perhaps," Refractor said smoothly, "you don't know her as well as you think you do."

Nate half rose from his seat. "You don't know her at all, light bulb."

"Your blatant desire to prompt an antagonistic response by the use of insults is extremely childish."

"Will you two shut up?" snapped Libby, rubbing her temples. "God, I've got such a headache. I can't think anymore."

The last twenty-four hours had been hard on her, too. "You need rest, Lib," said Nate with concern. "We both do. We can't do anything else tonight. Things will be better in the morning. We'll find a way home. I swear it."

To his relief, her anger disappeared, replaced by a mixture of gratitude and amusement. "Since when did you become such an optimist?"

"Maybe I simply don't relish the thought of another rock thrown at my head," he said lightly.

"The caretaker's bedroom is off the living area," said Refractor. "It is small, but comfortable."

"Take it, Lib," said Nate. "I'll sleep on the couch."

She thanked him with another warm smile that lit his insides. They rose from the table. Nate bid Libby goodnight. She paused a moment as if expecting him to add something more. He tried to think, but fatigue had set in, dulling his thoughts. In his befuddled state, he garnered a quick impression of disappointment. Most likely, it was only his imagination working overtime.

Refractor's glowing visage followed Libby as she shut the door to the bedroom.

Nate's teeth set on edge. "You have something to say?"

"I merely observe you don't share a bedroom with Elizabeth, yet you call her Libby, which denotes a certain level of familiarity."

"I don't see how our relationship is any of your business."

"A blanket and pillow are in the cabinet," he said, disregarding Nate's antagonistic response. "I assume you don't need my assistance tucking yourself in."

"I'll manage," he huffed. Nate wondered idly how brightly Refractor would shine with his head stuffed in a toilet.

Refractor strode to the spiral staircase. He paused at the first tread, his gaze drifted in the direction of Libby's bedroom door. Nate tensed, but then Refractor continued on his way.

****

Nate awoke to the mixed aroma of bacon and fresh coffee. His stomach growled in anticipation. He threw off the covers, puzzling over the heavy wool quilt on top. Man, he must have been tired. Nate vaguely recalled becoming chilled during the night, but had no recollection getting off the couch to scrounge for more covers. He didn't even remember seeing this quilt in the cabinet. Arms stretched overhead, he arched his back and yawned. Another whiff of food teased his salivary glands. His lips twitched in a smile at the thought of Libby waiting in the kitchen. "Something sure smells good," he called out.

"Thanks," responded a woman's voice. "Coffee's on. Breakfast will be ready in a few minutes."

Nate frowned. Not Libby's voice. He stumbled into the kitchen, halting in surprise at Kristie Williams bent over the stove. "What are you doing here?"

"Follow-up interview," she said brightly. "Your jail break was the lead story in the paper. Chief Peevey tried to make light of it, of course. Denied having anyone thrown in jail and said the hole in the wall was due to a gas leak. Threatened to sue me if I ran it. Screw her. I ran it anyway. Gas leak..." She snorted. "Man, how lame is that? Actually, I called Bobbie and begged to help. She filled me in, and I offered to bring supplies. Isn't that tunnel under Smuggler's Cove wild? Who knew all that hid beneath Second Chance City?"

Nate had forgotten how Kristie talked a blue streak. "Ray showed you the lab?" he managed to get out when she finally paused for breath.

"Cool, huh?" she said. "I swore not to tell anyone. Trust me, I only want to help, and I've got plenty of connections. I'm already useful. I figured you'd be hungry. Sit down, and I'll get you some coffee."

"Aren't you forgetting something?"

Nate turned around. Libby stood behind him, toweling off her hair. She smelled fresh from the shower and was dressed in a cotton shirt and jeans instead of Mrs. O'Reilly's old clothes. The slight dampness remaining on her body plastered the blouse to her breasts, outlining the delicate lace bra underneath. Nate forced himself not to stare even though he really wanted to. "Might want to throw on a pair of pants," she added dryly.

Nate glanced down. He had removed most of his clothing last night and slept on the couch in his underwear.

"I brought you a change of clothes," said Kristie. She tossed him a duffle bag that sat on the floor and then studied his muscular athletic shape with obvious approval. "I'd say I got the size right."

Flustered, Nate went into the bathroom. Kristie had packed toiletries as well as clothing. He showered and shaved, and then threw on the clean outfit. When he returned to the kitchen, to his disappointment, Libby wasn't there. He poured himself a cup of coffee and casually asked Kristie where she had gone.

She piled a plate high with food. "Smuggler's Cove. I told her we'd come over for a strategy session as soon as you finished eating."

Strategy? That was good. Maybe Ray had concocted something. Nate dug in while Kristie kept up a stream of chatter, filling in the details after his escape from prison. She had brought a copy of *The Times* with her. Prominently displayed on the front page was a sketch of a studly stylized police officer using his fists to knock Mega Mole into his hole. A bright red *ka-pow!* detonated in the air. The grandmother with the auburn curls standing behind the police officer witnessed the scene with adoring approval. The headline read "Good Citizen Strikes a Blow for Justice."

"That's not how it happened," Nate sputtered. "Libby is not a little old lady, and her flashlight had the ka-pow. She saved me."

"Journalistic license," said Kristie, waving off his

protest. "You want the public behind you. A strong superhero adds more punch to the story. Mighty Light has less visual appeal."

"Because Libby was drawn like she's waiting for a ride to the hospice." This Kristie had definite differences in comparison with the one in Coldwater Bay. At home, she obsessed over getting the details correct and would have freaked over a single typo. "Isn't this a newspaper?" said Nate. "Aren't you supposed to be guardian of the truth?"

"Truth is in the eye of the beholder." Kristie leaned toward him. "Like right now. The truth is you seem tense."

Nate froze as her hand massaged his knee. The grope took him completely by surprise. Definitely not Coldwater Bay Kristie. He slid away from her to the edge of his seat. "So how's Logan?"

"Logan who?"

"Logan Emory."

"Never heard of him." Kristie's hand slipped between his legs. "I've never been this close to a real superhero."

So much for that second cup of coffee. Nate stood up. "Gotta get to Smuggler's Cove. The others are waiting."

"A superhero needs the public on his side," Kristie said, rising from the chair. "I can make your life much easier."

"I don't plan on staying in Second Chance City."

"What if you can't return to your own dimension? Life holds no guarantees, Good Citizen," she said with all seriousness. "Sometimes you have to make the best of a bad situation."

Her words brought a sudden chill. Not return?

Kristie led the way to the tunnel. "Think it over. Mighty Light seems happy here. She and Refractor have hit it off nicely."

The chill grew colder. "What do you mean?"

"They went together to Smuggler's Cove while you were in the shower."

He gaped at her in disbelief. "Refractor left the lighthouse? I thought he was still up top moping."

Kristie examined her nails. "Mighty Light rose early. She was with him when I arrived. I heard their voices. She came down from the lighthouse to shower and change right before you woke. Wonderful, isn't it? Bobbie told me Refractor was a recluse, but Mighty Light has had quite a softening effect on him. As a matter of fact, he seems very much taken with her. He had her arm when they left. He can have sex, you know," she added brightly.

"What?" Nate said weakly.

"I asked Ray—a necessary part of investigative journalism is to get all the pertinent facts. He told me Refractor's junk is all there." Kristie slipped her arm through his. "Shall we go, too?"

Nate escorted Kristie into the tunnel, her words ringing in his ears. Could Libby possibly be attracted to Refractor? She couldn't...not yet. Nate had this all worked out. They were going home. He would ask her out. He would give her a reason to stay in Coldwater Bay. A mental image of Refractor and a naked Libby clasped together popped unbidden into his mind. She was lit from the inside and groaning in ecstasy.

Stop it! Stop thinking of them! Nate substituted another image of him giving Refractor a swirly in the toilet. His mood immediately improved.

Nate tensed as they approached the laboratory. He scaled the ladder, anxious about what sight would meet his eyes. To his relief, Libby didn't have Refractor's hand, although he hovered nearby. Her flashlight was tucked into her belt. "Hey, Lib," Nate called out, shooting Refractor a dark look.

Libby matter-of-factly nodded toward Kristie. "I see you two are getting acquainted."

So intent on Libby, Nate failed to notice Kristie had linked her arm with his again. Flustered, he removed it. Damn, she was growing to be a nuisance. Was it his imagination or did he catch a quick sparkle from the flashlight?

Ray huddled over a bank of electronic equipment while Bobbie tapped on a keyboard. He called out a greeting and motioned everyone near. "We have been discussing a plan of action."

"Any idea how to track down Scribe?" Nate asked eagerly.

"We think so. Mega Mole has used his services in the past. He may know Scribe's new hideout or, at the least, a way to contact him."

Refractor peered over Ray's shoulder at a computer monitor. "It appears to be some sort of sensor."

"Yes. I got the idea a while ago, but put development aside. After the explosion in O'Reilly's, it didn't seem necessary anymore." He looked down, abashed. "Sorry, I was wrong."

"We all were," said Refractor. His head turned toward Libby, gaze softening. "Until someone set us right." She smiled at him.

Nate tore his attention from them and focused on

Ray. "What does it do?"

"It measures seismic movement in the earth. The sensors are quite delicate. The trick was getting them calibrated to differentiate between Mega Mole's movements and other disturbances to the ground like construction or even heavy traffic." He flashed Bobbie an admiring glance. "With Bobbie's help, I have been able to make the necessary adjustments. I believe the next time Mega Mole excavates, we can intercept him."

"What's the range?" said Nate.

"That's the machine's drawback. Not far, I'm afraid—less than half a mile and Mega Mole tunnels damn fast. We'll have to jump on the trail as soon as his movements register or he's gone."

Ray regarded Nate with interest. "I've got something else you might like. I finished a new invention a while ago, but never got a chance to use it." He went to a cabinet and retrieved a metal case containing a pistol and shoulder holster. The gun was roughly the same size and shape of his 9mm. Nate hefted it experimentally. The weight and grip were similar, too.

"I started with a standard police issue," said Ray, "and then added my own modifications. Frankly," he admitted sheepishly, "it's better off in your hands. I'm not much of a marksman and would probably shoot my foot off...put your finger on the trigger and point it at the wall."

Nate aimed the gun. A red dot appeared. "Laser-guided firing system?"

"Yes," said Ray. "It activates with the slightest pressure."

Nate examined the clip with interest. "These aren't

standard."

"Sonic rounds. They deliver quite a kick. A regular bullet can wound Mega Mole or Time Bomb, but won't stop either for long. These should render them unconscious, but the wave dissipates the farther from a target, so you have to be fairly close. Be careful, though," he warned. "The discharge emits a heavy recoil. If you're not prepared, it'll knock you flat on your ass."

"Duly noted," said Nate. He had tucked his own weapon into his waistband before leaving the lighthouse. Now he put it in the metal case and slipped on the holster and sonic gun.

"We need to stop Mega Mole as quickly as possible," said Ray. "Right now, only Time Bomb is with him, but he always had a knack for recruiting henchmen. I don't want to confront any more. Remember Lorelei Del Fuego?" he said to Bobbie.

Nate's jaw dropped open. "Lorelei Del Fuego was a villain?"

Bobbie nodded. "An arsonist extraordinaire, and one nasty bit of work, but she disappeared a while ago. We must have proven to be too much," she added proudly, "and chased her out of town."

Ray jabbed Nate in the ribs. "It got too hot for her here. Get it?"

Refractor rolled his eyes. "That joke has become tiresome, Ray."

Nate was in a daze. "Lorelei Del Fuego? I can't believe it."

"You dated her, too?" asked Libby deadpan.

Bobbie patted his arm in sympathy. "I'm sorry for your loss."

"No," Nate sputtered. "At home, Lorelei Del Fuego owned Write Away. She also wrote romance books known for groaningly bad dialogue. Sweep me to paradise, my prince. Let passion ignite the flames of love…that kind of crap."

"Sounds kinky," Kristie purred. "I'm game for role play." Libby didn't seem amused.

"I don't read them," protested Nate. "I saw a display of her books in Write Away."

Bobbie frowned. "I don't carry them." Her expression brightened, and she added helpfully, "Perhaps you're thinking of your own copy."

"The other Write Away!"

"Lorelei Del Fuego was a snap," said Ray, "compared to someone like Time Bomb. Although, Araña gets my vote as the worst."

Bobbie nodded an agreement. "No argument there. Good thing we had Refractor on our side. I don't know what we would have done alone."

Libby was bewildered. "Who is Araña? She wasn't in the comic."

"Araña the Venomous," said Bobbie. "Her skin was deadly to the touch. She also ejected a particularly vicious poison—one drop resulted in a slow horrible death unless treated immediately."

"Let me guess," said Nate, "she was bitten by a radioactive spider." Bobbie's surprise told him he had scored a hit. Nate leaned over and whispered triumphantly in Libby's ear, "Even I know that trope."

Libby's attention, however, was fixed on Refractor. He hadn't said a word and appeared deep in thought. She touched his arm. "Did you think Araña was the worst?"

Refractor seemed perturbed by the question. "What does it matter?" he said harshly. "She is gone."

A strident buzz emanated from the seismic sensor. Ray pounced on the machine. "Mega Mole is in range!"

Chapter Eight

Nate was instantly on alert. "Got a location?"

"He's directly underneath Main moving in a southerly direction. Can't tell the objective."

Libby hazarded a guess. "Maybe he's returning to Cara Tyson's jewelry store to try again."

Bobbie checked the readings over Ray's shoulder. "Could be..." She held a tablet computer and tapped on the screen. "I've transferred the display to this device. We'll take it with us to track his movements. Let's go."

"How do we intercept him?" said Nate. "We came here by boat, but Mega Mole is moving fast under the city. We need a car to catch up. We don't have one."

"Use mine," said Kristie to Nate with an inviting smile. "It only seats five, but I can sit on your lap."

"You stay behind," he ordered. "It's too dangerous." Did she not get the concept of personal space?

Much to Nate's relief, Ray announced he had a vehicle. At a run, they followed him to a garage. Bobbie let out a gasp at the sight of a nondescript white van. "You told me you were going to sell it."

Ray jumped into the driver's seat. "I couldn't. It held too many good memories." Pink rose to Bobbie's cheeks as she climbed into the passenger seat.

Nate and Libby exchanged an amused glance. Obviously, the same thought occurred to both. *Ray and*

Bobbie so used to do it in the back of the van.

The cargo bay was lined with built-in storage units. By a less than polite shove to Refractor, Nate maneuvered next to Libby. Kristie moved to climb in with them. "Sorry," he said, "too dangerous." Nate shut the door before she could argue.

Ray reached into the glove compartment and tossed Nate a pair of manacles. "Take them, Good Citizen. They emit a frequency to temporarily disrupt the nervous system of anyone exposed to zayton radiation. Slapping the cuffs on Mega Mole or Time Bomb will weaken them considerably."

Nate tucked them into his waistband. "Only one pair?"

Ray's face reddened. "That's the last one I had left. I didn't expect to need more." He turned the key. The engine roared to life. "I haven't used the van lately, but keep it tuned and ready to go." He gazed at Bobbie, full of yearning. "Some old habits die hard."

The pink in her cheeks deepened. "Thankfully."

Nate's lips twitched in a smile. *They so did it last night at Smuggler's Cove, too.*

Ray gunned the engine and tore out of the driveway. Bobbie kept her attention glued to the tablet's display as they raced down the access road. "Mega Mole continues south on Main. He just passed the intersection of Center Street. Signal strength is increasing. We're closing in…wait. Mega Mole took a hard right on Oak Avenue."

"Not Cara Tyson's store, then," murmured Libby. "What's he after?"

"He's approaching the intersection of Oak and First," announced Bobbie.

Nate tensed in his seat. "Ray, take the next left. We'll cut him off."

"You know where Mega Mole is going?"

"I've got an idea. Is there still a bank on First?"

"Of course. Where else would Second Chance City Fidelity be?" The tires squealed as Ray turned hard left.

Bobbie remained focused on the tablet. "Mega Mole went south onto First and is slowing down as he approaches the bank. Nice work, Good Citizen."

Libby's hands clenched the flashlight, holding it out in front. The soft illumination washed over her, making her skin appear to glow from within.

As Nate watched, her breathing rapidly increased. Damn, she was beautiful. Suddenly, she swallowed hard and licked her lips. He recognized the signs. As a police officer, he'd felt nervous tension often enough. A little was good, but too much threw off judgment. He nudged her. "Nervous, sidekick?"

She made a face. "I'm not your sidekick, no matter what the newspaper says."

"Nope," said Nate. "You're my partner—your costume is still lame, even though you changed. Superheroes don't wear sneakers."

Her tension visibly eased. She flashed a smile. "So is your handle. Good Citizen sounds like a crossing guard."

Bobbie reached into the glove compartment and removed two woolen ski masks, both midnight blue in color with a bright yellow R embroidered on the foreheads. She and Ray slipped them on.

Nate gawked. "Ski masks?"

"Bobbie's own design," said Ray proudly. "She knitted them herself. Clever, no? They hide our appearance perfectly."

Beside Nate, Libby shrugged. "Beats black horn-rimmed glasses."

Ray slammed on the brakes. The tires screeched to a halt in front of the bank.

"Ready?" said Nate to Libby, drawing his weapon.

Her eyes took on a determined gleam, all nervousness cast aside. "Ready."

They burst from the van. The street was quiet. "Where is he?" said Refractor.

Bobbie checked the readout. "He stopped."

Nate tensed. "Could he suspect we're here?"

"I-I don't know." Bobbie tapped the palm of her hand briskly against the side of the tablet as if a pointless gesture would somehow make a confusing readout more understandable. She pointed north. "He appears to have halted two doors down."

"The family health clinic?" said Nate. "What does he want there? Supersize condoms?"

"Health services is in front," said Ray, "but the hospital's lab and storage facility is in the rear."

"Storage facility?" echoed Libby. Her interest riveted on the clinic. "What do they store?"

"Drugs mostly," said Ray, "and radioactive isotopes for use in medical research and treatment."

Libby narrowed her eyes. "By chance, would any of the isotopes contain zayton radiation?"

"It's possible, I suppose," Ray said haltingly. "The use of zayton is highly restricted because of the danger, but a secure lab like that one should have the means to implement proper safety protocols."

Libby smacked herself upside the head. "Oh, no. How could I have been so stupid?" She jumped in the van. "Ray—to the lab. Move it!"

They all piled in, and Ray hit the accelerator. As they approached, the ground rocked underneath the tires. The van jumped the curb and tore across the lawn to the parking lot in the rear of the building. Ray slammed on the brakes. Mega Mole stood in a hole near what had once been the metal security door. Twisted smoking wreckage at his feet was all that remained— Time Bomb's work, Nate had no doubt.

They bolted from the van. "Give it up, Mega Mole!" yelled Refractor. "Your crime spree is over."

Nate tensed, finger on the trigger waiting for the beast to attack. The laser sight made a tiny red dot on Mega Mole's massive chest.

Instead, his little piggy eyes grew wide. "Okay, I surrender. Help me, please," he begged.

Refractor stared at him in stunned disbelief. "What did you say?"

"Please..." Mega Mole climbed out of the hole with hands held high. "Let's get out of here."

Before the astonished Refractor could respond, a muffled explosion came from inside the building.

"Keep him covered," Nate ordered Refractor and the others. He glanced at Libby. She nodded tersely and then raced ahead. At the intersection of the first corridor, Nate drew Libby flat against the wall. Sounds of movement came from down the hall.

"On three," he whispered to her.

"One..." A shimmery shield of light formed in front of the flashlight.

"Two..." Libby gritted her teeth, her face set in lines of grim determination.

"Three!"

They charged into the hallway. At the other end, Time Bomb exited a room marked Lab 3. Nate got the peculiar impression he was relieved to see them.

Instantly, Time Bomb raised both hands. "I surrender."

"No, you don't," said a man behind him. Time Bomb grimaced and dropped his arms.

"Hello, Payton," said Libby with a cold angry voice. She didn't sound surprised.

"Elizabeth?" Debolt stepped from behind Time Bomb, fury mixed with astonishment colored his expression. He carried a silver case in one hand marked Radiation Hazard in bold red, and his pen device in the other. "Well, well, I can honestly say, you are the last person I expected to see here." He sneered at Nate. "And you brought Officer Numbnuts, too? What a pleasure."

"Scribe, what's the hold up?" barked another voice. A third man exited the lab. He was dressed in a gray utilitarian uniform with a quasi-military appearance.

Libby gasped. "Syr?"

"Who are they?" growled Syr. "How do they know me?"

"What the hell do you think you're doing, Payton?" said Libby. "What's going on?" The star's glow increased. The shield shimmered in the air as Nate's finger tightened on the trigger.

"I'm surprised at you, Elizabeth," Debolt, said snidely. "You've already forgotten the first three rules for any successful villain. Never monologue, never explain, and never let the good guys live…Syr."

Syr opened fire with some sort of laser weapon. Light beams bounced harmlessly off the shield, striking the wall. The blasts left smoking holes in the cinderblock.

Nate took aim. A bright red dot zeroed in on Debolt's chest. "Drop the pen and the case. Raise your hands."

Debolt glowered at them. "Well, this is a goddamned frustration. You'll have to die the old-fashioned way. Time Bomb, kill them."

Agony wrenched the henchman's visage. "Sorry…" The explosion rocked the corridor.

Libby grimaced, holding tight to the flashlight as the shock wave slammed into the star's force shield. Debris jarred loose from ceiling and walls, deflecting off the protective shell. The dust settled with no sign of Debolt, Syr, or Time Bomb, but a new gap in the wall led directly to outside.

"This way!" shouted Nate. "We'll head them off at Mega Mole." They retraced their steps to the rear and exited as Time Bomb appeared around the corner of the building. Nate dropped to a crouch and fired. The blast from the sonic round hit Time Bomb dead center in the chest.

Ray hadn't exaggerated the recoil. Even after Nate had braced himself, he staggered, barely able to keep from being knocked on his rear. Time Bomb, meanwhile, catapulted across the parking lot, slammed into a tree, and then crumpled to the ground.

Debolt shouted. "Mega Mole, attack!"

All hell broke loose.

Mega Mole, who had been placidly standing with raised arms, suddenly went berserk. He ripped up clumps of earth, tossing them with abandon. Libby dove to Nate's side and fired up her protective shield an instant before a boulder slammed into him. It ricocheted aside.

Syr's weapon exchanged rapid fire with Refractor who shot concentrated energy bolts from his fingertips. Bobbie's armband sent out electric charges shaped like lightning bolts. They slammed into Mega Mole with little effect, but one clipped Syr in the shoulder. He cried out in pain. Refractor stretched out his hand toward Syr. Energy crackled at his fingertips.

"Araña!" bellowed Debolt, clenching the pen tight.

A dark-haired woman dressed all in black climbed out of the hole. Glistening web-like striations mottled every inch of her skin.

Refractor froze in place, his gaze riveted to the woman in black. "Aña."

"Forgive me," she begged in a choked voice. Her head snapped back. Fangs erupted from inside her mouth.

"Take cover!" he yelled.

Ray yanked Bobbie inside the van as a fine spray shot out from Araña's mouth. Droplets spattered against the star shield. They evaporated with a sizzling hiss.

Libby grunted, holding tight to the flashlight. She pressed her lips together. "Damn, that stuff smarts."

Nate coughed as a foul, acrid odor filled the air. After several moments, the mist cleared. The noxious odor was gone. So were Debolt and the others, including the woman in black. Mega Mole's tunnel had been filled in, covering their retreat.

Libby dropped the shield, her complexion pale and sweaty. She took a stumbling step. Nate holstered the revolver. He put his arms around her shoulders and pulled her close. "You okay?"

She leaned against him with a sigh. "I am now."

"You sure?" He held her tight. "You look like hell."

"Wow," she chuckled. "You sure know how to worm your way into a girl's heart."

"Yeah," he said gently. "Mr. Smooth Talker, that's me."

Libby nestled against Nate's chest as if comforted by his heartbeat. "Man, that was foul stuff. Worse than Time Bomb's explosions—Time Bomb! He's still here!" she cried out in triumph. They ran to the unmoving form under the tree. Nate nudged him none too gently with his toe. Time Bomb stirred and groaned.

"Not dead, yet," Nate grunted. "We got ourselves a prisoner to question." He slapped on the cuffs. "You're under arrest or whatever it is they do here. You don't have the right to remain silent. Try it, and I'll knock you silly again." He scanned the parking lot. None of the others were visible. "Is everyone all right?" he called out.

Bobbie and Ray emerged from the van, unharmed. Tiny blisters of paint on the hood bubbled up where Araña's spray had landed.

"General Syr is in Second Chance City," said Bobbie, obviously shaken. "I thought I was safe here."

Ray took her hand. "I'm sure he didn't recognize you, and he'll have to get through me, first."

"Over here!" Refractor's call came from around the building. "Hurry!"

Refractor knelt beside Kristie. The camera lay at her side. She was unconscious and barely breathing, her skin discolored with bright red welts. Refractor motioned to a sedan. "She must have followed us in her car and then took position here for pictures. Unfortunately, a drop of Araña's poison landed on her skin. She needs medical attention immediately."

Libby gasped. "All this from one drop?"

Nate was stricken. He lifted Kristie into his arms. "This is my fault. I should have suspected she'd follow and kept an eye out for her."

Bobbie had already started Kristie's car. "Put her in. I'll get her to the hospital." Nate placed Kristie gently in the front seat and started to climb in the rear when Bobbie stopped him. "Stay here," she said firmly. "The police are still on the hunt for you."

"You shouldn't go alone, Bobbie," Ray insisted. "Not with Syr in the area."

"I'll go," said Libby, jumping in. "They don't know me."

Nate grabbed her arm. "Debolt does and he wasn't overjoyed to see us—"

"Don't worry," Libby said, shaking off his arm. "I'll make sure Kristie gets the best treatment." With a roar, the car tore out of the parking lot.

Nate watched the women leave, a heavy feeling in the pit of his stomach. Debolt allied with Mega Mole and Syr. That couldn't bode well.

A siren wailed in the distance. "We need to go," said Ray. "I don't care to answer awkward questions when the police discover smoking holes in the building."

Refractor and Nate grabbed Time Bomb and tossed him in the van. "That was quite a crash landing," Nate said, as they drove from the lab. "Are you sure he'll recover enough to talk? I don't feel particularly charitable right now and would just as soon dump him on the side of the road for the police, if he isn't any use."

"Need I remind you," said Refractor. "Time Bomb is a man who explodes and reforms at will. It would take more than a little knock on the head to do permanent harm."

"Point taken. You sure those manacles will hold, then?"

"They should," said Ray, who had been listening in. "Of course, they've been sitting in the van for a while…and the power pack only carries a limited charge…and it always had a tendency to overload quickly and shut down."

"Thanks, Ray," said Nate sarcastically. "I'm overflowing with confidence in your inventions." As the van tore down the street to Ray's lab, Nate glowered at the captive. "Will Kristie live?"

"Difficult to say," said Refractor. "It all depends on how much of the poison penetrated her skin. She is young and strong, and the hospital only minutes away. There is every hope. I'm sorry…you and Ms. Williams had formed a bond?" For once, his tone seemed sympathetic.

"I wouldn't say that." Nate grimaced, recalling the crotch grab. "I'm friends with the Kristie at home, but don't want to see anyone hurt. That poison is horrific stuff. How did you defeat Araña before?"

"I didn't. I assumed Aña was killed in the explosion at O'Reilly's."

"Aña?"

"I meant, Araña."

A nickname? Nate suspicions rose. As Refractor had pointed out not to long ago, a nickname denotes a certain level of familiarity. What exactly had gone on between those two? "So you don't know how to defeat her?"

"No."

"A smoking hole in the head from your laser beam might have done the trick. Ever think of trying that today?"

The pause was only an instant, but enough for Nate to take note. "I never had the chance. She moved too quickly."

Did she, really? Nate sat in edgy silence. There were definitely some interesting dynamics going on here. He prodded Time Bomb with his toe. "He and Mega Mole seemed relieved to see us. That's not what I expected, especially after our first encounter."

Refractor's bewilderment was obvious. "I don't understand.   Mega   Mole   even surrendered…surrendered." He shook his head. "I can't explain it. He didn't even try to fight until Scribe ordered him."

"His name is Payton Debolt," Nate spit out.

Ray glanced at him in the rearview mirror. "Scribe is definitely the man you seek?"

"Yeah, Debolt was an illegal alien from this dimension all along. His disappearance from Write Away must have been on purpose, but he certainly didn't expect to see me and Libby. No matter…he traveled from Coldwater Bay to Second Chance City, so he has a way to send us home. We have to find him."

"Elizabeth surmised his plan to steal the zayton," said Refractor. "How did she know?"

"No idea." Nate's lips twisted in a wry smile. "I'm going to have a long hard talk with her when she gets back."

Refractor motioned to the unconscious form of Time Bomb. "I'm sure our guest can be persuaded to part with information." Although his warm glow hadn't decreased, his voice could definitely be described as cold.

Time Bomb had begun to stir by the time they returned to the lab, his only visible wound a swollen lip. Refractor dragged him to a chair. Nate pulled out the gun and poked him sharply in the forehead with the muzzle. Time Bomb emitted a muffled groan.

"Wakie, wakie," said Nate, poking harder.

"Ow," he yelped. "That hurts." His eyelids fluttered open. A bleary gaze focused on Nate. "You."

"Yeah, me. You're our prisoner."

Nate expected a struggle, sullenness, or at the very least a few hurled obscenities. Instead, Time Bomb displayed a mixture of relief and joy. "I can't explode. I want to follow orders, but I can't. What did you do to me?"

"The cuffs," said Nate, at a loss to understand the lighthearted reaction. "They keep your power at bay."

Time Bomb leaned back in the chair with a happy sigh. "Thank you. You don't know how stressful this has been."

Nate gawked at him. "You're thanking me?"

Time Bomb shuddered. "These past twenty-four hours have been a nightmare...oh, hey, Refractor. I see you came back to town."

"Never left," he said icily. "I see you survived O'Reilly's. What happened that night?"

"Mega Mole spotted you going in. He and I planned an ambush—no offense," he added, "but you had become a real pain. Unfortunately for us, when Mega Mole came through the floor he must have ruptured a gas main. My explosion turned into a firebomb. We got knocked underground, tons of debris on top of us. We barely escaped. It took months for Mega Mole and me to recuperate." He spoke as if he expected sympathy and seemed put-off when none was offered.

Ray regarded him with disgust. "A dozen people died in that explosion."

Time Bomb shrugged, completely unconcerned. "Shit happens."

"What became of Araña?" demanded Refractor.

"Beats me. She wasn't with us that night. As a matter of fact, Araña hadn't been around for days. She kept to herself and stopped answering our calls. Told us to get lost. Pissed me the hell off—after all we'd done for her. Chicks," he snorted out in disgust. "Completely disloyal. Totally unreliable for man's work, probably had PMS or something. Yesterday was the first time I'd seen her since before O'Reilly's."

"What exactly," said Nate snidely, "did you do for her that deserved loyalty?"

He bristled as if the question was an insult. "Gave her a job, of course. After she got infected, Araña wasn't exactly Junior League material anymore. You'd think she'd have been more grateful."

Nate snorted. "For a life of crime?"

"Man, you really are new here," Time Bomb sniped. "What the hell else are we supposed to do?"

Before Nate could insist on an explanation, Refractor jumped in. "What is Scribe's involvement?"

All the color drained from Time Bomb's face, the

bluff and bluster vanished. "We got back from our thwarted robbery of the jewelry store. Mega Mole gets a call on this phone he hadn't used in months. It was Scribe, he wanted to meet. When Mega Mole returned, Scribe was with him, but something was off. I couldn't place it at first, and then I realized the truth. Mega Mole was afraid." Time Bomb shuddered. "Do you understand what I'm saying? Mega Mole was afraid. In all the years I've known him, he's never been afraid of anything—not even death."

Time Bomb swallowed hard and touched his swollen lip. "Out of nowhere, Mega Mole sucker punched me. I woke with blood dripping from my mouth and everything changed." He turned wild eyes on Refractor. "You should have killed Scribe when you had the chance. Now, you're doomed with the rest of us."

"You're speaking nonsense," snorted out Refractor. "What could Scribe have possibly done?"

"That thing he's got—that pen device." Time Bomb's tone took on a note of hysteria. "It makes people like us do whatever he says. You can't fight against it. God knows we've all tried. His first order is to obey. You do. The second order..." He wore a haunted demeanor. "If captured, kill yourself."

Nate's finger went to the trigger. The little red dot of light shone on Time Bomb's forehead.

"Don't worry." Time Bomb displayed his shackled hands. "I can't. The cuffs prevent it, but the compulsion is there." He grimaced as if experiencing intense pain. "I can hear it, even now. His voice is in my head ordering me to die. I need to get out of here. Far away, where the voice can't reach me."

"A mind control device," scoffed Ray. "You expect us to believe that?"

Some of Time Bomb's bluster returned. "Fine," he sneered, "be happy in your little castle of denial. Scribe already has another playmate. He's is in league with a guy named Syr who is hunting some chick named Princess Robella."

"How did Scribe even know about Syr," Ray demanded, "or Robella for that matter?" Nate was startled by the intense hatred in the tone of the usually genial Ray.

Time Bomb snorted a derisive laugh. "Are you kidding? Syr hired him months ago to find Robella's location. Scribe tracked her as far as Second Chance City and then contacted Mega Mole to be on the lookout. Apparently, Syr offered quite a paycheck because Scribe is still on the trail."

"And Araña?" demanded Refractor.

"Scribe sent her a message. I didn't think she'd come, but whatever he said lured her out of hiding. Now she belongs to Scribe, too." He raised the manacles and sighed in relief. "Not me anymore though, I'm safe."

Refractor leaned in. "Only for as long as I allow it. Where are Scribe and the others hiding?"

Time Bomb glowered at him. "If you want any more information, then first get me the hell away from Second Chance City. Far enough so Scribe's power can't reach me. Once this place is nothing but a tiny dot in the rearview mirror, I'll tell you everything."

"I'll turn you over to state police headquarters," said Ray. "Is that far enough for you?"

"Make it two states over," he answered sullenly,

"and you have a deal."

Ray grabbed Time Bomb by the arm, yanked him roughly to his feet, and shoved him ahead toward the door. "What does Scribe want with the zayton stolen from the lab?"

"Damned if I know," jeered Time Bomb. "When you meet him in person, be sure to ask."

Nate and Refractor followed. The van was parked in front, keys still in the ignition. Despite Time Bomb's agreement to cooperate, apparently old habits die hard. In one swift move, Time Bomb elbowed Ray viciously in the stomach and raced toward the driver's seat. Nate aimed the sonic gun, but Refractor stayed his hand. "They never learn."

Time Bomb started the engine and with spinning tires peeled out from Smuggler's Cove.

"Uh, Refractor?" said Nate. "He's escaping."

Refractor raised his hand. A beam of concentrated energy shot out, hitting the rear tire with pinpoint accuracy. Rubber exploded from the rim. The van skidded out of control before coming to rest at the edge of the driveway. "You were saying?"

"Never mind," said Nate with an approving look. "Nice shot."

Time Bomb leapt from the van and ran toward the bay. "Hey!" yelled Nate. "Where the hell do you think you're going?"

"Stop him," gasped Ray, struggling to recover his breath. "The boat is at the dock."

Nate raced after Time Bomb. "Stop or I'll fire!" he yelled.

Time Bomb ignored the warning and bolted to the stairs leading to the beach. Nate braced himself for the

145

recoil as he pulled the trigger. The shock wave hit Time Bomb dead center, knocking him in a high arc over the cliff.

Nate halted at the top of the stairs. Time Bomb had landed in the water. He bobbed to the surface, coughing and sputtering. Enraged, he let out a string of curses and raised his manacled hands overhead. "All right, I give. Stop shooting—"

A blue flash emitted from the manacles, followed by a puff of smoke.

"Damn," muttered Ray. "He probably shouldn't have gotten those wet."

Without warning, Time Bomb screamed. Panic replaced sullen rage.

Nate watched in stunned horror as Time Bomb vibrated in the ocean, the oscillations so severe, they sent ripples of sea water splashing against the shore.

"Help me," he howled. "I have to…I can't stop."

Nate moved to descend the stairs, but Refractor grabbed his arm. "Where is Scribe hiding?" he yelled.

The only response was a gut-wrenching shriek. The savage vibrations created a waterspout, turning Time Bomb into nothing more than a shadowy shape trapped within a whirling blur.

The concussive force of the explosion knocked them all to the ground. An instant later, Nate was hit by a splash of cold salty sea water. He opened his eyes, and immediately rolled across the lawn. A jagged piece of wood speared the earth right where his chest had been a moment before. Nate staggered to his feet and peered down to the dock—or what was left of it. The first three-quarters were gone. The Sea Spray was still moored to the one remaining section at the end that hadn't been destroyed in the explosion. The boat bobbed wildly in the churning water, straining at the lines.

The three men raced down the steps. A series of waves crashed against the shore, shooting water and spray into the air. They scanned the turbulent surface of the bay. Eventually, the waves settled to lap gently on the beach. Nate waited for Time Bomb to reform.

He didn't.

Chapter Nine

They trudged up the steps and returned to the lab. For a long time, no one spoke. Eventually, Nate managed, "What the hell?"

"Indeed," breathed out Refractor.

Ray stared in shock at the ceiling. "Gone… He's simply gone. I didn't think it was possible. He said Scribe commanded it, but I thought he was being overly-dramatic. I never thought he'd do it. I didn't think he could." He turned to Refractor. "Did you?"

"No," said Refractor. "I must admit, the thought crossed my mind he lied about Scribe's hold on him. I was wrong."

"I wouldn't be concerned with an apology," said Nate, still reeling from witnessing Time Bomb's demise. "I'd say he's past it."

Ray's phone rang, and they all jumped. He held a hurried conversation before hanging up. "Bobbie and Mighty Light are on their way here. Kristie received the anti-venom in time."

Nate met Libby at the door. Her footsteps dragged. She rubbed the back of her neck. It had been a long day for both of them. "Coffee's on," he said. "How about a cup?"

She flashed a grateful smile. "Sounds good."

"How's Kristie doing?"

The smile tightened ever-so slightly. "The doctors

are confident of a full recovery, but she'll be hospitalized for a while. You mentioned coffee?"

"Sit down. I'll bring you a cup." When he returned from the kitchen, Libby was seated next to Refractor, her hand on his arm, talking to him in a low voice.

Nate glowered. Damn it, he had only turned his back for a second. What kind of moves did this guy have?

Ray filled the women in on Time Bomb's death. Bobbie wore an expression of shocked disbelief. "He's dead?"

"Not a trace," said Ray. "If I hadn't seen the explosion, I wouldn't have believed it possible."

Nate turned to Libby. "How did you know Debolt would be at the lab?"

"The zayton isotopes." She gave her head a disbelieving shake. "I should have seen it coming. Every comic has one—call it krypton, gamma rays, the source, whatever. It's energy that has an unnatural effect on people or objects. Here, it's zayton radiation. It's what changed Refractor—all the others, too, I'm guessing."

"She's right," said Ray. "Zayton radiation can be beneficial, but only under stringent controls. Mega Mole and Time Bomb were overly exposed during medical procedures and developed mutations."

"Same with the spider that bit Araña?" said Nate.

"Yes," said Refractor. "She was at the clinic that day. The creature must have been subjected to zayton by accident in the lab and then escaped to the other part of the building." His voiced dropped. "She was the tragic consequence of human error."

"Zayton poisoning is nasty stuff," said Ray. "Once

the radiation infects an individual, it bonds to their cellular structure. Every blood corpuscle is loaded with it. I've searched for a way to return Refractor to normal, but haven't had any luck."

It all sounded ridiculous to Nate, but, after all, they had been sucked into a comic book. Who was he to judge?

"When you explained the lab had the ability to store zayton isotopes," Libby continued, "it suddenly hit me. Payton needed a power source for his transporter device. Nothing usual would suffice."

"Syr needs it, too," said Bobbie. "Traveling through space-time requires the type of energy zayton produces."

"Payton's development of the Refractor comic makes perfect sense now," mused Libby. "He didn't write original stories, only current events. All he had to do was spice up the characters a bit to make them sexier and more marketable. Ray became Pierce Powers, not some unknown guy in a ski mask. He used the rough image of Princess Robella to create Refractor's female helper—dumb luck on his part she really was Robella."

"All he had to do was give her huge boobs," said Nate, "stuffed in a leather bustier." He clapped his mouth shut after regarding the appalled visage of Bobbie and the less than pleased Ray.

Libby's lips twitched in amusement. "I was going to say, Princess Robella, a brilliant scientist who doesn't need to dress as an over-sexualized adolescent fantasy, became a supernatural bimbo able to control the weather."

Bobbie gave a derisive snort. "I can't control the weather. My invention is grounded in science, not magic. Who reads that nonsense?"

"Plenty of people," added Libby. "Debolt made a killing on Earth." She blinked in surprise. "I just realized why he never wrote a history for Refractor. He didn't know it and didn't have enough imagination to invent one."

"Didn't Syr have some kind of mind control helmet?" said Nate.

"Syr?" Bobbie raised a disbelieving eyebrow. "Ridiculous. He can't control minds—at least not through magical means. I'll agree he is a charismatic leader, and inspires almost fanatical devotion in his subordinates. I suppose in that way he controls minds."

A look of understanding passed between Nate and Libby. Syr wasn't a sorcerer or an evil scientific genius, only Mo'R'ees Six's version of Hitler.

"Why did Scribe bother to return to Second Chance City?" mused Refractor. "He obviously made a successful transition."

Libby shook her head. "I'm not so sure. Deep down, I always suspected Payton hated writing the comic. Only the money had appeal. Frankly, I think it killed him to make Refractor a hero. The publisher has been begging for the next installment, but Payton keeps putting him off. Don't you see? Payton was dumped in our universe soon after the explosion in O'Reilly's. That became the last issue because he didn't have any more stories."

The conversation was interrupted by muted rock music. Libby glanced in surprise at her pocket and then retrieved a cell phone. "It's Kristie's," she said. "She left it in the car." She peered at the display. "Abigail Franco."

Nate held out his hand. He put the phone on speaker. "Abby? It's Nate Hammond."

"Who?"

"Good Citizen," he said, repressing a sigh. Libby snickered.

"The very person I need." People chattered in the background. Her voice dropped to a whisper. "I have information, but am still at the station, and it's too dangerous to talk over the phone. Can we meet?"

"Frenchman's Creek. There is an old maple tree along the path, halfway between the bay and Main Street."

"I'll find it." One of the people in the background called for Sergeant Franco. "I'll see you there in an hour," she added quickly and then the connection ended.

Libby's skepticism was obvious. "Do you trust her? Maybe it's a trap."

"One way to find out."

"I'm going with you. Someone needs to watch your back."

Nate was pleased. "I wouldn't dream of going anywhere without my—"

"If you say sidekick," Libby warned, waving the flashlight. "I will blast you halfway to Jupiter—if this solar system has a Jupiter."

He flashed a grin. "I was going to say partner. Geez, you're touchy for a superhero."

"Take Kristie's car," said Bobbie. "You can drop me off at the bookstore. Everyone will wonder if I don't open up."

Ray blurted out an immediate protest. "You shouldn't be alone. Not with Syr in the area."

"He doesn't know I'm Bobbie Ballard or he would have come for me as soon as he arrived."

"Don't open the store today. It's too dangerous. Put a sign on the door that you're sick."

"No. I'm not afraid of Syr." Bobbie shrugged on a jacket to cover the wristband. "I have a weapon. I'm not defenseless. Syr may believe I'm in Second Chance City, but he certainly didn't recognize me today. He was much too busy dodging my lightning bolts."

She smiled warmly at Ray. "I'm not the same person who left Mo'R'ees Six. Shy, meek, scholarly, Robella would have ducked for cover when the shooting started and never thrown herself into a battle. You and Refractor gave me the chance to become someone more. Bobbie Ballard is a better person than Princess Robella ever was. I'm sorry, Ray," she said with deep regret. "I never should have left. I should have stayed with you."

"I wanted that, too." His voice filled with yearning. "It was too dangerous for us...for you. We agreed to split when Refractor..." He shot a glance at the superhero and paused as if searching for a polite way to continue.

"Had a breakdown?" suggested Refractor lightly.

"Needed time to reevaluate certain aspects of your life," said Ray firmly.

Bobbie placed a hand on Refractor's arm. "We were wrong. We should never have surrendered the fight. We should have helped you work through your issues."

"The problem wasn't yours, Bobbie," said Refractor. "I demanded solitude."

"I shouldn't have given it to you," she said. "A

friend needed help, and I walked away. It was wrong—like it was wrong for me to leave my planet. I should have stayed and fought."

"You are a symbol of freedom for them," argued Ray.

"I haven't even been able to make contact with the resistance for over a year. A symbol shut out of sight is no symbol at all. I'm tired of hiding. If Syr wants a fight, I'm going to give it to him. The war must be going badly or he never would have left. This is my chance to end him once and for all."

"How did Syr get to Second Chance City so fast?" asked Nate. "Debolt only arrived a day ago."

"He must have pushed his ship to the max," said Bobbie. "That takes a huge amount of power. The engines must be nearly depleted. Without the stolen zayton, it will be a very slow journey to Mo'R'ees Six."

Ray straightened in his seat. "An idea just occurred to me. Removed from secure storage in the laboratory, the zayton emissions are no longer shielded as effectively. I might be able to devise a way to track them to Scribe's lair."

"Excellent. Call me at Write Away if you find anything." Bobbie regarded Ray with a stubborn set to her expression. "I'm going. You can't stop me."

"Stop you?" His voice filled with naked yearning. "Who wants to stop you? All I've ever wanted to do was hold on."

All the defiance vanished. Bobbie wrapped her arms around his neck and kissed him. "That's all I ever wanted, too."

Nate and Libby dropped Bobbie off in front of Write Away and then drove to the waterfront. Nate parked the car in an inconspicuous spot near Frenchman's Creek. He scanned the lot, but saw no sign of Abigail. They hiked the path along the brook and waited at the old maple tree.

Bemused, Libby took in the surroundings. "Everything is the same as I remember—even the tree."

Nate ran his hands along the rough bark. Some things had changed. The carving was no longer there. A bittersweet memory washed over him.

Libby craned her neck, peering into the limbs. She shook her head in disbelief. "I can't believe we used to climb this thing. What were we thinking?"

Nate took every bit of her in with pleasure. Sunlight had always brought out the copper highlights in Libby's hair. He was glad she hadn't lost the freckles, too. Who would have guessed gangly Libby Parish would grow into a woman to take his breath away? He knew…even then his heart gave a leap when she called out to him from under their tree. Their tree… He patted the old maple fondly. Would he ever think of it any other way? Nope…a memory like that should stay etched in the heart forever.

Libby shook her finger at him with a teasing smile. "You should have had more sense and kept me from going up there."

"Not me," Nate said gently. "I never wanted to slow Libby Parish down. I liked her exactly the way she was."

A subtle pink colored her cheeks. "It's so peaceful here," said Libby, with a faraway look. "I always liked wading through the brook, although I remember the water was ice cold."

"Why don't you put your toe in and find out?" said

Nate with an innocently expression.

She laughed. "Oh, no, I'm not falling for that."

"Seems to me, I was the one that fell for it, and you were the one that pushed me."

"I'm sure you said something to deserve it...dork."

"Nerd..." Nate gazed out over the water. "Those were good times, Libby. Best I ever had."

"Long time ago," she said softly. "You're a different person. So am I."

"No, you're not," he whispered, stepping close. "I still see Libby Parish hiding in there." He brushed a stray lock of hair from her face. "You never could keep those curls under control."

The pink in her cheeks deepened.

"What are you hiding from, Lib?" he asked softly. Her curls slipped through his fingers as his hand moved to the back of her head.

For several seconds, neither drew a breath, then Libby dropped her gaze. Her voice filled with regret. "We'll be home soon, Nate, and return to our old lives. I-I know you'll be happy with the choice you've made."

Nate's hand dropped to his side. She was trying to tell him she could never be content with a small town cop. Once they returned to Coldwater Bay, her goodbye would be forever. Well, who could blame her? What the hell could he offer a woman like Libby?

"You don't have to worry," she added quietly. "Second Chance City Kristie will recover, and the Kristie in Coldwater Bay is fine."

"That's...that's great." Nate was confused. When did the subject switch to the two Kristie's?

Libby swallowed hard. Her voice betrayed a slight tremble. "I respect boundaries. I had a front row seat to watch my parents and know the heartache that occurs when a person crosses the line with another."

Boundaries? What line? Suddenly, he felt as if he had been dumped into the middle of someone else's conversation.

Before Nate could ask a question, a snapped twig jerked his attention down the path. Abigail Franco jogged toward them carrying a file folder. "Hello, Good Citizen."

"Hi, Abby." Nate motioned to Libby. "This is my partner, Mighty Light."

"I take it you're the one responsible for the jail break?" said Abigail with a grin.

Libby gave a slight bow. "Guilty as charged."

"Not the best words to use in front of a police officer," she said wryly. "However, considering the circumstances that bring me here, I'm probably breaking as many laws as you."

"What did you find out?" asked Nate.

"You were right about the explosion at O'Reilly's Tavern—the body count didn't add up." Abigail handed over the folder. Nate and Libby skimmed the paperwork. "The official police investigation," continued Abigail, "definitely stated parts of the bodies of Mega Mole and Time Bomb had been discovered and removed to the coroner's office. The coroner acknowledges receipt on the casualty list, but the records must have been altered. The explosion was violent, but enough remains were left. The body tissue attributed to Mega Mole and Time Bomb definitely belonged to somebody else."

"How do you know?" said Nate.

"All the testing entries are zero with null rads."

In response to their obvious confusion, Abigail pointed to an annotated list. "This is a separate lab report, not included with the coroner's paperwork. All remains were shipped to another lab for an additional test for zayton radiation. It's a standard screening procedure in the death of someone who has been exposed. Since zayton is so dangerous, remains that test positive must go through a rigorously prescribed disposal process. Even after death, both Mega Mole and Time Bomb would have emitted a radiation level off the charts, but every bit of biological material from O'Reilly's registered squat."

"Who altered the official report?" asked Nate.

Her expression grew stormy. "It must have been Chief Peevey. She's the only one with authority. She was also first on the scene that night and identified the remains of Mega Mole and Time Bomb."

"Why would she do that?" said Libby.

Nate scowled. "To stop the spread of panic. Florence told me so herself. She's worried about maintaining order, especially with Refractor out of the picture. What are you going to do with this, Abby?"

"I don't know." Her brow wrinkled in a worried frown. "Peevey was not the popular choice for chief, especially among the other police officers. For some reason, she was cozy with the mayor so the city council approved the promotion. After O'Reilly's, Peevey promised to maintain peace and order. As far as Mayor Templeton is concerned, she can do no wrong."

Nate startled. "Cordelia Templeton?"

Abigail nodded. "She's been mayor for the last ten years. Templeton and Peevey never had much to do with each other, but when the mayor's son came out of the coma after the car accident, she backed Peevey for chief. She now rubber stamps every one of her decisions."

"Bryce was in the car?" said Nate, bewildered. "I thought her husband died."

"Mr. Templeton died years ago. Bryce was all she had left. His recovery is pretty much a miracle considering the severity of the crash. No one at the local hospital ever expected him to regain consciousness. Mayor Templeton moved Bryce to a private sanitarium out of town. She reported his new doctors expect an eventual return to health, although he will have a long convalescence. Everyone thinks the emotional turmoil caused by Bryce's fragile condition affected the mayor's decision-making," added Abigail. "It made no sense to support Peevey for chief—just like it made no sense she bought the old factory and turned it into a nightclub."

Nate raised an eyebrow at the thought of Cordelia Templeton mingling with the club set.

"Surely," said Libby, "the attack at the lab this morning must have frightened the town council."

Abigail started. "The chief told us it was a gas leak."

Nate gave her a rundown of the fight and Time Bomb's death.

"The lab stored zayton isotopes?" Abigail scowled. The chief can't hide this theft. People must be warned about the danger loose in the city." She checked her watch. "I have to go. These files need to be returned to her office before she notices they're gone." They walked down the path toward the bay and the parking lot.

"What's your plan, Abby?" Nate asked.

"I'm not the only person on the force who's isn't crazy with the way Peevey handles things." She smiled slyly. "Maybe it's time for a coup, whether the chief has the backing of the mayor or not."

As they reached the parking lot, wailing sirens in the distance broke the silence. All three froze as the intensity of the sound rapidly increased. A bevy of patrol cars sped their way. Abigail scowled and shoved the files in Nate's hand. "Take them and get out of here."

"Come with us," said Nate. "We can protect you."

"Peevey has nothing on me. I can do more good inside the station—Go!"

Nate and Libby darted into the brush as Abigail leaned nonchalantly against her squad car. An instant later, several police vehicles roared into the parking lot. Brakes screeched in an abrupt halt. Half a dozen officers jumped out with Chief Peevey in the lead.

Chapter Ten

Nate and Libby crouched in the bushes watching as Abigail casually examined her nails. "Oh, hey, guys," she said to the arriving officers. "What's up?"

"You didn't answer your radio, Franco," Chief Peevey snapped. "I had to use GPS to track your car."

Abigail blinked as if in surprise. "I'm off duty, Chief."

"You didn't answer your phone, either."

Abigail yawned. "Like I said—off duty."

"What are you doing out here all alone?" the chief demanded. "Who are you waiting for?"

"No, one. I'm enjoying the view." Abigail inhaled deeply. "Gotta love that sea air."

Irina Duval stepped forward. "Files are missing from the chief's office."

"Really, Lieutenant?" said Abigail, completely unconcerned. "Maybe you stuck them in the wrong drawer."

"I saw you skulking out of her office corridor," said Irina. "What were you doing there?"

"I wasn't skulking. I had to use the bathroom."

"You know the rules," Irina snapped. "The bathroom for patrol officer use is on the other side of the building."

"Sorry, Lieutenant. Had to use that one. Someone cut the cheese in the other." Abigail wafted her hand in front of her face. "Big time."

Chief Peevey scowled. "Get your ass back to the station, Franco. I have more questions." She turned to the other officers. "The rest of you fan out...search any cars in the parking lot. Check the woods, too, for anyone suspicious."

Forget Kristie's car, it was time to go. Nate and Libby jogged along the path, jumped across a narrow spot in the brook and then cut to the south, keeping well out of sight of the coastline.

"I can't believe Irina ratted out Abby," said Nate. He couldn't get over the change in the cheerful demeanor of the dispatcher he had known. "Irina bakes cookies for the station, for God's sake. She's not a...not a..."

"A weasel?" suggested Libby, mischievously.

"Yeah, thanks. I was hunting for a word, but the only one that came to me was more insulting and started with a 'b.' It makes me very uncomfortable to think of Irina that way."

"Need I point out she's not Coldwater Bay Irina?"

"You got that right," said Nate. "The sooner we get out of here and return to where everyone was normal, and their actions understandable, the better. Like Cordelia Templeton. I can picture her horror at the suggestion she throw hard-earned money into a club."

"So nothing in Second Chance City appeals to you?" Libby said with a teasing grin. "Not even being a superhero? Come on, admit it. It's kind of cool."

"You like pushing people around with that flashlight, don't you?"

"It has its moments."

"And the fighting for your life part?"

"Meh. Maybe, not so much." She rubbed her thumb along the flashlight. "I wonder if the star will disappear for good in Coldwater Bay."

"We'll find out when we get home."

"Yeah, when we get home..." Her voice trailed away.

Suddenly, Nate was ill at ease. Libby almost sounded unsure. Did she really have doubts about leaving Second Chance City? Having superhero powers dangled in front of her would make the choice to stay mighty tempting, but she wouldn't really consider abandoning real life to live out a comic book fantasy.

Would she?

Libby had made it painfully clear Nate didn't have a shot, but the thought of a future without even a possibility of running into her again cut unbelievably sharp. Disquieting thoughts continued to percolate as Smuggler's Cove came into view.

Ray was in the lab working diligently on a conglomeration of electronic equipment. Refractor was nowhere to be seen. Nate tossed the files on the table. "Refractor returned to the lighthouse," said Ray with a frown. "I hope he's not getting all moody again."

Libby immediately volunteered to check on him. A rush of irritation gripped Nate. Why did she find him so damn fascinating? So he glowed and could shoot laser beams from his hands. So what? Nate had a sonic gun and a flashlight.

"Thanks, Mighty Light," said Ray, relieved. "You're good for Refractor. He likes you, I can tell. You know, underneath all that radiance, he's still a man." He nudged Nate in the ribs. "What man doesn't like a pretty girl paying attention?"

Kristie's words concerning all Refractor's parts in working order floated back. Nate's irritation rose. He followed Libby to the tunnel entrance. "I'll come with you."

"There's no need." To Nate's mind, her response came a tad too quickly.

"Refractor doesn't need you to hold his hand," Nate blurted out, more sharply than intended.

Libby bristled. "What Caleb really doesn't need is an unsympathetic ear right now."

"Oh, and you know exactly what's best for him?"

"I understand what he's going through better than you," she said, clearly irritated. "I spent time talking with him. You should hear the stories he has to tell—over two hundred years' worth, each one a gripping adventure…hiding, developing his powers, slowly reaching out to others." She gushed with admiration. "Caleb is an amazing man to have overcome such adversity and still retain an innate core of decency and honor. He's a real superhero."

Shut up, Nate. Shut up, shut up. Brain, however, was tired of hearing Refractor's sterling qualities. "Maybe you like basking in his glow a little too much."

Libby shot him an exasperated look. "What is wrong with you?" Without waiting for a response, she disappeared down the opening.

Nate shoved his hands in his pockets and wandered into the lab. *Damn it.* How had he developed the knack for always saying the wrong thing to Libby?

Ray clapped him on the arm. "Let's be honest, Good Citizen, chicks dig superheroes. Although, it's been a long time since Refractor has taken interest in anyone."

"Really?" muttered Nate, sourly. "Do tell."

"I know what you're thinking," said Ray cheerfully, "but you don't have to worry that Refractor has dishonorable intentions. Deep down, he is still an eighteenth-century gentleman at heart—a little old-fashioned and courtly even. He would never force himself on any woman. She must show mutual interest."

That's exactly what Nate feared. He had counted on severe nutlessness as a side effect of zayton radiation. He swallowed bitter disappointment that wasn't the case.

Ray returned to work, tinkering with his electronics while Nate glared at the stairway to the tunnel. Could Libby have developed feelings for Refractor already? Would he press her to stay? How could Nate compete against a superhero when all he had was a lame nickname?

The truth smacked him in the head. That's why all his previous relationships eventually dissolved without regret. He wanted them to end. No other woman ever measured up to Libby Parish.

Several hours later, Bobbie returned. She had picked up her car and stopped for groceries. Nate offered to assist with dinner, but she chased him from the kitchen. He wandered outside to glare at the lighthouse and wonder what Libby and Refractor were doing there.

To keep his mind off Libby, he changed the tire on the van and then parked it in front of Smuggler's Cove. The engine ran, but the body needed work. The windshield had been shattered by falling debris from the exploded dock. The side panels were dented. Acidic spatters from Araña's venom pockmarked the hood.

Bobbie called him to dinner. Disappointment set in when Libby hadn't returned. Even more so when Bobbie informed Nate he had just missed her. Libby had stayed only long enough to fill a tray and take it through the tunnel to Refractor.

Nate ate an uncomfortable meal. Bobbie and Ray were so focused on each other they barely knew Nate was at the table, while Nate's imagination ran wild at what went on in the lighthouse. He left early and made his way through the tunnel. The door to the spiral staircase was shut. So was the door to the bedroom. No sound came from either. He raised his hand to knock at Libby's door and froze. What if Refractor's voice called out? His hand dropped. He stretched out on the couch and quickly fell asleep.

****

Libby's door was still closed when Nate awoke. He returned to Smuggler's Cove and made breakfast and coffee, but ate without tasting either. As the hours ticked by with no return of Libby, the walls closed in on him. Nate wandered aimlessly through the building. Ray and Bobbie were hard at work in the lab. Every now and then they would reach for the same tool, touch hands, and smile at each other. Nate couldn't help but notice the rumpled covers on the bed and the indentations in two pillows. It didn't improve his mood one bit.

Nate offered to help, but both Ray and Bobbie politely refused, probably just as well. The tangled mass of wires and electronic parts and the calculations on the white board made as much sense to him as Egyptian hieroglyphics.

With a sudden longing for fresh air, Nate strolled outside. He sat on the steps to the beach and gazed out to sea. The sun beat warm against his skin. No doubt, in any world Smuggler's Cove was in a beautiful location. With no fog, he had a clear view of the bay all the way to Peregrine Island. Nate squinted against the glare, peering down the coastline to Second Chance City's harbor. The three-story TIDC building stuck out like a sore thumb.

Nate's thoughts drifted to Cordelia Templeton. She had always been a force to reckon with, but underneath had a heart of gold. Here she was a hard-nosed corporate CEO and mayor. Sad that her husband was still gone, but at least Bryce survived the crash. His miraculous healing must all be due to Cordelia's intervention. It certainly helped to have a mother who had pockets full of cash and a determined nature. He frowned in thought. Although, this Cordelia sounded more ruthless than determined.

Someone used to getting her own way.

Someone who wouldn't take kindly to the word no.

Someone who could easily sway the town council to put the unqualified Florence Peevey in as police chief. Florence would certainly be beholden to her. Beholden enough to always look the other way?

Nate rose from the chair, an idea buzzing in his head. He had to speak to Cordelia, but getting there unobserved posed a problem. Who knew how many officers Florence Peevey had hunting for him? Regular patrols undoubtedly canvassed the streets, but would they bother with more than a cursory pass through the harbor? His focus turned to the bay. Secured at the end of the half-demolished pier was the Sea Spray. It was only a short swim from shore.

Darting into the house, Nate grabbed a towel and a large plastic trash bag. Ray was so deeply absorbed in work he only nodded absent-mindedly when Nate asked to borrow his house keys. On his way out, Nate shot a glance at the secret entrance to the tunnel. For an instant, he considered letting Libby in on the scheme.

Is she busy with Refractor? Do I really want my worst fear confirmed? Definitely not, he decided.

Nate ran down the steps to the water. A quick scan of the beach offered assurance he was alone. He peeled off all his clothing and stuffed everything along with the sonic gun and holster into the plastic bag, securing it tightly against any water seepage.

Lifting the bundle over his head, Nate stepped into the water, sucking in his breath as icy cold waves lapped against his naked skin. There was really no good time of year for skinny-dipping in a place called Coldwater Bay. He dog-paddled to the boat and climbed onto the deck. Teeth chattering wildly, his shaking fingers untied the bundle. Nate quickly toweled off and threw on his clothes. He zipped the hoodie jacket to the neck, covering the holster.

After securing the anchor and line, Nate started the engine and sailed out into the bay. A stiff breeze sheared the tips off choppy waves. Wisps of sea foam twisted and curled, dancing across Sea Spray's wake.

Nate steered to the slip in front of Ray's house. He used the key to unlock the door and then used the phone to call Templeton International. The secretary stated Mrs. Templeton wasn't in the office today and offered to take a message. Nate declined and then dialed city hall. Mayor Templeton wasn't downtown either. Nate's spirits rose. With luck, Cordelia was home. The trick would be to get her to open the door.

The Templeton house was a short walk. The basic structure of the old Victorian could still be discerned, but this reality included luxurious touches such as a swimming pool, tennis court, and three car garage. The yard was extensive and obviously expertly tended by gardeners. To Nate's mind, the whole appearance was sterile—the perfect magazine house. Pretty in pictures, nothing out of place, but lacking any suggestion a real family with all their imperfections lived inside.

Nate jogged across the lawn to the front door, mindful of any security personnel, but no one was in sight. He rang the bell. Footsteps shuffled in the hall. The door remained shut, but the camera mounted off to the side gave any occupant a clear view of the visitor. He faced the lens. "You will want to hear what I have to say."

The knob turned. Cordelia Templeton was immaculately dressed, identical in outward appearance to the woman from Coldwater Bay with the exception of red-rimmed eyes. Something other than Nate's sudden appearance had obviously caused her distress today. "You're the one they call Good Citizen. Chief Peevey is searching for you." Her voice carried an uncharacteristically hard timber.

"We need to talk."

"We have nothing to discuss." She made a move to shut the door.

The time had come to play his hunch. "I know the truth about Bryce."

Cordelia's breath caught in her throat. She motioned Nate to a study off the foyer. Her hands betrayed a slight tremble, but by the time she sat at the desk, composure had returned. Straight-backed, fingers interlocked, thumbs pressed tight against each other, not a single betraying emotion visible. Cordelia Templeton was one tough nut. "Explain yourself," she demanded.

"It's not a miracle Bryce is alive." Behind Cordelia's façade of arrogant bluster, powerful emotions stirred. This woman had been pushed to the emotional brink. Nate experienced a rush of pity. He was about to push even more. "You gave him zayton radiation."

Her complexion turned the color of ash. "How could you know?" she gasped, sinking in the chair. "You couldn't possibly know."

"Mega Mole and others attacked the lab. They didn't tear the place apart, but went directly to one particular room. No side trips. Someone had already told them the zayton isotopes were there. You did. You knew because that's where you must have gotten it for Bryce."

Cordelia gripped the arms of the chair so tight her knuckles turned white. "He's my son," she said, her voice a harsh whisper. "He is all I have. What would you do to save the life of someone you loved?"

Nate regarded her with sympathy. "Kristie Williams nearly died from the attack at the lab. More people will get hurt. A trail of innocent blood is not the legacy you want to leave for Bryce. He deserves better."

"Yes, he does." Cordelia wiped a hand across her eyes. "I only wanted to help him. I never meant for anyone to get hurt. He promised me."

"Scribe?"

"Yes. He lies." Her voice dripped hate. "He lies about everything."

Nate placed a gentle hand over hers. "How did you know the zayton's location?"

Her shoulders sagged. "After the doctors gave me no hope for Bryce's recovery, Florence Peevey approached with an offer. Several months before, Mike Williams had assigned her to the security detail at the lab during the transfer of certain classified material. Florence figured out it was zayton isotopes. She's cleverer than people suspect. Zayton was the only hope for Bryce, and I had no way to procure it legally."

"Florence offered a deal?"

Cordelia nodded. "She came to me after the explosion at O'Reilly's. She would hand over a vial of isotopes. In return, I had to support her for chief of police and hide Mega Mole and Time Bomb with Bryce while they recuperated. She would announce to Refractor and the public they were dead."

"Why would Florence help them?" he said, dumbfounded.

"Mega Mole and Time Bomb promised to leave Second Chance City forever once they healed, and Florence would get all the credit for keeping the peace. She didn't believe Refractor could defeat them. The fighting would continue. More would get hurt. Florence and Mike Williams were intimately involved. When he died…well, I guess this was the only way she saw to fix the problem."

Her gaze strayed out the window. "The agreement worked well. Mega Mole was particularly kind to Bryce. I was grateful."

"Things changed though, didn't they?" said Nate. "Mega Mole and Time Bomb started to make forays into town again."

Cordelia stiffened. "They didn't say and I didn't ask, but as they healed Mega Mole grew more reluctant to leave. I suppose he read rumors in *The Times* alluding to Refractor's disappearance from Second Chance City and decided to risk venturing out. You can thank Kristie Williams for that."

She swallowed hard. "Bryce had been improving, but without warning took a drastic turn for the worse... I-I thought he needed more zayton. I went to see Peevey, but she refused to help. So I went to Mega Mole. A man named Scribe was with him."

Cordelia shifted in her seat. "Mega Mole and Time Bomb were...they were different...they didn't speak...Mega Mole peered at me with those beady eyes." She clasped her hands tight in her lap as if to still the trembling. "Fear, desperation, hopelessness...I know those emotions, Good Citizen. I have lived with them for a while, now, and I saw both in Mega Mole and Time Bomb. Not Scribe, though," she added harshly. "Nothing disconcerted him. He was most anxious to get hands on the zayton. He promised to share."

"Did he?" asked Nate.

Her voice dropped low. She took a deep breath as if to keep it steady. "Yes. I received one vial. Scribe swore it would cure Bryce. It didn't. It only made him worse."

"Where is Scribe now?"

"I don't know. Months ago, I bought the old abandoned factory for redevelopment. I planned to turn it into condos, but when Bryce and the others needed a hiding place I put the club on top to divert suspicion. Underneath is an old cellar where they healed in secret. The last time I saw Scribe he was there, but they're all gone now except for Bryce."

"Take me to him," said Nate. "Bryce might know where they went."

Cordelia gave a bitter laugh. "He can't help you."

"I have to try. Cordelia..." Nate took her hand. "Scribe must be stopped. You know whatever use he plans for the zayton can't be good."

With a sigh of resignation, Cordelia nodded numbly and led him to the car. It was a short drive to The Factory. Staff hadn't arrived yet to prepare for the evening and the building was empty. They went directly to the rear where Cordelia unlocked a door. "It's my private office," she said. "No one else is allowed inside."

She slid open a panel in the wall to reveal a secret staircase. Nate rolled his eyes. What was it with this city and hidden staircases? He followed Cordelia to a large room at the bottom, outfitted with a kitchen and living area. On one wall hung an old-fashioned brass key next to a heavy oak door.

A half-inch gap existed between the bottom of the door and the threshold. Light spilled out from underneath. It faded in and out....in and out. Someone on the other side continually paced across the room.

Nate's heart hammered. Bringing backup hadn't seemed necessary when he left Smuggler's Cove. Why had he violated standard police protocol and done such a dumb thing? Oh, yeah. He'd been ticked at Libby.

Cordelia knocked softly on the door. "Bryce? It's

mother."

From the other side came shuffling movement followed by a soft moan.

"I've brought someone to see you." She slipped the key into the lock and turned. "We're coming in."

Nate unzipped his jacket. His fingers rested lightly on the pistol grip. The light from a single bulb overhead illuminated a figure huddled in the corner. Nate was shocked by the change in the man he had known. Bryce Templeton was barefoot and shirtless, chest and head crisscrossed by old surgical scars. Eyes bulged from the sockets in a blank stare while his mouth twisted across his face in the agonized caricature of a frown.

Cordelia choked back a sob. "After the first treatment, he came out of the coma. H-he made steady progress, first talking, then sitting, then walking. Everything was going so well, but then he slipped, started losing the steps forward he had made. His mind became confused. He didn't recognize me. H-he started making these sounds…awful sounds." She drew a shuddering breath. "The zayton radiation wasn't enough. I-I thought…a little more."

Bryce's fingers clenched and unclenched in a mindless rhythm. He turned his head toward them. "Make it stop," he moaned.

"Cordelia," said Nate, tearing his gaze away. "He can't go on like this. We have to get him to a hospital."

Her chin trembled. "Bryce has been poisoned by zayton radiation. There is no treatment. People are afraid of the afflicted. He'll be thrown into an isolation ward—treated like a monster." She choked back a sob. "That's the way it's always been."

"Then change things," Nate demanded hotly.

"You're the mayor. You have influence with people. Look at him," he said harshly. "This is no kind of life. Nothing of Bryce is left. It's only a matter of time before the radiation kills him. Meanwhile he's dying by inches." He placed a comforting arm on her shoulders. "Raise a stink. Get Kristie Williams and the power of the press on your side to change public opinion. Force people to see Bryce not as an evil freak, but someone suffering from a medical condition. At least allow him to die with dignity in some clean safe place with his mother at his side and not rot in some damn hole in the ground."

Cordelia brusquely wiped her hand across her eyes. "You're right. This is no place for my son." She stepped from Nate's side and held out her hands. "It's time to go, Bryce."

Bryce retreated into a corner, eyeing them with distrust. He threw back his head and opened his mouth.

"Don't!" Cordelia shouted.

An ear-piercing shriek slammed into them like a 2x4. Nate and Cordelia were lifted off their feet and flung out the door. Cordelia crumpled to the ground as chunks of plaster dislodged from the ceiling.

"Bryce, stop!" Nate cried, drawing his weapon. "You'll bring down the whole building."

Bryce stumbled across the threshold. "Make it stop," he wailed. "Make it stop." He drew in a deep lungful of air.

Nate fired as Bryce let loose another scream.

The shock wave slammed into Bryce, cutting short the deafening shriek. Waves of energy careened through the room vibrating material loose from the walls. Bryce was lost in an avalanche of debris.

Cordelia lifted her head. "Bryce," she cried weakly.

Choking back the dust, Nate holstered the pistol and helped Cordelia to her feet. "We have to get out of here." They staggered to the staircase and climbed to Cordelia's office. A horrific roar issued from below followed by a billowing dust cloud. Nate slammed the bookcase shut, blocking the opening.

Cordelia lay on the floor, coughing and gasping for breath. Nate called 911 from the office phone. He grabbed a bottle of water off the desk and gently raised her head to take a sip. The coughing stopped. She thanked him weakly.

"Take it easy," said Nate. "I've called for an ambulance. They'll be here soon."

Her voice trembled. "All I wanted was to help my son."

"I know. I'm sorry." He rested a gentle hand on her shoulder. "The walls collapsed, Cordelia. He's gone."

She let out a tremulous sigh and dabbed at her eyes. "It's for the best. At least it's over now. Bryce isn't suffering anymore. He didn't want to hurt anyone, you know. He couldn't control what he had become." Her voice turned cold. "It was that damned zayton. It poisoned him. Scribe assured me I hadn't given Bryce enough in the first dosage. A second would cure him."

Nate clenched his jaw. Debolt was a real sonofabitch. He had no qualms taking advantage of a grieving mother. "He lied. He only wanted the isotopes for himself."

"How could I have been so stupid?" she moaned.

"Not stupid," he said with utmost sympathy, "only desperate. Scribe used that."

"I've lost everything…" Her voice drifted away.

"No," he said kindly. "I'm sure plenty of good people care what happens to you."

Iron determination filled Cordelia's expression. Nate had glimpsed it before in the Coldwater Bay version. "I'll do whatever is necessary to make amends," she said. "The zayton isotopes must be found before this happens to anyone else." A siren approached. "Go, before the police get here."

"I can't leave you alone," Nate protested.

"I'll be fine," she said with a glint of wry humor. "Templetons are made of stern stuff. How do I get in touch with you?"

"Call Bobbie Ballard. She'll get me a message."

She was puzzled. "The bookstore owner?"

"Yeah or Ray Quintero. Also, tell Sergeant Abigail Franco what you told me about Florence Peevey. I think it's long past time for a regime change at the police station."

"You have an interesting set of allies, Good Citizen." She gave him her hand. "Count me as one of them. Now go."

Nate darted from The Factory and hid out of sight. He watched until Cordelia was loaded into an ambulance. Secure in the knowledge she would be cared for, he returned to the sailboat and cast off.

The water had a heavier chop on the return trip, wind gusted off the bay. Being out here always had a calming effect and eased Nate's most turbulent thoughts. He fought off the temptation to unfurl the sail and instead headed straight to Smuggler's Cove. Now was not the time for a pleasure trip. The others needed to know what happened to Bryce.

L. A. Kelley

Cruising past Peregrine Island, his thoughts drifted to the Summer of Libby, as he now thought of it. When time and weather permitted, they would steal off on his family's daysailer for an hour or two of carefree abandon on the bay. They had no deep conversations he could recall. They probably talked of comic books and superheroes and Libby described new adventures she had created for their favorites. He wished he could recall some of the stories, but supposed it didn't matter. The best part of those outings was the peacefulness of the sea. Nate could put his mother's cancer out of his mind, and Libby had a reprieve from her parents' constant arguments.

The last trip on the daysailer had been bittersweet. Libby had told him she was leaving. A hard cold knot settled in Nate's stomach, but all he could offer was one last trip around the bay. The air held a good stiff breeze like today. Neither spoke a word as they sailed, but Nate's anxiety grew with each passing minute. He had a burning desire to say something to Libby, but what? Words flew from his brain as fast as the boat over the water. The thirteen-year-old boy didn't recognize the strange emotion tugging at his heart. He didn't know he was in love.

They sailed past the picnic grounds on Peregrine Island and then returned to the pier. Nate moored the boat. He stood numbly in front of Libby. He remembered thinking her eyes seemed red, perhaps from the sunny glare off the water. "Well, goodbye then," she said. Without warning, she kissed him on the cheek and then she was gone.

Nate had only been a beginning sailor back then, but now had a boat of his own moored in Coldwater

Bay. He wondered how Libby would look at the helm with those auburn curls blowing in the wind. Damn fine he concluded. He gripped the wheel. He should have asked her to come with him to see Cordelia. Letting his pride get in the way had been a mistake.

"Not this time," he muttered to himself. No more stumbling around. He would tell Libby what was in his heart. Whether she rejected him or not, at least his feelings would be clear.

Arriving at Smuggler's Cove's damaged pier, Nate moored the boat and then stripped down once more. He slipped into the water and sucked in his breath—it hadn't warmed any. The swim to shore was more difficult. Wavelets slapped him in the face as he struggled to paddle with one arm while the other held tight to the bundle of clothing. He coughed out several mouthfuls of sea water.

Finally, his feet touched sand. Nate lifted the plastic bag over his head. Standing chest deep in the bay, he blinked to clear the salt water from his vision.

"What the hell do you think you're doing?"

Startled, Nate froze. So intent on the swim, he hadn't noticed Libby seated on a rock watching his approach. She held the flashlight in her hand. The star at the tip emitted a shimmering sparkle, nicely complementing the fire in her eyes.

Chapter Eleven

Libby wasn't alone. Refractor perched on a rock near her, watching the scene with undisguised amusement. "Greetings, Good Citizen," he called. "A little chilly for a dip."

"Where the hell did you go?" yelled Libby, storming down the beach to the water's edge. "You left without telling anyone. You didn't even write a note. You didn't answer the boat's radio."

"I was in a hurry," Nate said weakly. "I didn't turn it on."

"Do you know how worried I've...we've all been? Did you think of that? Ray's detectors observed some kind of underground disturbance and then it was gone—nothing." Color rose to her cheeks. "I thought you went to fight Mega Mole alone. I thought...I thought..." She swallowed hard. "How could you let me worry like this?"

Nate's heart warmed. Libby had been concerned about him. "I'm sorry, Lib. It wasn't Mega Mole, though," he offered as reassurance. "I had an idea and went to see Cordelia Templeton." He quickly related what happened at The Factory. To his concern, Libby's anger didn't dissipate. If anything, she was more upset.

"Why didn't you ask me to come?" she demanded. "Why did you go alone? I could have helped you."

Nate tried hard not to look at Refractor. "I

thought…you were…you know…busy."

"Busy?" she sputtered. "Busy with what? Dusting knickknacks? Polishing my nails?" The star flared to brilliance.

As the cold water lapped at Nate, he became acutely aware of standing there in the all-together. Only the waves masked the family jewels, and the tide was rapidly going out. "No, that's not what I mean," he stammered. "You were with Refractor. I-I didn't want to interrupt." He hoped he didn't sound as idiotic as he felt, but apparently he did.

She gaped at him in disbelief. "You didn't want to butt in on a conversation?"

"Conversation?" he echoed weakly.

"What the hell did you think we were doing? What kind of person do you think I am?"

Nate's heart gave a tug at the hurt on her face. Serious doubts crept in regarding her attraction to Refractor, along with a sneaking suspicion he had made one huge mess of things.

Libby glared at him. "All that talk of being your partner was simply talk, wasn't it? I'm only your sidekick after all. You don't want me with you. You don't think I can handle it." The flashlight trembled in her grip. Her jaw clenched. "I'm not good enough."

A tightly focused energy beam shot out from the star and struck the bag of clothing making a compact hole, smack dead center. Nate yelped and tossed the smoking bundle to shore. "How's that?" snapped Libby. "Good enough for you?" She turned on her heel and stomped up the steps to Smuggler's Cove.

"Libby, wait!" he splashed out of the water after her.

Refractor cleared his throat. "If you are going to apologize to Elizabeth, might I suggest more appropriate attire? Actually, at this point, any attire at all would be an improvement."

Nate halted in his tracks. "God damn it." He pounced on the bag of clothing and ripped it open, burning his fingers on the melted plastic in the process. "God damn it." The gun and holster had been spared. The other items all sported a tiny assortment of perfectly formed holes complete with singe marks. "God damn it," Nate muttered pulling on his jeans.

"You should have foreseen her anger at being left behind." Refractor spoke with a know-it-all tone that set Nate's teeth on edge. "Elizabeth is a woman whose passions run deep."

The last thing he wanted to hear was Refractor ramble on about Libby's passions. "I care more for Libby than you ever could."

"Then why do you act such a fool? Why haven't you told her so?"

"Not that it's any of your business," he sputtered, hopping on one foot as he tried to wiggle into his shoe, "but it's complicated. We're from two different worlds. She deserves better than a small town cop."

"What Elizabeth deserves is her decision," Refractor said mildly. "She was very upset when you left without her. Once we realized Sea Spray was gone, she stood at the top of the stairs, attention focused on the water, refusing to eat or drink, or stir from the spot until you returned. Her relief was evident when the boat appeared once more—not to mention she could hardly tear her gaze from your little striptease."

Nate straightened up. "She saw that?"

"Oh yes. I'd say her attention was riveted. I found it most unpleasant, myself," he added lightly. "The whiteness of your ass shone like the lighthouse beacon across the bay. Why I do believe it sparkled as brightly as I do."

"Very funny, glow stick," Nate grunted, putting on his other shoe. "Seriously, I'm dying inside."

"The first night you were here, I heard movement below," said Refractor. "I came down to investigate and saw Elizabeth place the quilt from her bed on you while you slept. She appeared embarrassed to be caught and merely said you seemed cold." He peered sharply at Nate. "A woman does not check on a man in the middle of the night, nor place his comfort over hers, unless she cares for him. Was Elizabeth correct in her assumption? Don't you want her?"

Libby had given him the extra quilt. "I thought she..." he stammered. "I mean, you and she...damn it, do I have to spell it out?"

Refractor cocked his head and scrutinized Nate as if seeing him for the first time. "I understand now." He rose to his feet. "Elizabeth's advice and support have helped me return from the black depths of despair, but neither of us desire more than friendship."

Nate gawked at him. "You don't? She doesn't?"

"No. You care for her." It was more statement than question.

Care for Libby? Had he ever wanted a woman more? Unconsciously, his gaze strayed to Smuggler's Cove.

"Why don't you speak your heart to her, then?" said Refractor.

"I told you, it's not that simple. There are

obstacles—"

"The path to love can be strewn with many pitfalls, Good Citizen."

"You don't understand," Nate argued. "I don't have anything to offer Libby. I'm a cop in a small town. She's has a life in the big city. We lead very different lives."

"Even the most polar opposites can find common ground—if the heart is willing to reach out." Refractor paused as if to consider a course of action. All of a sudden, he clapped his hand on Nate's shoulder. "You and Elizabeth will come with me. I have something to show you."

"Now?" Nate shot a rueful glance toward Smuggler's Cove. "I don't think Libby is willing to be seen with me at the moment."

"I can be very convincing. You will simply tag along…as our sidekick."

Refractor bounded up the stairs with Nate at his heels. As they reached the top, Libby was visible at the window. Nate lifted his hand in greeting. She glowered at him and flicked the curtain shut.

"Perhaps it would be best," said Refractor lightly, "if you waited for us by the lighthouse. I have no desire to see the effect of her flashlight on my delicate anatomy."

Nate strode to the front of the grounds and paced up and down. He had really messed up with Libby. A simple apology wasn't going to cut it now, but he had messed up with her once before and made amends. Nate rubbed the back of his neck and smiled. The last time had been painful, but worth it. He examined the area at his feet and selected a smooth weathered stone that fit perfectly in the palm of his hand.

Footsteps crunched along the shell-strewn path from Smuggler's Cove. A moment later, Libby appeared with George Styles, the long-deceased lighthouse keeper at her side. Refractor's imitation was spot on.

Libby instantly caught sight of Nate and stopped in her tracks, glaring. "What's he doing here?"

"I asked him along," answered Styles with Refractor's voice.

Before she could let out another protest, Nate stepped forward. He pressed the rock into her hand. Libby regarded it with suspicion. "Go on, wing it at my head," he pleaded. "I deserve it. I won't even flinch—okay, maybe a little."

Her harsh look softened slightly. "This one is bigger than the pebble I threw when we were kids."

"I'm a bigger jerk now. I deserve a bigger rock."

"I don't need you," she blurted out, waving the flashlight in his face. "Me and my little magic light will be fine all by ourselves."

"I know," Nate said, gently wrapping her fingers around the stone, "but I won't be fine alone." She regarded him in surprise.

"I should have told you where I was going," Nate said. "I shouldn't have gone by myself. We started this thing together, and we have to end it that way. I need you with me, Lib." Why were the words in his heart so hard? Nate struggled to explain. "None of it is any good without you." He pointed to his forehead. "Go ahead…right here."

Libby hefted the stone. Her lips twitched in a slight smile. "I should, you know."

"You definitely should." He braced himself.

The last bit of anger died. "Stop grimacing, you big baby," she said jokingly. "You take all the fun out of it."

Nate grinned. "Can't help myself. You have quite an arm when you're steamed."

Libby shoved the rock in her pocket. "No fun if you know what's coming," she said slyly. "I'll wait until you least expect it."

Refractor folded him arms. "You have an interesting method of apology, Good Citizen. Most men would have brought flowers."

"Libby gets more satisfaction from a rock."

"When we were kids," explained Libby, "Nate swiped my special notebook full of stories no one was allowed to read. I meted out fair and just punishment on the back of his head."

"You are a writer?" said Refractor.

"No," Libby answered quickly.

"Yes, she is," protested Nate. "She's a terrific writer and artist. She even wrote and illustrated her own comic called *Crazy Ass Freaks*."

Pink rose to Libby's cheeks. "Can you really call yourself a writer if no one wants your stuff?"

"They will," said Nate. "Your work is amazing. Don't give up. A market for you is out there. You'll find it."

"Indeed," said Refractor, "if I have learned anything in over two hundred years of existence it's that talents should never be kept to oneself."

"Speaking of talents," said Nate, eyeing him askance. "What's with the George suit?"

"We will take a short walk," he said, striding away.

"Follow me."

Nate motioned to Smuggler's Cove. "Should we tell Ray?"

"Oh, so now you want to let everybody in?" said Libby with amusement.

"I've learned my lesson."

"Good, but I already told Bobbie we were leaving. She and Ray are working on the zayton sensor. I have her phone. Ray will call if they need us."

Refractor led them off the lighthouse grounds and then west on Pine Avenue. Nate zipped his jacket so the holster was hidden. He and Libby warily scanned the surroundings, but none of the cars or pedestrians paid them any attention. Libby asked where they were going, but Refractor wasn't inclined to talk.

Nate relaxed when they left the business area behind and entered a residential zone. After a mile of walking, they came upon heavily wooded lots, far from the noise and congestion of downtown. Refractor turned at a sign pointing to a picnic area, and Nate and Libby followed him along a well-worn path. Ahead, a body of water glistened through the underbrush.

"Willow Lake?" whispered Libby.

Nate nodded assent. Willow Lake had a park with a popular public swimming hole and picnic spot. Nate had been here often. Cottages dotted the shore, surrounded by mature trees offering privacy from any nosey neighbor's prying.

Refractor walked directly to a bungalow on the lake. Nate frowned. Something had changed. This building had no counterpart in Coldwater Bay. At home, the parcel of land was for sale and filled with nothing more than trees and brush.

Bright yellow shutters on the little house stood out against cedar shakes muted gray with age. Scattered spikes of green poked through the unkempt flower garden, perennials trying desperately to answer the call of the summer sun. Nate's parents were avid gardeners, and he took in the piles of leaves and overgrown tangle of grasses with a knowing eye. The flower beds badly needed tending. No one had been here in months.

Refractor bent over to lift the welcome mat and remove a key hidden underneath.

"He has a vacation home?" muttered Nate to Libby.

Her expression softened in understanding. "It's not his."

Before Nate could press for details, Refractor unlocked the door and motioned them inside. Most of the downstairs walls had been removed to make a large open space. Refractor doffed the Styles persona and became the glowing figure again, although his illumination wasn't needed to brighten the interior. Light poured in from skylights above and large windows fronting the lake.

In the center of the room was a cloth-covered easel. Canvases hung on every part of the remaining walls. The colors were striking, the energetic visuals breathtaking. "Oh, my God," cried Libby in shock. "They're comic book panels."

Each one had a different view of people and places in Second Chance City. Some buildings in the area Nate recognized immediately. There was the lighthouse, Peregrine Island, and an art festival in the park—all set off with vibrant colors and dynamic views. Nothing was static or uninteresting in this artist's world. These pictures screamed life.

A series of panels on the wall showed Refractor walking the streets of Second Chance City. Even without the captions, the sense of isolation and enforced solitude came though. "A hero walks the streets alone," Nate read, surprisingly moved. Other panels showed Refractor gazing at an art display in a window. Behind him was another shadowy figure reflected in the glass. Refractor turned. His demeanor underwent a subtle alteration. The caption now read, "Comfort is found in the most unexpected places."

Nate studied the other canvasses. All had strong elements reminiscent of comic books and graphic novels. Propped against the wall were unfinished pieces showing winter scenes as if the artist abandoned the works in a hurry.

"Whose place is this?" Nate asked.

Libby placed her arm on Refractor's. "It's hers, isn't it?"

"No," said Refractor. "It's ours." He yanked the cover off the easel to reveal the portrait of a beautiful dark-haired woman joyously wrapped in sunlight.

Nate sucked in his breath. Whoa...not sunlight. The image of Refractor and Araña together was so intimate, so personal, the truth was immediately clear. Nate regarded him sympathetically. No wonder Refractor understood complications. "I thought Araña was the enemy."

"No." His voice dropped. "Only another unfortunate cursed by zayton radiation poisoning. We met at an art gallery before she was infected. Some nights, the walls of the lighthouse seemed particularly close, and I wandered through the city in the persona of

George Styles. One evening, I was drawn to a crowd gathered for a local show." He motioned to the panel of Refractor walking the streets. "This hung off to the side out of the way, ignored by everyone else, but I was intrigued. The form was so different, the colors and perspective perfectly capturing my loneliness confined in the lighthouse watching the world below. The artist put on canvas what I couldn't put into words; I was part of Second Chance City and yet separate."

Refractor turned to the painting of the two together. His finger traced the outline of her hair. "Aña noticed my interest and told me the work was hers. She said she was not a real artist. Critics didn't accept her unique style, and she never sold anything. I told her she was wrong, how much the painting moved me. Only a real artist could do that. We talked until the gallery closed. Then we strolled the waterfront and talked nearly all night. The next day she came to the lighthouse and brought me the painting as a gift. I was so touched by her kindness, I revealed my true self." A slight smile played on his lips. "She had already guessed."

Refractor gazed into the distance as if recalling pleasant memories. "We became friends. It deepened into love. For months, we spent many happy hours visiting secretly at the lighthouse. Not even Ray and Bobbie knew. I have never felt so connected to someone. I had known women in the past, but meetings were brief. Physical needs quickly satisfied and then an exit without regret. But Aña was different. With one look, we knew the other's thoughts. It was truly as if we shared a single soul. Aña made it plain she wanted to take the relationship farther, but I refused."

He hung his head. "Do you understand the curse of

immortality? To know you will be forced to watch everyone you love eventually wither and die? What could I offer her in return? Not children, not a normal life, not even protection. If my enemies suspected Aña had captured my heart, they would hunt her down to punish me. My love was dangerous. In the end, I realized the only gift I could give was the same one I had once given my wife. Say goodbye and bid her find someone to offer the life she deserved."

"But you didn't stay apart," prodded Libby gently. "How did she become Araña?"

"Aña was at the clinic when she was bitten by a spider and then transformed into what you saw at the lab. People rushed forward to help, but several died before she realized her touch was fatal. Aña was devastated."

Refractor sighed. "People assume because you have monstrous powers, you are a monster. Thus you are branded a criminal before ever becoming one. Once everyone knew Aña was toxic, she had to hide. Unlike me, she had no way to cloak her appearance. To survive, she had to live alone and apart. I found her making preparations to leave Second Chance City before she was hunted and killed. She begged me to go, but her agony tore at my heart. The possibility of death held no concern. All I wanted was to ease her pain. I took her in my arms and kissed her. To our amazement, the venom had no effect."

His voice softened. "I was immune. In joy, we gave into our need. That night I took her to the lighthouse. In the guise of Styles, I bought this place for us, but knew I couldn't protect her forever. If people chanced upon our refuge, Aña would receive no mercy from their harsh judgment. I told her the next time I discovered Mega Mole's location, I would let her know. She would meet me there and pretend to take their side in battle. After that, she would offer to join him."

Libby gasped. "You told her to become a criminal?"

"Yes," he said harshly. "I make no apologies for my decision. I knew Mega Mole and Time Bomb would instantly see her as a powerful ally. They would respect her talents and keep her safe."

Refractor went to a sideboard and opened the drawer. Inside were several pieces of jewelry. "Items from the last robbery."

Nate scanned the lot. He was no expert, but none appeared particularly valuable. "That's all she stole?"

"No," said Refractor. "That's all that remains. Aña only worked with Mega Mole and Time Bomb long enough to gain their trust. She had to appear to be in full agreement with their criminal activities, so would pocket a few trinkets at each robbery and later return them anonymously. She never kept anything. We would meet here when we could for a few stolen hours of happiness. When these weren't returned, I assumed she was dead."

"So the superhero was in league with the villains," said Libby with a shake of the head. "Who would have seen that twist coming?"

"People will do the most incomprehensible things for love," Refractor said wryly.

"You never considered intervening in the robberies?" asked Nate. "After all those years of helping people, how could you simply stand by and watch them commit crimes?"

"I've discovered much concerning others infected with zayton," said Refractor, "especially since meeting Aña. Do you know Mega Mole's history?"

Nate looked at Libby. She shrugged. "Payton never bothered with his backstory either."

"Mega Mole's name was Jack Keller," said Refractor.

Nate blinked in surprise. "I know him. He was my high school biology teacher in Coldwater Bay."

"He was also a kind and loving father and a devoted husband before zayton radiation poisoning. Once transformed, he was rejected by his family and friends and hunted like an animal. What other choice was there, but to turn to crime to survive? I became more desirous of protecting innocent bystanders, than caring if Mega Mole and his gang made off with a few baubles."

"You didn't turn to crime," Nate pointed out.

"Nonetheless, I hid for decades, slowly building a reputation as protector of the innocent. Even in Second Chance City, I'm not fully accepted and must stay hidden. The effects of zayton are feared that much. Ray and Bobbie, dear friends that they have become, would never suggest differently. They know others would not be so tolerant of my existence, no matter how much good I do. Those poisoned by zayton are always set apart. Aña suffered the same fate. Wild tales soon spread of unprovoked attacks on innocent people. All lies," he snorted. "Except for two unfortunate deaths at the clinic the day she was bitten by the spider, Aña never poisoned anyone."

"Kristie would disagree," said Nate.

"I had no wish to harm her," said a soft voice. They

all turned their heads. Aña stood in the open doorway.

"Aña," Refractor breathed out her name as a sigh. He crossed the room and gathered her in his arms.

Nate pulled out his gun, but Libby laid a hand on his arm. "Don't," she whispered. "She's not the enemy."

"How do you know?" he asked out of the corner of his mouth.

"Trust me. I'm sure." Libby spoke with complete confidence. The star didn't emit a single stray twinkle. Nate returned the gun to the holster.

Aña buried her face in Refractor's chest. "I couldn't disobey Scribe's order, so I unleashed the finest spray and hoped the wind would dissipate the poison. I had no idea Kristie was near. Please…" Her voice trembled. "Tell me she lives."

"She'll be fine," said Libby. Aña's expression filled with relief.

Refractor laid his cheek against her hair. "Why did you let me believe you were dead?"

"When several items I stole showed up again, Mega Mole started to ask questions. His suspicions rose about us. He began to follow me. I always managed to give him the slip, but realized after the explosion at O'Reilly's I was your greatest liability."

"He can't cause me any harm," he protested. "I am immortal."

"Those around you are not. Mega Mole searched for me that night and saw you go into O'Reilly's. I heard the explosion and ran toward the carnage. I saw your grief. Others would use me to find you and more innocents might suffer the same fate. You would never have willingly let me go, but our love could bring you nothing, but pain. The explosion was my chance. I decided it was best for you to think I had died, too."

Abruptly, Aña pushed him aside. "You must leave here at once."

"Debolt," growled Nate. "Where is he?"

She grimaced in pain. "I-I can't tell you. He won't let me. He has control."

"How does he do it?" demanded Nate.

"I approached Scribe months ago seeking a cure. He contacted me again...said he found one to lure me out...he lied. I can't...I can't say anything more..." She turned to Refractor in despair. "I would rather die than hurt you, Caleb, but I can't fight him." Each word seemed a struggle.

"It's all right, love," said Refractor. "I will find Scribe and make him pay for what he's done."

Aña turned to Nate and Libby. "He can't control you." Her expression showed the strain of fighting whatever mental imperative Debolt had planted. "He doesn't understand why you're here."

"I do," said Libby fiercely. "I just figured it out. We're here to stop him. Right, Nate?"

His lips formed a cold tight smile. "Damn straight."

Aña's hands went to her head as if fighting to hold back the pain. "Forgive me," she whispered to Refractor. "I have to...I have to..."

Refractor's arms went around her. The emotional distress in his voice echoed hers. "My love—"

Aña's hand reached inside her jacket. All heard the *snick* of the switchblade an instant before it plunged into Refractor.

Chapter Twelve

Refractor fell back with a cry against Nate and Libby. Aña yanked the knife from his shoulder and darted to the door. Nate made a move to follow, but Refractor grabbed his wrist. "Leave her be," he commanded. "Aña is not to blame. I swear Scribe will pay."

Libby pressed a hand over the wound. "I feel it bleeding." As she spoke, a drop of light spilled beneath her fingers and hit the floor.

"Do not worry," said Refractor, standing erect. "The wound is shallow. I will heal. I always do."

"We should return to the lighthouse," said Nate. "Can you change into Styles?"

"I can." A moment later the elderly lighthouse keeper stood before them.

Libby went to the kitchen for a clean dishcloth to press against the injury, but the bleeding had already stopped. They made their way through the woods. Refractor walked at a slower pace, but if that was due to minimal blood loss or the emotional toll of seeing Aña again, Nate couldn't tell. What he did know was something wasn't right. Nate felt it deep down in his gut. He scanned the woods repeatedly for any sign of trouble, but all was peaceful and quiet. Aña's arrival made no sense. Why did she come to the house alone? Why stab Refractor? Both she and Debolt knew any injury would be superficial. What was the point?

The sun had set by the time they returned to the lighthouse. Refractor resumed his normal appearance. Libby insisted he lie down and rest. She wouldn't accept his protest that he had completely healed.

"Is she always this stubborn?" Refractor asked with amusement.

"No," said Nate, lightly. "Generally, she's much worse."

As Refractor climbed the spiral staircase, Libby regarded Nate kindly. "You should get some rest too. It's been a long day."

Nate stretched. "Can't. I'm wired to the hilt. Aña's arrival made no sense."

"Could she have broken from Payton's hold for a bit?"

"Not a chance. You saw the way she acted. She warned us to escape, so what was she doing there?"

"Haven't a clue, but you're right it makes no sense. If Payton sent her, he knows they're in love. He must also know a knife wouldn't do any lasting harm. Did he think an attack from Aña would shake him up?"

"If so, he completely misjudged. All he did was piss off glow stick even more."

Libby sighed. "It's so sad, don't you think?"

"Yeah. They deserve better. Refractor said love often involves complications. He wasn't kidding. Did he mention Aña?"

"No, but I had a feeling. When we first got here, he was in mourning. I thought it due to the deaths of Chief Williams and the others, but it ran deeper than that, like a part of his soul had been ripped away. After his reaction to Aña's appearance at the lab, my suspicions grew."

Nate rubbed the back of his neck. "I can't think straight any more. Let's take a break. Do you want some coffee?"

As he brewed a pot, Libby scrounged a jar of peanut butter and some crackers from the cupboard. "Not much of a dinner I'm afraid," she said, sitting at the table with Nate.

"I don't mind. The company makes up for it."

She looked down at the table and smiled.

Nate shot a surreptitious glance as Libby nibbled on a cracker. Could Refractor be right? Did Libby harbor feelings for him? She was ticked when he left. She had worried about him, so Refractor had said. She also got the full monty of Naked Nate with his Private Parts at ease and didn't seem repulsed—again, so Refractor had said.

He shifted in his seat. They were alone. He should say something to Libby, but what? That he fell in love with her all over again as soon as he spotted her at Write Away? Yeah, right. That sounded like he was only trying to talk his way into her pants. Nate cleared his throat. "Crazy, huh? All this stuff with Debolt, I mean."

Libby chuckled. "If we ever get home, I'm so going to be much pickier accepting another job. No way will I fetch coffee for a supervillain ever again."

Nate cradled his steaming cup, his hands suddenly cool and clammy. "You could stay in Coldwater Bay—write that comic book. Do what you were always meant to do."

Libby startled.

"I mean it, Lib." He leaned forward, heart

pounding. "You have talent. Why waste it making assholes like Debolt successful?"

The pink tint in her cheeks deepened. "I-I don't know…"

Nate reached out and took her hand. Her fingers trembled under his touch. "Please, Libby. Stay." He leaned forward, his eyes sought hers.

Stay with me. Damn it, why won't the words come out?

Libby's breath quickened, and then her expression filled with regret. "When we return, it would be better for me to immediately leave town." A tight painful knot grew in Nate's chest. Someone already waited for her at home. *Too late again.*

"Oh. Right." Nate dropped her hand and stared into the coffee cup wishing he was anywhere, but there.

A melodic chime broke the awkward silence between them. The cell phone Bobbie had left with Libby had an incoming text. She checked the display and then returned the phone to her pocket. "Bobbie says Kristie is doing better." Her voice tightened. She shot him an inquiring glance. "She can have visitors now."

"I'm glad to hear it. I wonder if Logan Emory is in this reality?" he added dryly. "He'd probably enjoy being fondled under the table."

"Fondled?" repeated Libby, obviously perplexed.

"Second Chance City Kristie is a bit grabby. I've got to be honest, she kind of creeps me out. She's like Coldwater Bay Kristie on speed. Like I said, though, Logan might appreciate it."

Libby's confusion deepened. "Who's Logan?"

"Kristie's boyfriend."

Libby's mouth dropped open. "What?"

Now it was Nate's turn to be puzzled by her confounded reaction. "Yeah, he's a doctor, finishing his residency at the hospital. Nice guy."

"I-I thought…I heard…" Libby cleared her throat. "At Write Away, I heard Kristie tell you not to be late for your big date."

"Oh, that. She's been planning a surprise birthday party for Logan for weeks. When Kristie gives a command to attend," he added lightly, "all are expected to obey."

"So you aren't…in Coldwater Bay….you and Kristie…" Libby flustered. "You know…together?"

"My girlfriend? No, we're only friends. She'll ream me good if I miss the party, even though I have a perfectly legit excuse, being trapped in another dimension and all—"

The confusion left Libby's face, but some other emotion seemed on the verge of breaking through. Could it be relief? Nate took a steadying breath. "I don't have anyone waiting for me at home."

"Oh," Libby said weakly. "Oh." Her gaze softened. She smiled at him, freckles splayed across the bridge of her nose.

Hope sprouted in Nate, growing stronger with each beat of his heart. "Does anyone wait for you?" he finally dared ask.

Sssssss

A wispy smoke curl rose from a glowing dot on the wall. Nate half rose from his seat. "What the hell—?" A beam of light missed his head by inches. He dove across the table and hit the floor, pulling Libby down with him.

As Nate drew the sonic gun, Libby activated the

flashlight's shield. Refractor stepped into the doorway, holding his head. "I can't stop it," he groaned. One hand reached out, trembling. A light ray blasted from his palm.

Libby grimaced, holding tight to the flashlight, as energy pulses slammed against the barrier. "Caleb, stop!" she cried.

"Scribe…" Refractor spit the name out between gritted teeth. "Voice in my head…ordering me to kill you both." The beam from his hand burned white hot. Ripples of protective force danced across the surface of the shield nulling the effects of Refractor's ray.

"Forgive me…" Refractor's face contorted in agony. "I told him Princess Robella was at Smuggler's Cove. They'll find her." He grabbed one hand with the other. Muscles strained as he forced his arm away from Libby. The beam didn't cut out, but instead tore into the wall. "Run!" he commanded. "I…can't…stop." Laser bolts raked the ceiling sending chunks of debris raining down on them. This whole section of the keeper's quarters would soon be nothing more than rubble.

"The tunnel!" cried Nate.

Libby and Nate dashed to the hidden opening and scrambled down the ladder. As Nate slammed the trapdoor shut, a roar came from above. Tons of bricks and mortar collapsed. The hinges on the trapdoor groaned under the weight.

"Move!" shouted Nate. They darted down the tunnel. With a crash, the trapdoor gave way. Wreckage tumbled in, blocking any return to the lighthouse. The lights in the tunnel winked out.

The soft glow of the flashlight was now the only illumination. Libby dropped the shield, waving away the dust cloud. "No going that way."

The ground shifted violently under their feet. Nate grabbed for Libby and steadied them both against the side of the tunnel. "That's either an earthquake or Mega Mole."

The earth vibrated again. Both tensed waiting for an attack; Nate with his finger on trigger, Libby's hand clenching the flashlight. The narrow confined space was not the best place to mount a defense especially with one end already blocked. Slowly, the residual vibrations moved off and then died completely. Seconds passed with no more tremors.

Nate eyed the tunnel warily. "He's gone. He's not coming after us."

Libby gasped. "Bobbie and Ray!"

Without a word, they took off at a run, but within a dozen yards stopped short. Rocks and dirt clogged the tunnel.

"We're trapped," cried Nate. "No way forward, no way back."

Libby ran her hand across the surface of the cave-in. "Maybe not. I think I can shift the debris. It's risky, though. More movement might bring the whole thing down on our heads."

"Have at it, Lib." Nate spoke with complete confidence. "You can do this."

"All right then." Intense concentration defined every inch of Libby's body. As she touched the flashlight to a large boulder, the star glowed bright white. The rock quivered, and then inch by inch shifted aside. He watched uneasily as more dirt dislodged from the walls.

Nate offered encouragement. "Steady, Lib. You got

this."

The power of the star blazed like the sun, lighting the tunnel. Dirt and more rocks were drawn out and repositioned. Slowly, carefully, tons of debris moved aside, clearing a path. The strain showed in Libby's pale complexion.

Nate regarded her with concern. "Maybe you should take a break."

Libby wiped her brow. "No, I'm almost through. I can feel it. There's not nearly as much weight pressing against the flashlight anymore." She aimed the star against the rocks. "One...more...shove...will...do... it!" The rest of the debris tumbled aside. With a crow of triumph, she stepped through the new opening.

The air was musty. Nate coughed, and then excitedly pointed to an offshoot from the main tunnel. "That's the route to the beach. We're not far from Smuggler's Cove."

From ahead came a moan. "Ray!" Nate called out, breaking into a run. "Hang on, we're coming." They reached the end of the tunnel directly under the entrance to the lab. This section hadn't fared too well. Part of the floor above had collapsed.

"Ray!" Nate called again.

"Here..." came the weak reply. Ray was shoved against a wall. He had made it as far as the bottom of the staircase before the whole structure fell apart, pinning him underneath. "They came..." He grunted. "Couldn't stop them."

"Lie still," cautioned Libby. "I'll get you free in a second." She shifted the staircase out of the way.

"They ambushed us," he said. "Out of nowhere. Syr took Bobbie. I have to find her."

"Don't try to talk," said Libby. "You need a doctor."

"I'm all right." Ray struggled to sit up. "The whole house started to break apart. I bolted for the staircase, but only made it halfway down. Was trapped underneath, couldn't move. It's lucky you found me."

"Ray, we have to get you to the hospital," said Nate. "That arm is broken. You could have internal injuries."

"I'm not going anywhere," he said harshly, "except after Bobbie. Syr is going to kill her. It's the only way for him to maintain control. He'll take her to Mo'R'ees Six for a public execution..." His voice choked off.

"We'll get her back," Nate promised. "First, we need to find a way out of here."

A creaking noise issued from overhead. Libby warily examined the ceiling. "Not that way. It's too unstable to clear the opening."

"The cliff exit then," said Nate, helping Ray to his feet. "Let's go before the rest caves in."

As they retraced their steps, Ray described the attack. "I had switched on the seismic monitor to search for Mega Mole, but it didn't give any warning until he was right outside. He must not have traveled underground. Scribe and Araña were there along with Syr and a dozen of his men. Refractor was with them." The tone of his voice relayed complete shock. "He watched while Mega Mole grabbed Bobbie... He helped them... I-I couldn't believe it."

"Debolt found a way to control him, too," said Nate. "Time Bomb even warned Refractor. He told him he was as doomed as the rest of them."

Libby drew in a sharp breath. "Of course, his

blood! When Mega Mole met with Payton, he was bleeding from gunshot wounds. When he returned, the first thing he did was knock Time Bomb out and give him a bloody lip. Aña must have stabbed Refractor for a blood sample. Payton could have easily gotten a sample of hers, too. After all, she went to him for a cure."

They turned down the secondary tunnel, but within a dozen yards came to a dead end. "It's a solid wall," cried a disheartened Nate.

With a crafty look, Ray pointed to a lever attached to the wall. "Pull that." A hidden door slid open. The blast of fresh sea air instantly raised Nate's spirits. "Secret entrance," bragged Ray. "Bobbie and I put it in."

They carefully made their way down the rocky slope to the beach. The trek was slow going. Ray moved with stumbling steps, and a thick fog now blanketed the coast. A short walk brought them to the stairway and then back up to Smuggler's Cove.

"I'm sorry about the lab, Ray," said Libby, surveying the grounds with sympathy. Half the building was unrecognizable rubble.

He grimly viewed the devastation. "Everything can be rebuilt. The only thing that matters now is to find Bobbie."

"We'll go to Connor's," said Nate to Libby as they skirted the debris field. "No one knows about the place except us." He stopped in his tracks. "Damn it, the van is gone. They must have taken it."

"Bobbie parks her car behind the shed," said Ray, smiling slightly. "She always leaves the keys in the ignition even though I tell her not to."

Once safely at Connor's, Nate tended to Ray. "I don't suppose you'll change your mind and let me run you to the hospital." He eased the injured arm into a makeshift sling.

"Not a chance." Ray grunted, shifting in the chair to find a more comfortable position. "We're running out of time. Syr must be recharging his ship's engines as we speak."

"How long will that take?"

Ray was grim. "Not long."

"Did you have any luck with the zayton monitor?" asked Libby.

"Some. It honed in on frequency clusters, but before I could fine tune the reception for a tighter read, Mega Mole arrived and all hell broke loose. Now it's smashed into a thousand pieces and buried under Smuggler's Cove. I've got nothing left to build another. I don't have the seismic monitor anymore, either." Ray couldn't hide the despair any longer. "How will I find Bobbie?"

Nate thought hard. Time was against them. Debolt and the others could be anywhere in the city. Searching every building was impossible. With no clue where to begin, he clenched his fists in frustration. "We're missing something, Lib."

Libby didn't respond, apparently deep in thought. Her complexion was still pale. She had put out a lot of effort to save them this evening. Maybe too much, but she wouldn't complain. It wasn't her style. Nate went to the sink. He returned with a glass of water that he pressed into her hand. "You should drink something."

She nodded absentmindedly and slowly sipped. Abruptly, Libby slammed the glass down, sloshing water on the table.

Nate leaned in. "You have an idea."

"Maybe," she said with growing excitement. "This is a comic book, right? At least, for you and me. If so, the way to find Payton's hideout is to consider comics for the answer." She turned to Ray. "Where did those frequency clusters point before the signal cut out?"

"Somewhere off to the east."

Libby's lips twitched in a slight smile. "Perfect."

"The only thing east of here is water," said Nate.

"Not exactly. You're forgetting Peregrine Island."

"That's a park and picnic area."

"In our world—yes…Ray, what's on Peregrine Island?"

"Nothing, now. It used to be an old Coast Guard station, but it's been inactive for years, since they built the new facility. The whole place is off limits. No visitors allowed."

Libby chuckled. "Couldn't ask for anything better. Next to a dormant volcano or a vacant warehouse, an abandoned government facility is the most popular place for a villain's hideout."

Ray wasn't convinced. "It's not far from the mainland. People would spot increased activity on the island. If boats landed there, someone would have noticed."

"Not if Scribe and the others traveled underground," said Libby. "Mega Mole would have had no trouble excavating a tunnel under the bay."

Ray rose from his seat. He paced the floor with growing excitement. "The location of the entrance into Second Chance City is the only question."

A suspicion jabbed at Nate. "On the day Scribe

stole the zayton, where did you first pick up Mega Mole on the seismic monitor?"

"East of Main Street near the harbor."

"The Factory," Nate announced in triumph. "It makes perfect sense. Mega Mole was there for months. He could have dug a new tunnel to Peregrine Island while he and Time Bomb hid with Bryce. Cordelia said he was reluctant to leave Second Chance City. He probably planned a new headquarters at Peregrine Island. Once Bryce died, Mega Mole and Time Bomb could have easily disappeared. Cordelia certainly wouldn't have hunted for them." Nate turned to Ray. "How many buildings are on the island?"

"Only a handful."

"Anything big enough to hide a spaceship from curious onlookers?"

Ray's expression brightened. "Yes. One of the buildings is a large concrete block structure; half set aside for storage, the other half a maintenance facility. It had sliding bay doors on one wall—big enough to get a ship though." He struggled to his feet. "We have to go."

Nate placed an arm on his shoulder. "Not so fast."

Ray shook him off. "We're wasting time sitting here!"

"Ray, there are only three of us, and you're injured. We need help to go against Refractor and the others under Debolt's control." Nate held out his hand to Libby. "I need the phone."

"Who are you calling?"

"Abby Franco."

Libby said nothing and handed over Bobbie's cell. Abigail answered immediately. Nate gave her a quick rundown and their location.

"Are you sure you can trust her?" asked Libby once Nate hung up.

"I guess I'll find out."

Nate kept an anxious watch out the window. A short time later, clusters of headlight beams cut through the fog. A dozen patrol cars came to a sudden halt in front of the house.

Libby's nervousness showed through. "Were you expecting a party?"

"Not exactly," he admitted with growing unease. "Let's go say hi." Had he misjudged Abby? It was too late to run now as Sergeant Franco approached the house with others in uniform. However, none of the police drew a weapon and none were Florence Peevey. Nate relaxed. "Where's the chief?"

"Warming a cell with Duval and a few more of her buds. You should have heard their language," Abigail added dryly. "Learned a few new words myself. I reckon we're all under arrest tomorrow, but for tonight Second Chance City's finest is all yours. What's the plan, Good Citizen?"

"I'll fill you in on the way to The Factory."

They drove off with Abigail leading the line of patrol cars. The Factory was dark and buttoned up tight. No welcoming neon sign shone through the fog, but Nate's spirits rose upon catching sight of a battered white van parked in front.

Police tape still stretched across the door. Abigail ripped it off and then signaled two officers gripping a small battering ram. Within seconds, the entry gaped open. The interior was quiet. Nate wrinkled his nose. A strong smell of fresh earth mixed with alcohol wafted out. To his right, Abigail pressed flat against the wall. She waved the other officers back. "On your mark, Good Citizen."

Startled, Nate realized he and Libby were expected to lead the charge and clear any dangerous obstacles out of the way. He grimaced. So much for the perks of being a superhero. Libby held the flashlight tight, her determined face lit by the faint glow of the star. She was never more beautiful.

Nate drew his gun. "Ready, partner?"

Libby flashed a smile. She stepped beside him, shoulder to shoulder. "Always."

Nate's heart hammered out a ferocious beat. Together they crossed the threshold and entered the dark interior of The Factory.

Chapter Thirteen

No explosion greeted their arrival. No ray gun beams shot from shadowy corners. Libby slowly panned the star back and forth for a complete view of the interior. "What a mess," she murmured.

Floorboards had exploded up from the dance floor creating a gaping hole wide enough for Mega Mole to crawl through. Ejected debris had crashed behind the bar, shattering rows of liquor bottles. Smashed glass littered the ground. A steady *drip-drip-drip* filled the air. Bottles on the shelves that had been tipped over dribbled the remains of their contents, forming spreading puddles on the floor.

Nate peered over the edge. "I'm no expert," he remarked dryly, "but I'd say we found another entrance to the tunnel."

Libby played the flashlight into the hole. "The sides are fairly smooth. Can't see much from here, but I believe this new tunnel takes a hard right at the bottom. Mega Mole must have opened a secondary passageway bypassing the cave-in under Cordelia's office. We should have a clear shot to Peregrine Island."

Nate found the light switch and gave Abigail the all clear. She entered with Ray and the other officers. Several carried sturdy ropes. He regarded Ray with concern. "You'll never be able to climb with that arm."

"I don't plan to." Ray replied with firm resolve.

"You'll need a distraction. I'll take a boat from the harbor to the island."

Libby let out a protest. "The fog is thick now, but won't hide you forever."

"It'll get me over there without being observed. Once ashore, even with a broken arm, I can lead them on a merry chase."

"You'll be alone," warned Nate. "If the other end of the tunnel is blocked...if we can't get through..."

"I won't be left behind," he said stubbornly. "Not when Bobbie needs help."

Nate clapped him on the shoulder. "Wouldn't think of it. Watch your step, though. Debolt is in a shoot-first-ask-questions-later mood."

"So am I." Ray checked his watch. "I'll start the diversion in exactly one hour. That should give you enough time to cross underneath the bay."

Abigail handed him a pistol. "Can you shoot one-handed?"

"Almost as poorly as I do with two," Ray admitted with a weak smile. "But even badly aimed gunshots can distract." With that, he headed out the door.

Officers lowered two ropes into the hole. Abigail activated a chemical light stick and tossed it over the edge. "Good twenty foot drop," she murmured to Nate and Libby, stepping back. "Be careful."

Nate and Libby eased over the rim and slowly inched down the shaft. The sides crumbled at the slightest touch, dislodging rocks, pebbles, and soil. At the halfway point, a loosened clod from above fell and smacked Nate in the face. He spit out a gritty mouthful of dirt. "Not that this isn't super fun and all, but the comic book gig is getting real old real fast."

"Why are you complaining?" joshed Libby. "You're only the sidekick. I'm the superhero with the magic light."

Their feet finally touched the bottom. Nate wiped the sweat from his brow on a shirtsleeve. The star's gleam revealed a newly excavated tunnel heading in the direction of the bay.

"All clear," Nate yelled up.

As they waited for the others to descend, Nate and Libby explored ahead. After a dozen yards, they came to an offshoot half-clogged with rubble. Nate tossed aside a few rocks. Libby shone the star inside. The light clearly revealed a larger opening. "That must lead to the room underneath Cordelia's office." He sighed. "Bryce is buried not far from here."

Libby's expression filled with pity. "What a horrible way to go."

"Better a quick clean death, than the miserable life he suffered."

She laid a gentle hand on his arm. "When we return tell Cordelia we found another way. At least, she'll be able to retrieve Bryce's body for a proper burial. That may offer some small comfort."

Nate leaned against the wall. "It's another thing to remind me that Second Chance City isn't home. It's not only Cordelia and Bryce," he added solemnly.

Libby nudged him playfully in the ribs. "Don't tell me you miss the other Florence Peevey, too."

Nate's lips twisted in a half-smile. "Let me tell you a story of the real Florence Peevey—the one she keeps hidden. Not long after Mom started chemo, she and Dad stopped at Valenti's Automotive to get the oil in the car changed. By then Mom wore a scarf to cover her balding head. She wasn't well, but forced herself to get out with Dad and not always be a prisoner to the disease at home.

"While Dad waited outside, Mom sat in a chair by the register because she was too tired to stand. Florence was behind the counter doing a daily crossword. Mom mentioned how she got stuck on three down. Turns out they were both puzzle fanatics. They chatted a bit, and then Mom got a phone call to confirm her chemo appointment for the next day. Dad came in to tell her the car was ready, so they paid the bill and left."

"The following day, my sister and I were off somewhere running errands. As my folks got ready to leave for the doctor, Florence arrived with a mop, broom, and bucket-load of cleaning supplies. 'Sorry you're sick,' she grunted. 'I'm here to clean your house.' Note, she did not ask permission. She simply pushed passed them and got to work."

"That's so sweet," said Libby, touched. "What did your parents say?"

"Nothing. They were too stunned, plus they were running late. So they left Florence alone with all our stuff, not knowing if they'd opened their door to the mastermind of the local burglary ring."

"I take it they were wrong?" said Libby, amused.

"When they got home, every item in the house was exactly as they left it, except spotless. Even the laundry had been done. From that point on, Florence showed up every time Mom had chemo. I don't know how she knew, but that's the way it is in a small town. Florence never said anything much beyond hello and growled if anyone tried to thank her."

Nate shook his head. "When someone gets

diagnosed with a devastating illness, the entire family's lives get turned upside down, not just the patient. Everything revolves around the disease. People send cards and flowers, wish them well, but what the sick person really needs is someone like Florence to barge in without asking, clean the house, and do the laundry. She took a big burden off of us that summer. Not to mention the psychological lift it gave Mom to always return to a clean home. Don't get me wrong, Florence has continued to be Coldwater Bay's resident pill, but a pill with a good heart. The Florence here...I don't ever see her putting herself out like that for anyone." He leaned against the wall. "No matter how many similarities exist between Coldwater Bay and Second Chance City this place will never be home."

"There's a lot that's right with Coldwater Bay," said Libby softly. She leaned against the wall next to him.

Nate raised an eyebrow. "I thought you hated it there. I distinctly recall that summer the many times you stated a clear intention to leave small town life behind. I believe the exact words were, 'This place sucks.' "

Libby chuckled. "I did say that often, didn't I? I realized years later it wasn't Coldwater Bay that sucked—only my parents constant bickering. In my mind, the two were fused together, as if somehow leaving Coldwater Bay would make life better."

"Did it?" he asked kindly.

"Yes, but that was due to my folks' divorce, not because the town was so awful. It took a long time for the truth to sink in." Her voice took on a wistful quality. "Big cities didn't have everything I needed, either. I hadn't planned the signing tour to include Coldwater Bay, but something inside forced me back." Her voice betrayed a slight tremble. "As if that's where I could find the missing piece of my life."

Nate drew in a breath. This was neither the right time nor place, but none of that mattered anymore. "You never answered my question in the kitchen. Is someone waiting for you at home?"

The glow from the flashlight cast soft illumination over Libby's face, but it was enough to see the color rise to her cheeks. Her voice dropped to a whisper. "No. None of my relationships ever stuck. Why is that, do you think?"

Heart pounding, Nate slid his hand to the nape of her neck. Her face tilted toward his. "None of mine have, either. The memory of one little kiss on the cheek never let me go."

Her lips met his, eagerly and with no hesitation. The star flared to brilliance. The air was calm and still. So was Nate, his path and purpose now perfectly clear. He nuzzled her ear. "Would you like to have dinner?"

Libby gaped at him. "What?"

"You know...when we get home to Coldwater Bay. Someplace nice."

To Nate his question was perfectly logical. He wanted to celebrate and show Libby off to the whole world, but she simply gawked at him as if for no apparent reason he abruptly grew a second head. "We're preparing to confront impossible odds," Libby sputtered, "against an enemy who has made it abundantly clear he would be happy to have us both dead at his feet, and you're asking me on a date? Now? Are you insane?"

God, she was beautiful even when her expression held stunned disbelief. All that was left was for Nate to admit everything. Now, before the battle began. Now, before he faced a deadly enemy—perhaps for the last time. Now, before an eternal silence might claim them both. Don't leave any regrets behind.

Nate ran his hand through Libby's hair; those beautiful, impossible, untamed curls. "Yes, I am. Completely. Utterly. Totally insane about Libby Parish. I've held you in my heart since the day we met. Back then I was too young and stupid to understand those feelings. Then you showed up once more out of nowhere flooding every lonely place in my soul with your impossibly bright light."

The words flowed so easily now. *Too Late Nate will never delay speaking his heart again.*

"I love you, Libby Parish. No other girl ever measured up to your memory. No one ever will. So, go out with me?"

Her brilliant smile warmed him like a roaring bonfire on a cold winter's night. As if in answer, her lips pressed hard against his. Nothing mattered anymore; not the insane circumstances that brought them here, not unknown danger lurking ahead. All that mattered was Libby in his arms.

"Mighty Light! Good Citizen!" Abigail called down the tunnel. "We've all made it to the bottom."

With reluctance, Nate and Libby stepped apart. "Good Citizen," murmured Libby, eyes glistening, "your timing sucks. Let's find Payton and get the hell out of here."

"My thoughts exactly, Mighty Light." With a happy grin, Nate called the others over.

Abigail jogged to Nate's side. "What's the plan?"

"If luck holds," he said, "we'll have a clear shot to Peregrine Island. Our one advantage will be surprise, so we have to get to the other end before Ray makes his move. Once inside the compound, we find Scribe and disable the pen device that controls Refractor, Mega Mole, and Araña."

Abigail frowned. "Is that wise, Good Citizen? If the device has control wouldn't it be best to use it to force them to turn on each other? We could rid Second Chance City of Araña and Mega Mole once and for all."

Libby voiced an instant protest. "Absolutely not! They're as much prisoners as Bobbie."

"Bobbie is like us," Abigail said coolly, "and she is the ruler of a planet. Saving her would be beneficial to Second Chance City. Refractor has proven his worth, but Araña and Mega Mole are dangerous." A rumbled accord from the police officers behind them showed agreement. "I won't order my people to stand down if they're attacked," she added. "They will defend themselves."

"We're not asking for surrender," sputtered Libby, "only don't charge in guns blazing. What is wrong with you people—"

"Mighty Light and I will deal with Araña and Mega Mole," Nate assured Abigail. "You take care of Syr."

The group trudged through the tunnel. Chatter consisted of hushed whispers. Light from the flashlights and the star cast spectral shadows on the wall amplifying the eerie atmosphere. As they moved farther from The Factory, the ground had a definite downward slope. The air grew even more dank and chilled and now contained an unpleasant mustiness. Nate wrinkled his nose. How much oxygen was in here? The sooner they were all out in the fresh air, the better.

"I'm worried for Aña's safety," Libby whispered. "Abby's people are liable to be trigger happy when up close and personal with a supposed villain. They'll never believe she means them no harm."

"I agree. We have to get that device from Debolt deactivated, and get her out of there fast."

"How far do you think we've come? I'm beginning to get claustrophobic."

"So am I, but I'd say we're halfway to Peregrine Island." A drop of something very cold and wet hit the top of his head. Nate stopped short and grabbed Libby's arm. He motioned Abigail and the others to a halt.

"What's wrong?" whispered Libby.

He pointed to the ceiling. "Shine the star right there."

A black jagged gash ran lengthwise along the rock. As they watched, a drop of clear liquid oozed out and plunked into Nate's outstretched palm. He touched the moisture to the tip of his tongue. "Salt water," he said grimly.

Libby pointed the star ahead. The light flashed on a reflective surface. Her voice dropped low. "More puddles."

Abigail played her flashlight along the crack. "We'd better pick up the pace. I don't like the condition of that ceiling."

They jogged down the tunnel. Every now and then, Nate shot an anxious glance upward. To his relief, the cracks didn't appear to worsen. On the nerve-wracking side—they didn't disappear either.

Talk was kept to a minimum, the necessity for speed weighed hard on everyone. Eventually, Libby broke the silence. "Is it my imagination," she panted, trotting by Nate's side, "or are we now going uphill?"

"No, you're right," said Nate, spirits rising. "We must be close to Peregrine Island." At that moment, a blast of fresh air hit his face. He stifled a shout of relief and motioned for everyone to stop. He passed the order to douse all light except for the star. Nate and Libby led the way at a brisk walk. Ten yards down the tunnel, the ground took a sharp upward angle. Another few yards and the star's light revealed an abrupt end.

They stood in the bottom of a pit. A metal ladder had been propped against the wall. Abigail and her officers clustered around, waiting expectantly.

"Douse the light, Lib, and follow me," he whispered.

Nate scaled the ladder pausing at the top to listen. Other than his own labored breathing, everything was quiet. He hauled himself over the edge and then turned to give Libby a hand. The room was dark except for the dim illumination provided by an exit sign over a door at the far end.

As their eyesight adjusted to the gloom, the surroundings came into focus; a large open space with a few broken desks and chairs scattered about. Lined against the walls were bulletin boards and old file cabinets. A glass-paneled door under the exit sign led to an interior hallway.

"This must be the old admin office area," Libby whispered. She motioned to the exit light. "Someone must be on the island. The electricity works."

Nate crept to a window covered by a closed venetian blind. He cautiously separated two of the slats to see outside. The ground was cloaked in thick fog. In the distance came a muted flash, and then the muffled drone of a fog horn.

Libby peered around his shoulder. "Can you tell where we are?"

"West side of the island. I can see the lighthouse beacon, so the tower was undamaged. Refractor's attack must have taken out only the caretaker's living quarters."

Voices approached. They pressed flat against the wall as two uniformed guards armed with laser pistols strode past.

"Syr's men," said Libby. "Let's hope he didn't bring too many more."

Nate watched as they disappeared past the corner of the building. "They're not coming inside. I wonder what's over there."

Libby jerked on his sleeve toward the door to the hallway. "Let's find out."

They pressed flat against the wall and listened, but no sound came from the corridor. Nate glanced at Libby. "Light 'em up." The star glowed faintly, the shield ready to activate at the first sign of trouble.

Cautiously, Nate stepped out. Other doors, visible from their position, only revealed additional empty offices. "All clear," he reported.

"I don't think there's anyone except us in the building," whispered Libby.

"Then why are you whispering?" Nate whispered with a mischievous grin.

Her chuckle eased the tension. "Shut up. You're

such a dork."

They jogged down the hall to an exit. Nate pressed his ear against the door. "I hear sounds, but they're muffled. With luck, no one is right outside. Ready?"

Libby doused the star. "Whenever you are, Good Citizen."

Cautiously, Nate cracked the door enough for them to peek out. Across an open space was a large two-story concrete block building, the entrance set in a recessed alcove. Two more of Syr's men stood guard. Light poured from every window. "That's promising," he muttered. "I guess they don't care about being noticed from Second Chance City anymore."

"Besides," noted Libby, "no one on the mainland can see much in this fog."

A man strode past a second floor window. Nate's jaw tightened. "Debolt...what do you want to bet Refractor and the others are there with him?"

He craned his neck a little farther. Barely visible through the fog was another structure, similar in size to the two-story building. However, this one had large sliding double doors. The guards who passed by earlier stood in front. Each grabbed hold of one side. With a squeaky rumble, the doors spread apart to reveal the interior. Floodlights illuminated a shiny metallic cylinder with stylized fins nearly filling the cavernous space.

Libby drew in a breath. "Syr's spaceship."

Underneath the rocket was an open hatch. Several of Syr's men huddled closely around a portable monitor, deep in conversation. All at once, small running lights at the edge of the craft winked on. The air reverberated with a faint thrum. The soldiers appeared pleased.

"I'm no starship trooper," observed Libby, "but I'd say refueling is nearly complete. We can't wait much longer, Nate."

Nate shut the door. He and Libby returned to the opening in the floor and signaled for Abigail and the rest. Nate led them to a vantage point in an office on the other side of the building. From there, they could spy on the activity in the old maintenance bay.

"I count ten men," Abigail murmured. "All armed with laser pistols. No telling how many are inside the ship."

"Ray should start the diversion any minute," said Nate. "With luck, the shooting will draw out most of the guards. Keep them busy. That spaceship mustn't leave. We'll deal with Scribe and the others."

Abigail nodded tersely. "Good luck to you both." She and her officers slipped out a window and darted to the woods.

Nate and Libby returned to the door nearest Debolt's building. "No cover between here and there," said Libby. "They'll spot us before we're halfway across the yard and raise the alarm. So much for a sneak attack." She made a face. "Not very sporting of them."

"Why, Mighty Light," said Nate lightly, "one would almost think battling the forces of evil wasn't high on your list of priorities."

Libby snorted. "Believe it or not, storming a supervillain's stronghold is the last thing I hoped for in a visit to Coldwater Bay."

Nate regarded her with pride; auburn curls wild about her face, a fierce determination marked her every move. That's the Libby he held in his heart all these years. "Hard to believe," he whispered. "You're a natural." He turned his attention to the guards. "We've got to move before more of Syr's men show up, but I can't get a good shot from here. Have to draw them from the alcove first." Barely visible through the fog was a line of rusty oil drums ten yards from the guards' position. "Can you use the flashlight to nudge one of those over? The noise should lure them close enough for me to use the gun."

Libby frowned, examining the distance. "I don't know. It's pretty far. Can you hit two guards at the same time through heavy fog from here?"

"I guess we'll find out."

"Then I guess we have a plan."

Nate examined his weapon. "This has quite a kick. Once we're inside, I'll take out Mega Mole and Refractor—or at least slow them down."

"I'll go for Aña," Libby said without hesitation. "Her venom can't penetrate my shield."

Libby was so sure, so stubbornly set to see this through she would throw herself into the fight with no thought to her own safety. Creeping doubts drew a tight knot of fear around Nate's chest. He wasn't a superhero, but at least had police training. Libby was only a writer, the girl who captured his heart once and never let it go. "Libby—"

"Don't ask me to stay behind. I won't leave you, Nate. I've made my choice."

"I only want you to be careful," he said gently. "If anything happened—"

"Nothing will." Libby grabbed him by the collar. "Fight to stay alive, Nate Hammond. I'll never forgive you if you don't return to Coldwater Bay with me." Her fierce kiss took his breath away. "After all, you promised dinner."

Libby focused across the yard, lines of concentration etched deep into her brow. Through the fog came a tinny rattle as the oil drum wobbled back and forth.

The guards' heads jerked in the direction of the sound. One of them stepped from under the alcove. Nate brought the gun up to sight them in. "Come on," he growled impatiently under his breath, "the other guy, too."

The rattling increased. The guard in front said something over his shoulder to his partner. Weapons drawn, the two stepped into the open. Nate braced himself and fired. Syr's men slammed against the building with a thud and then dropped to the ground.

Libby and Nate raced across the clearing. The door to the building was unlocked, and they bolted inside. Nate peered at the array of rusty lockers and old bed frames. "This must have been the barracks."

Whoosh.

"Down!" cried Libby. An instant later, droplets spattered against her shield. The poisonous liquid raised an acrid plume.

Aña called across the room. "I'm sorry." Her expression twisted in anguish. "I have orders."

"Where's Scribe?" Nate yelled.

"Upstairs with the others." She grimaced again. "I can't let anyone pass. He won't let me."

Nate and Libby ducked behind a row of storage cabinets. "Get Payton's device," she whispered. "I'll keep her busy. Hey…" She tugged at his sleeve. "This restaurant—someplace fancy? No paper cups or heat lamps?"

"Whatever you want."

With a grin, Libby concentrated on the star. Gathering energy crackled around the top of the flashlight. The star blazed to brilliance. Nate edged past her and then, heart pounding a ferocious beat, ran toward the stairway.

With an ear-deafening *clang!* the star rocketed a storage locker into the air. It tumbled toward Aña, forcing her to jump aside. Libby moved forward tossing stray tools and pieces of furniture to herd Aña to a far corner of the room. She returned fire with her poisonous spray. Caustic venom splashed against the wall, instantly turning the paint to a sludgy mess.

Nate darted up the stairwell to the top of the landing. Pressing flat against the wall, he edged to the opening. Finger on the trigger, he peered cautiously into a large open space with several long tables. At the back of the room through another open door, he glimpsed the stainless steel deep sink, open shelving, and stove of the old galley.

Debolt strode from the galley to the center of the room. He stopped next to a table piled high with electronic equipment. At his feet sat a familiar silver box with bright red letters warning of a radiation hazard—the zayton isotopes stolen from the lab. The lid was open, every vial gone except for one.

Nate eased across the threshold and sighted on target. The little red dot centered on Debolt's chest. No one else was in the room.

Although Nate made no sound, Debolt's head swung toward him. Some sort of violent emotion played out across his face, but he made no aggressive moves. Nate tensed. Where were Refractor and Mega Mole? Why did Debolt just stand there? Something wasn't right. Nate squeezed the trigger.

The sonic blast would have knocked any normal man flat on his rear, but Debolt merely took a slight step as if he hardly felt the blow. The wall of the galley exploded as Mega Mole rammed through and thundered across the room. Nate fired three shots in rapid succession, hitting him dead center. With a horrific wail, he collapsed.

A stunning blast knocked Nate against a support column. He dropped his weapon and crumpled to the floor. A second Debolt strode through the gaping hole in the wall to stand next to his twin. In his shirt pocket was the pen-shaped control device, in one hand Syr's ray gun. "Useful little things," he said mildly. "I could have killed you immediately, but you're only stunned. Movement will return in a few minutes." He turned to his double. "Time to change the meat suit. Let's see how you do with Officer Numbnuts." An instant later, Nate stared at his perfect double.

"That should allow you to get close enough to overpower Elizabeth," Debolt said to Refractor. "Bring her to me. Judging from the racket below, I have a funny feeling she's not far." Debolt scrutinized Nate with cold dispassion. "She's going to confess all the secrets of her magic wand before I kill you both."

Chapter Fourteen

Debolt holstered the ray gun and retrieved Nate's sonic blaster. "Clever. One of Pierce Power's, I take it. Or should I say Ramón Quintero? You know, the joke is on me. I wrote Powers as smart, but frankly, that was a trope to please the fans. I never thought Refractor's mysterious sidekick was particularly bright—only some wonk in a mask who liked to hang with the cool kid so his dick felt bigger. And Robella, too? Unbelievable. She's flat chested, dumpy, and plain as all hell—not heroine material at all." Suddenly, Debolt turned on Nate and kicked him hard in the ribs. "How did you follow me here?" snapped Debolt. "It's that wand, isn't it?"

Nate glared at him and gasped out a wheezy breath. "I can honestly say, I haven't got a clue."

"Why am I not surprised?" he said lightly. "No matter. Elizabeth will tell me, all in good time. I can be quite convincing."

The cold chill in his voice sent a shiver down Nate's spine. "I don't get it, Debolt. You escaped to Earth. You were safe. You had a good life. Why bother to return?"

Debolt snorted in disgust. "Do you honestly believe that miserable backwater bunghole has the slightest draw for someone with my talents? You think I went there on purpose? It was an accident. I planned an escape across the galaxy to Mo'R'ees Six."

The stun effect began to fade. Nate nearly shouted with relief as he wiggled his toes. "You were in alliance with Syr to find Robella."

"He knew my reputation for locating hidden items," Debolt said smoothly. "Things weren't going well for him in the war. Instead of a quick victory, Robella's escape rallied the citizens. He was trapped in a long bloody conflict with no assurance of eventual victory. Syr was desperate. I like dealing with desperate people," Debolt said with a sly smile. "You can charge so much more."

Keep him talking. "You didn't only offer to find Robella," said Nate. "You offered a control device."

Debolt seemed amused. "So you're not that thick. I stumbled upon something intriguing while doing business with Lorelei Del Fuego. Certain frequencies from my transporter interrupted the brain wave pattern of those infected with zayton radiation. Poor Lorelei's head exploded, but I believed, with fine tuning, I could perfect the mind control aspect. Syr agreed to provide funding. It didn't take much to convince him having someone like Refractor at the end of a leash would bring his little war to a speedy conclusion."

"Refractor tracked you down first, though," said Nate. "Must have pissed you off."

"You've no idea." His words dripped with bitter agreement. "I had just finished incorporating the control unit into my transporter device when Refractor showed."

"But you couldn't control him because you needed a blood sample first."

His shoulders stiffened. "I may have misjudged

229

you, after all. I'm done talking."

"Then let me finish," said Nate. "Something went wrong with the transporter and instead of across the galaxy you ended across dimensions. The bridge between universes collapsed. You were marooned."

A booted foot came down across Nate's neck, cutting off his air. "You really are very annoying."

The tingle spread up Nate's arm. "Yeah, sorry about that," he gasped. "So, I understand it's tough to be rich and famous in my dimension."

The pressure on his neck eased. "And a surprisingly easy process," Debolt said in an oily boastful manner, "as soon as I discovered comic books. I knew the recent history of Refractor and Second Chance City. Elizabeth was most willing to provide assistance with editing."

Understanding flooded Nate. "You're a real shit, Debolt. Libby wrote the stories. Not you. I bet she also drew the pictures."

"I dictated," he insisted smoothly, "and then allowed her to polish the panels. Elizabeth was so damn grateful for the job, she never complained. It would be her big break. Rather pathetic, really, but that's desperate people for you." He cast a disparaging glance at Mega Mole. "Like him. You should hear the way he moans over his wife and kids and the life he used to have—as if anyone gives a damn for a zayton-infused freak."

Footsteps shuffled up the stairway. "Speaking of freaks," Debolt added cheerfully, "here come some now."

Nate's heart sank as Refractor, Libby, and Araña came through the doorway. Refractor carried the flashlight and no longer wore Nate's disguise. Libby stood between them, one hand clenched tight. Too tight compared with the other. She met Nate's eyes—a call to action lurked behind her deadpan expression. She shot a glance down to her one clenched fist.

Nate held her gaze and gave a subtle nod of understanding. "You okay, Lib?" he called out. *Whenever you're ready.*

"Never better," she said. *When I make my move.*

"Elizabeth, how nice to see you," said Debolt. He placed the sonic pistol on the table.

Nate tightened his muscles, flinching as the prickling sensation increased. Feeling had nearly returned. *Not yet. You only get one chance.*

"Where is Bobbie?" she demanded.

"Her royal highness is safe for the moment on board Syr's ship. I'll be leaving as soon as it's refueled—thanks to the extra zayton isotopes that shouldn't take long. I'm sorry to say Princess Robella's homecoming will be short-lived. Syr believes a public execution is best to bring the rebellious citizens of Mo'R'ees Six under control."

He addressed Aña. "Keep an eye on Officer Numbnuts while Libby and I have a nice little chat. If he so much as twitches, give him a taste of your poison—not that he'll need more than a drop." Aña hesitated. Debolt displayed the pen. Pain distorted her face. "Don't make me ask twice," he said lightly. With a flash of intense hatred, she turned toward Nate.

Debolt grabbed the flashlight from Refractor and held it close, scrutinizing every detail. He made some adjustments to the pen device. A 3-D heads-up display appeared. Debolt ran the machine along the flashlight.

Formulas, graphics, and words danced in the air. None of it made sense to Nate.

Apparently, the same held true for Debolt. With a scowl, he turned off the display and jammed the controller in his pocket. "It's just a damn flashlight. Not a spark of zayton radiation registers." He peered closely at the words etched on the side. "Write your own ending? What the hell does that mean?" He barked at Refractor, "You're positive this is what she used to make the shield."

"Yes," he answered without hesitation.

Debolt focused on Libby. "How does it work?"

"Not a clue," she answered smoothly.

Without warning, he slapped Libby hard across the face.

"Keep your hands off her!" Nate roared. He made a move to sit, the temporary paralysis now completely gone.

"Please, Good Citizen," Aña begged in an agonized whisper. "I don't want to hurt you."

Hatred for Debolt flooded every last one of Nate's pores. *Not yet. You'll get your chance.*

Debolt grabbed Libby by the throat. "Do you think I'm joking?" he spit out. "You know me, Elizabeth. You know what happens when I don't get my way. How does that thing work? How did you get to Second Chance City?"

"I told you I don't know," she choked out. "Nate and I followed you to Write Away. There was a funny green light at the comic book display. We woke up here."

"It's the truth, Debolt!" yelled Nate. "Let her go."

Debolt released his grip, eyeing them both with

suspicion. "After all that time, my transport device suddenly reactivated in a bookstore. I never would have suspected a bridge to Second Chance City existed in a useless hole in the wall like Coldwater Bay, but there it was—right by the comic book display." His voice grew cold. "That doesn't explain why the bridge opened for you."

"I told you," said Libby, rubbing her neck. "We don't know."

Debolt studied the flashlight in his hand. "This thing is quite a formidable weapon. It stopped a laser gun, Araña's poison, not to mention Time Bomb's blast. It also appears to have allowed you to enter an interdimensional rift. I'm afraid 'I don't know' won't cut it."

Mega Mole staggered to his feet, the effects of the sonic gun now worn off.

"Mega Mole," said Debolt mildly. "Rip off one of Good Citizen's arms. Perhaps that will loosen her tongue."

"No!" Elizabeth yelled.

Mega Mole's focus didn't waver from Debolt. Pure unvarnished hate blazed from within his beady eyes.

"I said," Debolt repeated, "rip his arm off. That's an order."

Mega Mole doubled over as if in pain. He bellowed in naked rage.

"You can't fight it," Debolt mocked. "Why do you even try?"

With an agonized howl, Mega Mole took a stumbling step toward Nate.

Gunfire crackled outside the building. "Wait!" Debolt picked up a radio. "Syr!" he barked. "What's happening?"

A burst of static came through the receiver. "The ship is under attack."

"I'll send my pets," Debolt said coldly. "They'll take care of them—"

Libby let fly with the rock Nate had given her at the lighthouse. It slammed into Debolt's forehead. With a cry, he fell backwards, dropping the flashlight. Blood poured from a wound in his forehead. "Araña, kill them!" he shrieked.

Nate and Libby were already on the move. Nate grabbed the sonic pistol from the table as Libby pounced on the flashlight. The star blazed, forming a shield as Aña's poison splattered ineffectively over the top.

Debolt tucked the last vial of zayton in a shirt pocket and then drew the laser pistol from the holster. "Refractor, Araña—as soon they drop the shield, kill them both and then join me at the ship. Mega Mole, come with me." The behemoth followed him obediently out the door.

Libby grimaced as another blast of Aña's poison hit the shield. "I'm open to suggestions."

Nate gripped the sonic gun. The ray spread out and weakened across distances, but the damage done by an up close and personal blast inches from the floor should be damn near spectacular. "Get ready to jump." He aimed the muzzle straight down and pulled the trigger.

The explosion shook the floor, rocking Refractor and Aña off their feet. Nate bounced hard against Libby's shield, and then regained his balance. The charge made a perfectly round hole straight down to the old barracks room below.

"Go!" cried Libby. "I'll hold the shield."

Nate vaulted over the edge, landing with a hard thump. "Now, Lib!" An instant later, she plummeted into his outstretched arms. They took off at a run. Behind them, one of Refractor's laser bolts blazed through the hole and tore a jagged scar in the linoleum tile. Libby and Nate darted past the old lockers. Footsteps above pounded across the ceiling in the direction of the stairs. Refractor and Aña, still under Debolt's influence, weren't wasting any time.

Libby and Nate made a beeline through the exit. Outside was a battlefield. Gunfire exploded all around them. Beams of light from the laser weapons of Syr's men cut through the thick fog.

"We have to find Payton," she cried. "We need that control device."

A bestial roar echoed from the service bay. "Mega Mole is at the ship!" yelled Nate over the staccato of gunfire. "Debolt won't be far—this way."

They ran into the fog. A door slammed closed somewhere behind them. Refractor and Aña had made it outside.

Mega Mole stood in front of the open service bay doors, blood spattered on the ground from a dozen wounds. It didn't slow him down in the least. Razor-sharp talons raked across the ground, shredding chunks of concrete pavement. He tossed them like oversized confetti toward Abigail and her advancing party. The police scattered in all directions.

Bodies of several of Syr's guards lay unmoving underneath the ship. Syr stood at an open hatch firing a laser gun. He made a beckoning gesture to someone. Nate glimpsed Debolt making a dash for the hatch.

Debolt spotted them, too. He fired the laser pistol, but the beam bounced harmlessly off Libby's shield.

"Mega Mole," he screamed, "Kill them!"

Nate dropped to a crouch. Libby opened a section of the shield allowing Nate to fire the sonic gun.

The distance was too far for a direct hit. The sonic wave dissipated, but not before striking Debolt a glancing blow. He stumbled to his knees. The laser gun fell from his hand and skidded beneath the frame of an old rusted out jeep. Nate and Libby broke into a run.

Mega Mole ignored the gunfire tearing into him. He grabbed a corroded oil drum and lobbed it effortlessly toward Nate and Libby. The missile struck the shield and rebounded toward Mega Mole's head. In a flash, giant claws tore into the earth, and he disappeared. Debolt staggered to his feet as Refractor and Aña appeared through the fog.

"Get Payton!" shouted Libby, "I'll hold them off."

Nate raced ahead. His finger tightened on the trigger of the sonic gun only this time instead of the answering recoil, his reward was a subtle *click*. Nate yelped as a jolt of electricity stabbed his hand. A puff of gray smoke coiled up from the chamber. Nate tossed the weapon aside. The power unit had depleted and the sonic gun rendered useless.

Debolt dove for the laser pistol, as Nate barreled into him. The controller dropped from his pocket as they jockeyed for position, wrestling across the ground. Nate strained to reach the weapon, but with a savage kick, Debolt shoved him aside. His arm hooked around Nate's neck, cutting off his air.

Nate jabbed him in the stomach. With a yelp, Debolt eased his grip. Nate twisted, elbowing his ribs.

Squirming from Debolt's hold, his fist connected with a satisfying thud to the jaw. Debolt's neck snapped back, and he fell over. Nate stretched out his hand for the controller.

A booted foot came down on top of the device. Syr pointed a laser pistol at Nate's head. "Nice try," he smirked, "but too late—"

Syr dropped the pistol. His hands fell limply to his sides. He gawked in stunned disbelief at the smoking hole through his chest. An instant later, Syr fell forward into the dirt. Bobbie stood at the spaceship's hatch next to Ray, a laser gun in her hand, and immense satisfaction on her face.

Ray stood by her side. "I freed her after Syr left the ship," he yelled. "Lucky thing she's an excellent shot."

Libby! Nate scrambled to his feet.

A dozen yards away, Libby held Refractor and Aña trapped within the flashlight's force field. They struggled to break free, pounding against the unyielding barrier. Libby reeled with each blow.

Desperately, Nate scoured the muddy ground. *Where the hell was that pen?*

The earth heaved violently beneath his feet.

Nate stumbled. Mounds of dirt vomited up like an erupting volcano blocking his view of Libby, Ray, and Bobbie. Mega Mole exploded from the ground, grabbing Nate around the chest. Giant arms squeezed tight, cutting off the air.

Debolt staggered forward. Blood trickled from his mouth. One hand clutched Syr's laser pistol. "Drop him," he ordered Mega Mole. "I'll kill him myself."

Nate tumbled to the ground, gasping for breath. Debolt raised the ray gun. From somewhere nearby,

Libby screamed Nate's name. "Libby," Nate whispered, "I love you."

Mega Mole took a staggering step in front of Nate. "Get out of the way," Debolt roared. Mega Mole remained in place, attention fastened on Debolt.

Ray scrabbled over the mound of dirt. One hand held the control device aloft. "Good Citizen," he cried cheerfully, "I believe I turned it off."

With a raging howl, Mega Mole charged. Debolt fired. The blast tore into the mutant. The stench of singed flesh filled the air. Mega Mole shrieked in pain and barreled forward. Debolt sidestepped, but not before the massive paw hit his shoulder a glancing blow. Something snapped. With a scream, Debolt clutched the weapon to his chest.

Mega Mole pressed forward with a shambling gait, puddles of blood pooling in his footsteps. Eyes focused on Debolt, his expression infused with hate. Debolt continued to fire. Mega Mole lunged, impaling him on a talon. Debolt screamed. He fired again. Mega Mole jerked back and collapsed with a ground-shaking thud.

A bolt of light blasted through a mound of dirt and turned the old jeep next to Debolt into a rusty-colored slag heap. Refractor and Aña were also freed from his control. On stumbling legs, Debolt ran into the fog.

Libby raced to Nate and threw herself into his arms. "You're all right?"

He held her tight. "I am now."

A groan from Mega Mole drew their attention. Libby knelt beside him. "Lie still. You need help."

Mega Mole wheezed, struggling to draw a breath. "Y-you have to stop Scribe."

Jagged wounds from the laser pistol left no doubt

the words were nearly his last. "Take it easy," said Nate. "Don't try to talk."

His tiny eyes filled with understanding. The end was near. "Too late for me," he coughed out. "Better this way…I-I never wanted this life…"

"We know, Jack." Nate filled with pity. "This isn't your fault."

Mega Mole's breath came in ragged gasps. "Debolt has the last vial of zayton…don't let him use it again." He exhaled a long rattling sigh. His eyes closed a final time.

Abigail arrived, gun drawn. "The remainder of Syr's men headed toward the water and Ray's boat. My people are holding them off in the woods, but I have wounded."

"Bring them to the spaceship," said Ray. "Bobbie can ready it for takeoff and fly us to the mainland."

Nate snatched Syr's laser pistol and then turned to Refractor and Aña. "Help Abby round up Syr's men and get the injured to safety. Libby and I will find Debolt."

"Be careful, Good Citizen," warned Ray. "If an energy blast from the laser gun hits the vial of zayton, the resulting explosion will wipe out all of Second Chance City."

"Remind me to have a word with Ray on his timing," grumbled Nate to Libby as they ran after Debolt. "That information would have been super helpful a few minutes ago during our wrestling match for the ray gun."

They followed Debolt's blood trail directly to the old administrative offices. Cautiously, they entered, but the building was silent. The star's light illuminated dark spatter leading to the hole in the floor. Libby pointed to a red splotch on the ladder. "Fresh blood."

They made the descent, the faint glow of the star lighting the way. More blood on the ground bore witness that a wounded Debolt wasn't far ahead. They jogged through the tunnel. Near the halfway point, Nate and Libby abruptly halted. Instead of shallow puddles, they splashed ankle-deep into icy cold water. The long jagged scar across the ceiling was now crisscrossed by many others. A dripping spiderweb of cracks mottled the entire area.

Nate ran his hand along the walls. Water dribbled freely from a dozen different locations. He glanced at Libby. No words were necessary. The tunnel wouldn't hold much longer. They broke into a run, pressing hard to reach the exit.

Minutes passed. Libby panted at Nate's side. "We must be near The Factory by now."

Ahead, the light of the star illuminated a figure slumped against the tunnel wall. Libby engaged the shield. At the same time, Nate raised the laser pistol. "You can't use it while he has the zayton," said Libby. "The blast will set off an explosion."

"Better listen to Elizabeth." Payton Debolt's face was the color of ashes. Blood gushed from a jagged hole in his chest. One hand held the laser pistol in a trembling grip, the other hung at his side as if unable to move.

"You can't fire, either," said Nate. "It won't get through Libby's shield. Give it up, Debolt. There's nowhere left to run."

"Who says I want to run?" The chilling dispassion of his words set off every one of Nate's inner alarm bells. The muzzle of Debolt's gun turned from them and rested directly against the vial of zayton in his pocket.

"Payton, don't," cried Libby. "You'll take out the whole city."

"Prison is better than death, Debolt," yelled Nate.

Despite the paleness of his skin, Debolt's eyes glowed with a feverish light. "I won't make it that far. I'm dying. The least I can do is take both of you and this miserable city with me."

A wailing shriek rocked them all on their heels, shattering a section of the wall and blowing dirt and debris against Debolt. With a cry of surprise, he dropped the gun. Nate stared in stunned disbelief as Bryce Templeton reeled out of the darkness.

Bryce pinned Debolt against the wall. "I'll make it stop," he said with a sob. "I'll finally make it stop."

"Let go of me, freak!" Debolt struggled in vain to loosen his grip.

"Bryce…" Nate regarded the mutant's tortured expression with profound pity. "Come with us."

"You can't stop it." The agony in Bryce's voice vanished. His expression took on an air of peaceful serenity. "I'll make it stop forever."

Libby snatched the vial from Debolt's pocket.

"Elizabeth," he begged, "help me."

Libby stepped away. "Go to hell, Payton."

Bryce's voice dropped to a whisper. "Run." He threw back his head and opened his mouth.

"No!" Debolt screamed.

Nate grabbed Libby's hand as they raced down the tunnel. They passed the opening where Bryce had dug himself out. Only a little farther…

Bryce's excruciating howl blasted into them. The ground shuddered violently. Earth and rocks plummeted down as the roof of the tunnel collapsed. With a thunderous roar, a wall of water raced toward them, pushing ahead a battering ram of boulders and debris. It slammed into Libby's shield. Her whole body shuddered trying to hold back the flood. "Get out of here, Nate! I-I can't stop it."

Nate tossed the laser gun aside. He slipped behind Libby and wrapped his arms around her waist, pulling her close. "I'm not going anywhere."

Libby's grasped the flashlight so hard her knuckles turned white. Both arms trembled with the effort to keep the shield steady. "Nate..." Her voice choked out a sob. "Please go. I can't...I can't..."

He buried his face in those beautiful auburn curls. "No," he whispered softly. "You and I together, Lib, to the very end. That's how it's meant to be."

Behind came a deafening clamor. The tunnel to the exit collapsed, boxing them in. Chunks of dirt rained from the ceiling. Slowly, the strident clash of tumbling rocks ended and all was silent once more. The dust settled. They were trapped inside the tunnel within a small bubble of safety.

Nate grabbed Libby as her legs gave out. He lowered her gently to the floor and took her in his arms. Her hand clutched the flashlight. The light of the star faded to a dull flicker.

"No more energy," she whispered. "Can't get us out."

"Hush," he crooned, holding her tight. "Rest now. You've done enough." The air in the confined space rapidly grew thin.

Libby's eyes fluttered as she fought unconsciousness. "You are the missing piece in my life." She drew a shuddering breath. "Never been so happy as that summer…I gave you my heart with that peck on the cheek." She dropped the flashlight in her lap, and wrapped her arms around his neck.

Nate bent his head toward Libby. "All these years," he whispered, "I've kept it safe for you." Their eager lips touched. Nothing else held meaning; not the cold and damp, not the advancing dark, not the crushing weight pressing in on them from all sides.

Libby breathed a happy sigh and nestled against his chest. "I love you, Nate…" Her voice trailed off. She went limp in his arms. The light in the star dimmed to barely a glimmer.

His throat was tight. "I love you, Lib—always." He kissed her auburn curls, lightheaded, fear fading away with each struggling breath. Was it love or lack of oxygen? The answer held no concern. The only thing that counted was Libby in his arms. Slowly, the sights and smells around him disappeared.

The light in the star winked out. Nate buried his face in Libby's hair as they were swallowed by the dark.

Chapter Fifteen

"Nate?"

An anxious voice drew him from the darkness. Warm hands clasped one of his and raised it to a soft cheek. "Nate, please wake up."

His eyes opened. He squinted in the glare of sunlight and blinked to clear his vision. He was in a room somewhere, no longer underground. Sunlight streamed through an open window. Libby's anxious face peered down at him.

"Lib?" Nate's voice came out as a scratchy croak. "You're all right."

Her smile warmed like the sun. She kissed him tenderly on the lips.

"This better not be a dream," he murmured.

"How do you feel?"

"Alive…confused…thirsty." He kissed her again. "Pretty damn happy right now…what happened?"

"Have some water first."

Nate nodded with gratitude as he sat up. Libby handed him a bottle of water. He swallowed, rinsing away the fetid taste of dirt in his mouth. "I feel like I plowed half the soil in Second Chance City with my teeth."

"We almost did."

He downed another swig. "How did the flashlight get us out?"

"It didn't. You can thank Refractor and the others for the rescue. They captured the remains of Syr's army, and then Bobbie piloted the ship to The Factory. We actually weren't far from the exit. Refractor used his energy ray to blast through the rock. Luckily, our little safety bubble held long enough for him to pull us free."

"The vial of zayton?"

"In Ray's eager hands along with Payton's pen doohickey."

"Can he send us home?" asked Nate eagerly.

"Ray and Bobbie assured me with total confidence that with the extra vial of zayton they can probably get the device to work without blowing us apart...maybe."

"Well, that totally sets my mind at rest." He pulled her close. "You don't seem worried."

Libby crawled into bed and snuggled against his chest. "I'm with Nate Hammond. I'm not worried about anything...Smuggler's Cove."

"What?"

"That's where I want to go to dinner."

He nuzzled her ear. "Good choice."

"I'll order the most expensive item on the menu...and champagne. You'll have to spring for dessert, too."

"Wouldn't have it any other way."

Nate examined the surroundings with a puzzled frown. "Where are we? This place seems familiar."

"Ray brought us to Breezy Point." She chuckled. "Check the décor again."

Nate gaped at the nautical prints and blue silk curtains. "It can't be...is it?"

"Yup," said Libby with undisguised amusement.

"This was Payton's room in Coldwater Bay. Same furnishings. I guess some things never change even inter-dimensionally." She placed a cool hand on his forehead. "You slept so long. I was sick with worry. I tried to get them to take you to a hospital, but everyone treated me like I was crazy." She snorted in disgust. "Apparently, it's a well-known fact superheroes never need health checkups. God, the people here drive me insane."

He gazed at her with loving tenderness. "The only thing I need right now is you."

"You got that right." Enthusiastic lips sought his.

"Ahem."

They let go of each other. Refractor stood in the doorway. "Glad to see you have awakened, Good Citizen. All physical functions appear to have returned to normal," he added dryly. "I told Elizabeth she was unduly concerned, and you required no medical attention." Libby rolled her eyes.

"Thanks." He took Libby's hand. "I'm feeling better all the time."

"Good. Your presences are requested. Sergeant Franco has arrived with news."

Nate and Libby followed Refractor to what would have been Breezy Point Inn's dining area and communal space, but here was simply a large living room. Ray and Bobbie greeted them affectionately. Aña was there, too, off in a corner. She acknowledged their arrival with a pleased smile, her venomous toxin prohibiting any closer interaction. Immediately, Refractor went to her side. She leaned her head against him as if comforted by his touch.

Abigail waited with several officers. She gave Nate

and Libby warm handshakes. "Can't thank you both enough for all your help."

"Any casualties to your people?" said Nate.

"None thankfully and all wounds should heal. I can't say the same for Syr's men. Those that still live will be returned to Mo'R'ees Six to face punishment."

"So you're leaving to claim the throne, Your Highness," said Libby to Bobbie. "I feel like I should curtsey."

Bobbie blushed. "Please don't—and call me Bobbie. Princess Robella was only a title, one I gladly shed. All I ever wanted to do was be a scientist and help people." She glanced at Ray and the blush deepened. "Well...that's not all I want anymore. I've contacted the rebels with the ship's communicator. The death of Syr struck a devastating blow to his forces. They surrender as we speak. By the time we arrive, the war will be over. I will return home only long enough to help my people install a constitutional republic."

Nate regarded her with disbelief. "You want to give up the throne?"

"Yes. Being the monarch of a planet is highly overrated. If I've learned anything from my experiences with Scribe and Syr it's that the power to rule should never be concentrated in one person—or even one family. The people of Mo'R'ees Six will do much better without me."

Ray beamed. "When Bobbie and I return, we will rebuild the lab and start our own scientific research company. We'll call it Smuggler's Cove Incorporated."

"It has a nice ring to it," said Nate with a straight face, "even though I kind of saw a restaurant there."

Ray was obviously puzzled. "I'm afraid I'm not

much of a chef."

"Never mind," said Libby with a grin, slipping her arm around Nate's. "I'm sure your company will be a huge success."

"I have one more thing to ask before I go," said Abigail. "Florence Peevey has been recalled as chief of police. My officers and I would be honored if Good Citizen would accept the position."

"Me?" Nate was floored. "That's nice of you to ask, but I can't stay."

"Are you certain? Second Chance City has much to offer."

"For others," said Nate firmly, "but not me."

"I understand. Duty calls you elsewhere. Good luck to you both then. Now, if you'll excuse me, I need to speak with Refractor before leaving."

As she approached, Aña retreated into the corner. The other police officers in the room moved their hands close to their weapons. Abigail kept a wary watch on Aña while she and Refractor exchanged hushed words.

"Are you sure you want to say farewell to Good Citizen?" Libby said with dry humor. "Superhero-dom has perks, too. I'm told Mighty Light already has a fan club."

"Not a chance. You?"

"No way. Not that the adventure wasn't fun; desperate straits, evil villains, death waiting around every corner—it hasn't been dull, to say the least. I also have to admit, I got a real kick out of blasting things with my little light."

"Yeah, I'll miss the sonic gun, too," said Nate with honest regret.

After Abigail and her officers left, Refractor and

Aña joined them. Both Ray and Bobbie stiffened slightly as she neared. "How much time did Sergeant Franco give?" Ray asked.

"Twenty-four hours," said Refractor. "She was most generous."

Libby was clearly puzzled. "For what?"

"Aña has been given twenty-four hours to leave Second Chance City before the death sentence is reinstated. After that, she will be hunted and killed on sight."

Libby's jaw dropped open. "They can't do that," she sputtered. "She's not a criminal."

"To you," Refractor noted somberly. "The citizens of Second Chance City, however, do not agree."

"She's not evil." Libby's voice rose in anger. "Kristie Williams' poisoning was an accident."

Nate added his protest. "What about Peregrine Island? She fought for us."

"Only after I was freed from Scribe's control," Aña said in her soft voice. "My actions against Syr will not be remembered, only the effect of my venom." She gestured to the web-like striations on her skin. "I can't hide what I am. My appearance...the poison...my very touch is deadly. Everything I am marks me as a villain."

Libby exploded. "That's such a load of crap! Why do people here jump on anyone with zayton poisoning? Why are they instantly branded as criminals? Nobody tries to help or understand. It's not fair," she cried out in distress. "Your story deserves a happy ending."

Refractor took Aña's hand. "She won't be alone. I'm going with her. Ray kindly offered us the Sea Spray. It's moored at his dock outside. We already have supplies stowed aboard."

Nate let out a protest. "The rest of your lives will be spent as fugitives."

"We'll have each other," insisted Refractor. "Being together will be enough."

Nate beseeched Ray. "Can't you talk to Abby?"

Ray shuffled his feet, apparently uncomfortable with the suggestion. "I-I don't think…it's only that…"

"You're afraid of Aña, too," said Nate, aghast. He turned to Bobbie. "Can you take her with you?"

She didn't meet his eyes. "I won't bring a new danger to my planet."

"The law is the law, Good Citizen," said Aña. "Anyone helping me suffers the same consequences. Expulsion is a better option than immediate death—and safer for everyone else."

"What is wrong with this place?" Libby snarled. "Why does everyone jump to judgment? Why aren't people like Aña and Mega Mole given time to adapt and control their mutation? Not even one lousy counselling session? Seriously? It's all—let's just shoot folks who are different? Why won't anyone help?"

"Ray has tried to reverse zayton contamination," said Refractor. "Countless others have, too. It's hopeless."

"Then tell me it will be different someplace else," Libby pleaded. "Tell me, outside of Second Chance City you and Aña will find a safe place to live out your lives. Tell me you won't spend the rest of your days together running and hiding." Refractor and Aña stood silent.

"How can a whole planet condemn a person for a medical condition?" Libby shouted. Ray and Bobbie stared guiltily at the floor.

"Don't be angry with them, Mighty Light," said Aña. "You can't change the world. I am deeply grateful, though." She spoke with heartfelt sincerity. "You saved me from Scribe. The kindness and understanding shown toward me is a rare commodity. You and Good Citizen have great hearts."

A helpless feeling enveloped Nate. "Nothing can be done?"

"Aña and I will stay long enough to see you and Elizabeth off for home." Refractor clapped Nate on the shoulder. "For what it's worth, you have the eternal thanks of an immortal being. With Aña at my side, I am again free of the dark."

Ray cleared his throat. "Bobbie and I should have the transporter working in a few hours."

"All right then," said Nate. "Libby and I will get out of your way. We have a few things to finish before we go."

Ray offered his phone. "I'll text you when we're ready. Take my car. It's parked right outside."

As they drove away, Libby gazed wistfully at Breezy Point. "It's not fair, Nate. You saw the way Refractor and Aña stood off to one side with Abigail and the others. A roomful of people and yet so terribly alone. How long can they last on the run?"

Nate gave her hand a supportive squeeze. "I don't know," he answered truthfully.

Libby's voice dropped. "Yes, you do. So do I—not long. Refractor and Aña know, too. I saw it in their eyes. She'll be killed, and he'll be condemned for helping her escape. This time there will be no more safe places for him. He'll be alone once more."

Nate glared out the window in frustration. "We

thought all along this was a comic book. We were wrong. You would have written them a new ending."

Libby sighed. "Not all comic books end well."

"You'd have found a way."

Libby reached under her jacket for the flashlight. "Most kids dream of being a superhero—having all that power, being special. I know I did, but really, there's not much to be said for it. Power doesn't make you a better person—look at Payton. He was an absolute douchebag. Look at Aña. It ruined her life. Look at Refractor—over two hundred years in hiding. Being denied all of the common comforts of home and family is hardly worth the price." She gently ran her fingers along the shaft. "I'll leave the superhero life behind with no regrets."

Nate's hand gently stroked her cheek. "Has Libby Parish finally stopped hiding who she really is?"

"Yes," she said decisively. "I'm not Mighty Light. I'm a writer and a comic book geek, and I'm going to put *Crazy Ass Freaks* down on paper as soon as we get home. It will have a happy ending." Her voice tightened. "None of my characters will ever suffer for eternity."

"What will you tell the publisher about Payton Debolt?"

Libby flashed a wicked grin. "The complete and absolute truth. He tragically disappeared in a snow storm never to be seen again."

They pulled into the hospital parking lot and went directly to the gift shop for flowers. Nate paused at the threshold, staring intently at the clerk.

"Trouble?" asked Libby, alarmed.

He chuckled. "Not that kind. I recognize her."

"Geez, don't scare me like that...who is she?"

"Her name is Madison Taylor—not the kind of person you'd expect to see working in a hospital gift shop. Madison likes expensive things and, specifically, guys who have money and dole it out freely—if you get my drift."

"I do. This one doesn't seem all that interested in luxury."

Madison dressed plainly, her once stylish hair arranged in a simple bun. No heavy make-up, no bling, all evidence of a former flamboyant lifestyle discarded. Her shoulders sagged as if burdened with a heavy weight. Something in this Madison's life was definitely different.

Nate chose a card for Kristie Williams and wrote a note. "Going to deliver it yourself?" Libby teased.

"Not a chance in hell," he whispered.

Libby peered over his shoulder and read. "Call Dr. Logan Emory...funny sort of 'get well' greeting. You didn't even sign your name." She jabbed him in the ribs. "Should you warn Dr. Emory Kristie is on the way?"

"Nope. If he's anything like his counterpart, he'll enjoy the grope."

"My, my, Nate Hammond. I had no idea you were such the romantic." Her eyes held a wicked gleam. She shot a quick glance around the gift shop as if to be reassured no one paid any attention to them. Satisfied, Libby languidly slid a hand across his butt cheek and then down between his legs. "Are you always so violently opposed to a little fondle?"

Nate's breath caught in his throat. Lightning bolts of hot animal lust rocketed through his groin. "Nope," he managed to choke out.

Libby slid her hand from between his legs and into his back pocket. The warmth of her hand filtered through the denim. A delicious torture of exploding desire filled every square inch of Nate Hammond. He pressed his lips together to stifle a cry. *Dear-God-make-it-stop-no-wait-don't.*

She rose on tiptoes and whispered in his ear, "I'm not sure I believe you. I expect I'll need proof."

"Lib," he finally gulped out. "All you have to do is say the word, and we'll give the customers of the gift shop something to talk about for years to come."

With a chuckle, Libby removed her hand. "I can wait. Fair warning, though, Nate Hammond. Kristie Williams' groping is nothing compared to mine."

Nate was so ready to go home.

He waited with card in hand for Madison to ring up another customer. Libby motioned to a photograph by the cash register. Her voice dropped to a whisper. "She has a baby. That's what different in her life. Motherhood changes things." The picture showed Madison cradling an infant boy, a wistful sadness in her smile. Nate stared at the picture, suspicions rising.

The other customer left, and Nate stepped to the counter. The little makeup Madison wore didn't hide her red-rimmed eyes. Nate handed over the card and asked for it to be delivered to Kristie Williams. Then he ordered a bouquet of flowers for Cordelia Templeton.

"Do you wish them delivered, sir?" said Madison. Her face tilted down as if intent on the receipt, but she couldn't hide the tremble in her voice.

"No, I'll take them myself." Nate played his hunch. "You heard about Bryce. I'm sorry for your loss."

Madison's complexion paled. "You're Good Citizen, aren't you? H-How did you know?"

"That doesn't matter." He rested his hand lightly on hers. "Did you tell anyone?"

Madison shook her head. "Not even Bryce knew. I found out I was pregnant after the accident and kept the father's name a secret. I planned to tell him after he got out of the sanitarium. Now…" She swallowed hard. "If people knew Wyatt was Bryce's son, he'd be marked forever."

"Why?" said Libby, aghast. "He wasn't infected."

"It doesn't matter. Wyatt would always carry the stain of his father's curse. Mega Mole's entire family had to leave town. I have nowhere else to go," Madison said in anguish. "No one would protect us."

"I know someone who will," said Nate, "and she's not afraid of a fight—or what people will think. Close the store. You're coming with me to talk to Cordelia."

"Mrs. Templeton?" Madison gasped. "You can't be serious. She won't be happy to see someone like me." She glanced at the picture. "To see us."

"Don't be too sure," said Libby. "Becoming a grandmother changes things, too."

Libby waited outside the room with Madison while Nate went in alone. Cordelia greeted him warmly. "Good Citizen? It's kind of you to drop by…such lovely flowers. Thank you."

He put the vase on her nightstand. "You seem much better."

Her lips twitched in a wry smile. "Bullying the town council always has a positive effect on my well-being. I had them remove Florence Peevey as police chief."

"Abby Franco told me."

"Did she also offer you the job?"

"She did," said Nate. "I turned her down. Second Chance City doesn't need me when it already has Abby. Offer her the position. She'll be great." His voice softened. "I have something to tell you concerning Bryce."

Her eyes filled with tears as Nate explained how her son died. "At least he's at peace," said Cordelia with a shuddering sigh.

"He left something for you," said Nate gently. "Something precious you'll need to help keep safe. It won't be easy, but if anyone in this town has the balls to change public opinion, it's you." He told her about Madison and Wyatt.

Tears streamed down Cordelia's cheeks. "I want to see her—to see them."

"I hoped you would." He ushered in Madison and then left the room, shutting the door behind him.

Libby hooked her arm into his as they walked to the parking lot. "Big leap of faith there, Good Citizen. How did you know Madison's child was also Bryce's?"

"He's the spitting image of his father. Also, Irina knows all the gossip. Madison had a short-lived fling with Bryce after he came back to town."

"Any little Wyatt in the picture?"

"Nope. Madison moved on to bigger game a long time ago. She doesn't even live in Coldwater Bay anymore. Last I heard, she was working her way up to being the trophy wife of a rich lawyer."

"Do you think Cordelia and Madison will work it out?" asked Libby. "Become a family?"

Nate shrugged. "Honestly, I don't know. You're

the writer. What ending would you give them?"

"Definitely a happily ever after."

The cell phone chimed with an incoming text. Libby read the message with a chuckle. "Ray and Bobbie say they're almost ready to try the device and want us to meet them at Write Away in an hour."

"Naturally," said Nate with a grin. "That's where it all started."

They made a quick stop at Connor's apartment to change into their old clothes from Coldwater Bay and then to Smuggler's Cove to retrieve Nate's police issue pistol from the wreckage.

"Where did you leave it?" said Libby.

"In the metal box. It was on the table near the rear wall."

"One last time," she chirped. The star glowed in her hand. Debris shifted aside and the table emerged. To Nate's relief, the weapon was still inside the box and undamaged. He tucked it in the holster.

Nate kissed her. "Last chance to become a citizen of Second Chance City."

"No way," she laughed, returning the kiss with an enthusiasm that left Nate breathless. "How about you? Promotion to chief comes a lot faster here."

"No thanks. The police chief in a comic is always the secondary character. His only job is to arrive after the superhero is finished and clean up the mess."

"Then let's get out of here—I'm sweating like a pig in this winter coat and boots."

They made their way to Main Street. Write Away had already closed for the day, but Bobbie stood at the door to let them in. They went directly to the spot in front of the post card rack.

Aña and Refractor waited as promised. Aña stood aside as Refractor grabbed Nate and Libby in a crushing embrace. "We will never forget you."

"Same here," Nate wheezed out. "Good luck."

"And to you both," said Aña. "You've done more for us than we ever dreamed possible. I wish…I wish I could hug you, too." Refractor moved to her side and took her hand.

Libby blinked back a tear. "It's not right, Nate. There should be something more we can do. They won't have long together out there alone. In a few hours, the whole world will be hunting them."

Nate wallowed in the same frustrated helplessness. What comfort could he give? He simply held Libby close.

Ray huddled over Debolt's pen device, tapping it with a finger. Suddenly, a holographic readout again flashed numbers, figures, and three dimensional charts that made absolutely no sense. Ray and Bobbie, however, were transfixed. After studying the display, they shared an uneasy glance.

An anxious knot formed in Nate's stomach. "Isn't it working?"

"Yes," admitted Ray with obvious discomfort, "but we lack Scribe's experience with the device. The only test to see if it functions perfectly is to actually send you across the bridge. You must understand," he added quickly, "we believe the direction to your dimension has been reversed, but there is no way to know for sure. You could be trapped in nothingness, or the arrival on the other side could be…" He swallowed nervously. "Messy."

Nate got a cold chill. "How messy?"

"Parts added. Parts subtracted. Parts rearranged." He cleared his throat. "Messy."

"There's one other thing you should know," said Bobbie.

"Oh great," muttered Nate. "More good news?"

"This device," she said, "takes an enormous amount of power and the zayton from the last vial did not charge it to capacity. Plus, it was designed for only one person's travel. We can't be certain it will handle two. I would have more confidence if one of you agreed to stay behind."

"Not a chance!" cried Libby.

"Libby—"

"Don't you suggest it, Nate Hammond," Libby snapped. "Don't you even think it. If you go, I go." She held him in a tight embrace. "If you stay, I stay." The love flooding her words warmed Nate's soul. She would give up her privacy, her freedom, and any chance at a normal life to remain at his side.

"Consider a life here, Good Citizen," Ray urged. "Opportunities abound in Second Chance City."

"I don't want to stay," said Nate with absolute conviction. "I want to see my family, Ellie and Connor, Mike Williams, and all the friends who aren't here. Hell, I even miss Florence Peevey. Second Chance City doesn't need me to take care of it. There are plenty of good people already here who can do that. All I want to take care of is Libby Parish and Coldwater Bay. It's time for us to go home."

"A wise choice, Good Citizen," said Refractor. "You will have your happy ending."

"Happy ending?" Libby's brow wrinkled in a puzzled frown. She stared off in the distance as if deep in thought.

Ray handed Nate the device. "When you're ready simply click the button at the top."

"I guess we're all set," said Nate. "Right, Lib?"

She gazed out the window. "Happy ending?" she murmured again.

"Lib?"

A wild light danced in her eyes. She held out the penlight. "Nate, remember what it says on the side? Write your own ending. What if I create a better one?"

"Uh, okay by me," said Nate, not at all certain he caught her drift. "This one sucks."

"It does, doesn't it?" Libby said gleefully. "Payton would end the story this way, but not me. I have one crazy mad idea, Nate. It's insane…it probably won't work…but it's exactly how I'd write the ending if this was my comic book."

Her excitement spilled over to him. "Tell me."

"We'll probably end up as a mixed ball of gooey body parts."

"Not a bad way to go. I like all your parts, gooey or otherwise."

"Okay…" Libby turned to Ray and Bobbie. "You said the device hadn't filled to capacity. It needs more zayton."

"The other vials have already been used to recharge the engines on Syr's ship," said Bobbie. "We don't have another source."

"Actually, we do," said Libby triumphantly gesturing toward Aña and Refractor. "Their blood is loaded with it."

Ray and Bobbie gaped at each other. "I never considered that," said Ray. "Can it be done?"

"I don't know," said Bobbie, equally startled. "Mighty Light is correct, though. Their blood contains a pure source."

"Take as much as you need," chimed in Aña. "It's the least we can do."

"Thanks," said Libby. Her excitement had reached fever-pitch. "But that's not all I want. Zayton doesn't exist on our Earth. It can't. It's an impossible part of a comic book universe with no scientific grounding."

Refractor and Aña were obviously confused. "I'm not sure we understand," said Refractor. "If you could explain—"

"You and Aña return with us to Coldwater Bay," Libby burst out. "Zayton can't exist in our world. As soon as you step across dimensions, it will vanish from your systems. You'll be cured."

"Free?" Aña clutched her chest. "Is it possible?"

Refractor was equally shaken. He turned to Ray. "We could be normal again?"

Ray was bowled over. "I-I don't know. I honestly don't. There are too many unknown variables. I can only say with certainly," he added kindly, "neither Bobbie, nor I, nor anyone else on this side of the bridge, can help you."

Nate regarded Libby with pride. "I say Libby wrote a hell of an ending. It's worth a shot."

Refractor took Aña's hand and placed it against his cheek. "You must go."

She gazed at him in horror. "What are you saying? Leave you here? Alone?"

"I have to stay," he said tenderly. "My face...I no longer have human features. Even without the glow, I could never blend in, but you can have a normal life."

"No!" she cried out. "Better a few months together than none at all—"

Libby interrupted with a subtle cough. "Actually, I have another crazy idea for that, too." Their excitement grew as she outlined the plan. "You understand," she added at the finish. "There are no guarantees."

"Life never grants guarantees," said Refractor, "but without risk there is no reward. I'm willing to try."

"We both are," vowed Aña.

"Then let's get started," said Ray. After handing Refractor his penknife, Ray unbuttoned his shirt.

Refractor punctured his finger and dripped blood over the device's power cell. Aña did the same. Everyone held their breath while Bobbie checked the readings.

"It's working," she said at last, relief coloring her voice. "The device is fully charged."

Libby nodded toward Refractor. "You're up."

Refractor donned Ray's clothing. The light bent and twisted into a familiar visage. "Well?" he said.

Libby scrutinized Refractor's appearance from head to toe. A broad smile spread across her face. "Absolutely perfect."

"We're ready," said Nate.

Bobbie grew misty-eyed. "Since Ray and I have no way to know if you will arrive safely, I will simply say *bon voyage*...and thank you for everything."

Nate activated the device. A rectangular square of neon green light formed in front of them. The glow fluctuated, pulsing on-and-off in a hypnotic rhythm. The hair on Nate's arms rose to attention.

A droning hum filled the air. Somewhere in the distance, Nate heard Ray shouting, "Good luck to you all."

Nate took Libby's hand. Refractor clasped Aña's. Without a backward glance, the two couples stepped forward.

The world turned into green light.

Chapter Sixteen

Nate groaned. His eyelids fluttered. Blinking hurt. He remembered this feeling. He hadn't liked it the first time. He liked it even less now. "Lib?"

Someone next to him stirred and groaned. "Nate?"

He forced open an eye and glimpsed auburn curls. "You okay?"

"Think so. You?"

"Think so."

Nate struggled to sit. They were in a large dark room, Debolt's pen device still clutched in his hand. No hum, no green light. The transporter was dead.

Libby flicked on the flashlight. "It's normal again—no star at the top." She played the beam around the familiar interior of Write Away and froze at the sight of the last issue of Refractor displayed in a stand of comic books.

"We made it!" Nate shouted joyfully. He jumped up and helped Libby to her feet.

She peered around in growing panic. They were alone in the store. "Where are Refractor and Aña?" With a stifled sob, Libby clung to Nate. "They didn't make it."

His despair echoed hers. "Oh, Lib. I'm sorry…"

The lights flicked on. From the rear of the store ran a beautiful dark-haired woman and a grinning man in Ray's clothing.

"You're awake!" The spitting image of Payton Debolt grasped them in a firm embrace.

"I went to find the lights," said Aña. "Caleb…" She laughed. "I mean, *Payton*, wouldn't let me go alone." She pointed to the comic books in wonder. "I can't believe it. Except for that display, everything is exactly the same. The covers resemble my artwork, don't they? Although I've never seen breasts like that on a real woman."

"You're both okay?" cried Libby joyfully.

"See for yourself." Refractor/Payton spread his arms wide for their inspection. "The illusion bonded tight. I am now Payton Debolt."

"Perfect," Nate declared. "You're an exact twin to the sonuvabitch—without a single glimmer."

Aña chuckled. "He was so used to always having a light in the dark he ran right into a bookcase and stubbed his toe."

"How do you feel?" Nate asked Aña.

"Fine," she said uneasily. "Caleb touched me without harm, but he always could. I can't be sure the venom is gone, though."

"Trust the author. She put together a helluva ending." Nate and Libby exchanged a cagey look. Together they threw themselves at Aña. She froze as they hugged her tight.

"Not dead yet," said Libby cheerfully.

Aña relaxed and returned the embrace. "Thank you." Her voice caught in a sob. "Thank you."

Nate's radio crackled to life. "Nate, do you read me? Over."

"Irina!" he blurted out. "You're here. I mean, we're here. I mean, how's it going?"

"Nate?" The dispatcher sounded confused at his exuberant response. "Are you okay? You're blood sugar sounds low. I saved you a few cookies."

It's still Sunday.

"Hey," Irina continued, "the chief wants to know if you found that, and I quote, 'pain in the ass mucky-muck.' "

Nate regarded Refractor with a grin. "Yeah, I got him. He's fine."

"Great," Mike Williams' voice boomed over the speaker. "The storm has passed. We're not getting any more calls. Go home. I'll ring you if I need you."

"Okay...thanks, Chief...good to hear your voice again."

"What?"

"Never mind. See you tomorrow."

Refractor wore a dazed expression. "What now? I hardly know what to do next."

"For tonight," said Libby, "you have a room at the Breezy Point Inn."

"It's an inn?"

"Yeah," said Nate dryly. "Try not to stare at the innkeepers."

"Tomorrow," said Libby, "you will call the publisher and tell him the Refractor comic is going on a little hiatus while you reboot the series. The explosion caused Refractor and Araña to be sucked into the past. They are enemies at first, but, eventually, discover in order to get home they must become reluctant allies, then friends, then something more. It will take a long time and many adventures before they return to the present. Damn," she said with immense pleasure, "that's a couple of years' worth of issues right there."

Refractor scratched his head. "You wish me to write?"

"Why not? You have over two hundred years of stories. All you have to do is add the character Araña to them. Aña can do the artwork. I'll help with the editing." She snickered. "Meanwhile, you are free to spend Payton's money—trust me, he has a bundle."

"An intriguing plan," mused Refractor, "and one that should fit Aña and me well, but we will take some time to learn the ways of this world first."

"Of course," said Libby. "No need to rush. I can help you settle in."

Refractor's eyes twinkled. "That won't be necessary. Aña and I will manage on our own. Beside, you won't have time...this publisher is indebted to Payton Debolt?"

"Are you kidding? The Refractor comic is the company's cash cow, and Payton owns the rights. The publisher would stand on his head and spit out wooden nickels to keep him happy."

"Then he will, no doubt," said Refractor, "be amenable to any request from me."

"Absolutely, what do you want?"

"To have Elizabeth Parish sign a contract for her own series. I believe the name is *Crazy Ass Freaks*."

"If he refuses," said Aña, "I'm afraid no further Refractor stories will come his way."

Libby drew in a breath. "I-I don't know what to say."

"I do," said Nate, blowing on his hands for warmth. "She says yes, and it's too damn cold in here to chat. Let's go."

The storm had fizzled out. Stars sparkled from the

clear night sky. Nate's squad car was right outside where he had left it. He turned the heater on full blast and drove a shivering Refractor and Aña to the door of the Breezy Point Inn. "Sorry, we should have had you dress warmer, but we left in kind of a hurry."

"No complaints, Good Citizen." Refractor whispered a cheerful aside, "Aña and I will not require much in the way of clothing for the rest of the night."

Nate handed him the defunct pen device. "Here…a souvenir."

"The Neptune Suite is upstairs at the end of the hall," Libby called cheerfully. "The door is unlocked. I'll see you in the morning."

Libby leaned over and rested her head against Nate's shoulder. "You still owe me dinner. I assume Smuggler's Cove is closed for the evening, but we could go to your place. I have in mind a very special dessert."

Nate and Libby drove to town in contented silence, but when Nate parked in a spot on Main Street, Libby looked at him in confusion. "You live near here?" she asked. "I only see businesses."

"No, but I want to show you something first."

They walked along the path next to Frenchman's Creek and halted at the old maple tree Nate always considered theirs. His hand brushed away the snow. "Shine your light there." The thin tight beam revealed a crooked heart etched into the trunk.

Libby ran her fingers across the two sets of initials in the center, NH + LP. Her lips formed a tender smile. "Oh, Nate."

"Mike found me carving them into the bark on the day you left. In my little fevered brain, it was the only way to hold onto you."

"Not anymore," she whispered. "I'm here to stay."

Nate held her close, initials forgotten, their names now etched into each other's hearts forever.

Libby snuggled against him, melding into his arms. "Nate, I see the whole truth now."

He nuzzled her ear. "What truth?"

"This wasn't Refractor's story," she said with a contented sigh. "It was ours all along. We were sent to Second Chance City to find our happy ending and bring it home."

Nate took Libby's hand. Together, they walked to his squad car and drove off leaving Too Late Nate at the curb, never to be heard from again.

A word from the author…

I live in Florida, where the heat and humidity have driven everyone slightly mad. In my spare time I call in Bigfoot sightings to the Florida Department of Fish and Wildlife. They are heartily sick of hearing from me.

If you enjoyed *Second Chance City*, please take a moment to leave a review at your favorite retailer. No essay necessary, a few words is fine. Spelling and grammar will not count toward your final grade.

For more information about my books, visit my blog or drop me a line. I love hearing from readers.

Lurking spots:

http://lakelleythenaughtylist.blogspot.com

Twitter @AuthorLAKelley

Facebook www.facebook.com/l.a.kelley.author

l.a.kelley.author@gmail.com